THE MISTERS KURU

MAR '22

TO

ANOUSHIE
   I WISH U

WITH LOVE

NANU PEMAPPA

Praise for *Ms Draupadi Kuru*

'Das writes with great wit and imagination.'
— *Hindustan Times*

'A lively romp ... a commentary on how we perceive our role models in mythology. Draupadi serves as her own, and every diverse woman's inner monologue.'
— *India Today*

'A fun deviation from the serious for fans of mythology, *Ms Draupadi Kuru* is a refreshing take on the feisty queen.'
— *The Telegraph*

'An electrifying, fast-paced narrative that truly entertains.'
— Hello!

'Trisha Das' Draupadi is a defiant, courageous woman fully in control of her body and mind.'
— DailyO

'Das has rewritten the epic for the Snapchat generation.'
— *Indian Express*

THE MISTERS KURU

RETURN TO MAHABHARATA

TRISHA DAS

HarperCollins *Publishers* India

First published by
HarperCollins *Publishers* in 2021
A-75, Sector 57, Noida, Uttar Pradesh 201301, India
www.harpercollins.co.in

2 4 6 8 10 9 7 5 3 1

Copyright © Trisha Das 2021

P-ISBN: 978-93-5422-435-5
E-ISBN: 978-93-5422-436-2

This is a work of fiction and all characters and incidents described in this book are the product of the author's imagination. Any resemblance to actual persons, living or dead, is entirely coincidental.

Trisha Das asserts the moral right
to be identified as the author of this work.

All rights reserved. No part of this publication may be reproduced, stored in a retrieval system, or transmitted, in any form or by any means, electronic, mechanical, photocopying, recording or otherwise, without the prior permission of the publishers.

Typeset in 11/14.1 Bembo at
Manipal Technologies Limited, Manipal

Printed and bound at
Nutech Print Services – India

This book is Printed on FSC˚ certified paper
which ensure responsible forest management.

For R & J. You made me more than I made you.

1

She was the colour of burnt sugar—the kind they drizzled over milky sweetmeats in Hastinapur when he'd been a child in the mortal world. The dark syrup had added colour as well as a smoky, slightly bitter sweetness to anything it touched. It reminded him of his first wife, Draupadi.

Arjuna looked on lazily from the tousled bed as the naked nymph walked around his heavenly chambers, politely stepping around his sleeping dogs. Her hair was a lush black, falling in soft, shiny waves down to her knees. Her lips plump and pink, her eyes never-ending pools of darkness, her flawless, graceful body encased in skin so smooth and soft it almost didn't feel real. Every part of her smelled like light, breezy jasmine. *Every* part of her. She gasped and giggled at all the right moments, whispered the filthiest things into his ear when they made love, and listened in wide-eyed awe and amazement when he recounted his earthly exploits. She was, in all the ways that it was supposed to matter, the perfect woman. That precise combination of virgin and whore that every mortal man fantasised about.

It was so predictable.

Arjuna supressed the small sigh that almost slipped out. Instead, he sat up against his cushioned headboard and folded his arms behind his head, allowing his mind to wander.

A memory of his fourth and last wife, Subhadra, naked in the bed they shared as mortals, flashed through his head. She had an embarrassed smile on her face as she covered her womanhood with both hands, refusing to let him kiss her there. No amount of coaxing had ever made her comfortable enough to allow that act. In stark contrast was his first wife, Draupadi. There had been little that the two of them hadn't done. Unfortunately, Draupadi's uninhibitedness hadn't been restricted to their bedchambers—she'd been quite a handful outside them too.

That thought brought a wry smile to Arjuna's face. He imagined Draupadi splayed across the grassy forest floor, her long hair fanning her face, arching as he pleasured her with his mouth. Her husky, unrestrained moans had to be earned, each one a tiny victory, egging him on, challenging him to do better. The smell of fresh foliage mixed with lotus blossoms mixed with the earthiness of her womanhood. The saltiness of her swollen flesh, the expression on her face when she found her release. Or the scorn that spewed from her mouth when she didn't. There had been absolutely nothing predictable about Draupadi.

Except the fact that she would be his brother's wife within the year.

His head fell forward and he groaned. The nymph, he couldn't remember her name, turned around and smiled at him with questioning eyes. He wanted to ask her to leave, but even after thousands of years in heaven and the knowledge that nymphs had no earthly feelings, he couldn't bring himself to discard mortal etiquette.

Instead, he threw off the plush, silvery sheet that covered his legs and stood up. Donning the white toga that was the uniform of every mortal in heaven, he secured his shoulder-length hair behind his head with a tie, quickly kissed the nymph goodbye and left the chamber.

Walking with more purpose than he'd had in a while, he made his way on a fluffy path of clouds to Subhadra's chambers. They hadn't seen each other in a few hundred years, both agreeing that they needed time to cool off after their last disagreement. It wasn't a fight, oh no. Subhadra never fought—she was too much of a princess for that. Instead, she would go silent and pointedly ignore him until his anger turned into guilt for being angry and then the guilt turned into resignation, and he finally apologized. Then, she'd tell him about her hurt feelings in a soft, sad voice that made him feel like a monster.

Until the last time. Their last disagreement had been about Subhadra's decision to become a Vidyadhari, a demigod who owned the wisdom of the worlds, possessed magical powers, and supported the gods in earthly and heavenly management. She wasn't entirely sure how she would become one, since most Vidyadharis were either born into it or were mortals preordained by the gods. But Subhadra was convinced that if she did tapasya, an intense yogic meditation, for a few hundred thousand years, the gods would be convinced of her suitability. After all, in the old days on earth, if one did tapasya in a forest or on a mountain for a few years, there wasn't much the gods wouldn't grant you.

For the immortal soul of him, Arjuna couldn't understand why his wife wanted to become a demigod. Wasn't Subhadra happy sharing eternity with him? After all, this was what they'd dreamed of as mortals, what he'd promised Krishna, her brother and his mentor. Subhadra had been engaged to his cousin Duryodhana when Arjuna met and fell in love with her. When her family refused to let her marry him instead, they had eloped—not only creating a diplomatic crisis between kingdoms, but also effectively cutting off Subhadra from her relatives. That was when he'd made his promise to Krishna, the only person who had supported them. That he would always cherish Subhadra, take care of her. That they would be together forever. He'd given Krishna his word as a man of honour.

Arjuna was nothing if not an honourable man.

He reached Subhadra's chambers and stood outside the door for a few undecided moments. As her husband, he'd never knocked before. But, to be perfectly honest, in the last thousand years, he had felt less like a husband and more like a nagging, older brother around Subhadra.

He knocked.

'Come in,' her soft, sweet voice chimed from inside.

He entered her silken, peach-coloured chambers. Her golden bed glowed like a halo at the centre of it. In its folds sat Subhadra. She smiled at Arjuna and got up to greet him.

'I'm glad you came, my husband.' Her doe eyes and heart-shaped lips beamed up at him as she took his hands in hers. 'I thought I'd lost you forever.'

Arjuna pulled her petite body into a hug and felt her stiffen slightly, as she always did when he touched her. It usually took her a while to warm up to physical intimacy. He rubbed her shoulders gently and smiled back. 'I've missed you.'

Subhadra's smile broadened. 'As have I. But I have some news.'

'What is it?'

'I've decided not to become a Vidyadhari,' she said in a wispy voice.

Arjuna chuckled. 'Good. What made you change your mind?'

She disentangled herself from his arms and stood back, her eager eyes blinking excitedly. 'I've thought of something better!' she declared.

Now what, he thought, and then immediately felt guilty for feeling impatient with her. He sighed. 'Tell me.'

Subhadra gestured towards an armchair near the bed. In the old days, Arjuna would have ignored the chair and swept her up in his arms, falling with her on the bed. Laughing, touching, talking, easing out her studied formality. But today, he walked over and sat in the armchair, dread creeping over him. She wasn't going to announce that she wanted to become a nymph, was she? No, probably not. Nymphs were creatures of pleasure, and Subhadra hadn't taken hers in over a thousand years. At least, not with him.

'I think we should be reborn!'

Arjuna frowned. 'What?'

She sat on the edge of her bed and continued in an excited voice, 'We should be reborn as mortals! Think about it, my love. We could be farmers who live off the land, or travelling merchants who see the world, or maybe even gypsies!'

'Er... that's not how rebirth works anymore, Subhadra. Remember the announcement before the start of the Kalyug? You can't choose who you are or where you're born, and you certainly cannot choose your mortal companions. We talked about this,' said Arjuna, valiantly trying not to talk to her as if she were a child even while knowing he was failing miserably. The rules had been different for a while now. Only the truly enlightened could walk past heaven's silvery gates and become immortal now. The rest of mortal-kind was doomed to an endless cycle of birth, death and rebirth until the gods decided to destroy the earth and everyone on it. Although it was pretty clear, despite constantly threatening to do so, that they weren't in any hurry.

Subhadra waved her hands dismissively. 'Yes, I know we discussed it, but it turns out the rules are flexible. After all, your other wife and your mother have both done it.'

Arjuna blinked. '*What?*'

She nodded. 'Draupadi, Kunti and that lady who stood in your chariot during the Great War, Amba or Sikandi or whatever they called her back then, are all ensconced in the mortal world right now. I heard it on the grapevine. Apparently, my brother, Krishna, allowed them to visit the mortal world for thirty days and they decided to stay! Isn't that marvellous?'

Not in the least. 'That's not possible,' he replied, shaking his head.

Subhadra's lips twitched and her eyes twinkled. 'Have you seen Draupadi in court lately, my love?'

Arjuna stilled. He hadn't, not for at least a year. It was unusual, but he'd put it down to one of her antics—Draupadi periodically stayed away from court, trying to organize female tribunals or protests or some such thing. And his mother *had* become a bit of a recluse lately. Could it be true? No, they wouldn't have taken such a huge step without consulting him. Without consulting Yudhishtra.

'That's not possible,' he repeated, with more bravado than confidence.

'It's true. They really went down there. And we can do it too!' Subhadra squeaked. 'Imagine looking up at the night sky again. The warmth of a gypsy fire.'

He looked down at her, his recent shock temporarily pulling the veil off his annoyance as he asked in a sharp voice, 'You want to be gypsy? Really? You know absolutely nothing of mortal life outside the walls of a palace, Subhadra. It's difficult and dangerous, and there is no god-avatar brother to protect you at every turn. Don't let foolish romanticism overrule your common sense. You belong up here, in comfort, with your own kind.'

'But Draupadi has done it!'

Arjuna shook his head, frowning in disbelief, 'That's not confirmed, but even if it were ...' He held the rest of his words back with difficultly.

Subhadra didn't need him to say them. She looked up at Arjuna with a wounded expression and spoke in a deceptively mild voice, 'Even if it were, Draupadi is different. Draupadi is made of stronger stuff. Draupadi will succeed where Subhadra will fail.'

'Subhadra ...'

'Admit it, Arjuna,' she said. 'You always thought more highly of her.'

'Stop it. I will not discuss Draupadi with you.'

'No, you never did,' she replied sadly. Then she went silent on him. Probably for another few hundred years.

Arjuna stared at her for a long, hard moment before he turned around and walked out.

2

The infinitely sized crystal amphitheatre that was the heavenly court, with its countless white pillars and cushioned, shimmering crystal thrones that made even the most insignificant of divine creatures feel good about themselves, buzzed with its usual activity. Immortals of every kind gathered and talked in groups that seemed arbitrary in their arrangement, but Arjuna knew it was anything but. Power play, wheeling and dealing were as common amongst gods, demigods and former mortals as they were in the mortal world. Heaven was a cesspit of dirty politics.

He grabbed a golden chalice full of amrith, the nectar of immortality, from a passing nymph's tray and walked past a group of half-demon-half-gods with a studious nod of greeting. With the constant threat of battle between the demon and divine worlds, the cross-bred were perpetually caught in the middle. They were the best spies available, because they moved freely between both worlds, but their demon-like appearance meant that they were despised by all heavenly inhabitants and equally mistrusted by those in Mara's realm because they didn't look demonly enough.

Taking a sip of the slightly sweet liquid, Arjuna made a face. Amrith might keep him in the prime of youth for eternity, but it tasted like something you would feed a baby. What he wouldn't give for a hearty swig of wine, but alcohol was no longer provided to former mortals. Apparently, there had been an 'incident' a while back, a drunken mutiny of sorts, which no one ever talked about. Only the gods got to get drunk these days.

He sighed. At least the nymphs were still around. God knows his wives didn't want anything to do with him anymore.

Arjuna saw his brothers waving to him and smiled, walking over and briefly bowing in respect to his elder brothers, Yudhishtra and Bhima. In turn, his younger brothers, Nakula and Sahadeva, bowed to him. It was a mortal ritual that meant a lot to Yudhishtra, so they kept it up for his sake.

'We didn't see you at training today,' said Bhima.

Arjuna nodded. 'I was otherwise detained.'

They still trained for battle every day, to keep their bodies in prime condition. It was a habit they'd formed as mortals and would be a useful one if they ever had to fight demons in the future. He looked around at his brothers' faces and asked, 'Have you heard about Draupadi and Mother?'

Yudhishtra, Bhima and Nakula all returned his query with a blank look. Sahadeva, with his fair skin and eternally boyish face, blushed a light shade of red.

Arjuna frowned at him. 'You knew?'

'Knew what?' The question came from Yudhishtra in a moderate but authoritative voice that implied impatience at not knowing something of import immediately.

Yudhishtra was shorter and slimmer than Arjuna's tall, robust build and Bhima's even taller muscularity, but his voice had always held unquestioned authority. He stared at Arjuna with sharp intensity.

'Subhadra told me that Draupadi and Mother, along with the woman who stood in my chariot during the Great War, Sikandi, went down to earth and are now living as mortals,' Arjuna said.

Yudhishtra frowned. 'They've chosen rebirth? How can that be? They would have consulted me first.'

Sahadeva shook his head gently. 'No, not rebirth. My wife, Vijaya, told me that Krishna allowed them to visit Indraprastha for thirty days, and they decided to stay on in their current mortal forms. Vijaya heard the information directly from Gandhari, who accompanied them and returned after the allotted time. Apparently, Mother has decided to stay with Karna's reincarnation, a young orphan. Draupadi is apparently working for a living.'

Yudhishtra, Bhima and Arjuna stared at Sahadeva in shock. Nakula's handsome face broke into a bemused smile. 'As what?'

Sahadeva shook his head. 'Vijaya was unclear about the details.'

Bhima frowned too and then slapped his forehead, his eyes widening. 'No wonder I haven't seen Draupadi at any of my re-enactments of the Great War lately. I knew she wouldn't miss them on purpose!'

'This is ridiculous! How could they do that without informing anyone? Without asking my permission?' Yudhishtra asked angrily.

The other brothers stayed quiet, acknowledging Yudhishtra's seniority over them by not pointing out the obvious. That neither Draupadi nor Kunti, nor any of them, were obliged to ask for his permission or even keep him updated about their lives anymore. Yudhishtra might have been their king on earth, but heaven was a great equalizer. He had no authority left over his family. The fact that his brothers still afforded him a veneer of influence was only because of their love and regard for him. In the absence of a father during their mortal lives, Yudhishtra had been a father, brother, leader and king. They owed it to him.

Arjuna had a thought. 'They went to Indraprastha?' For a brief moment, he actually felt a tiny twinge of envy. He would love to set eyes upon the city he had worked so hard to build and establish with his brothers. What might it have become? Did mortals still remember them? Tantalizing thoughts teased his mind.

Sahadeva nodded. 'Gandhari says Indraprastha is now the capital city of Bharat Varsh, which has united into a single kingdom.'

That was the most wonderful thing he had heard in the last thousand years! A wave of unadulterated pride and joy washed over Arjuna.

Right before another wave of annoyance. He glared at Sahadeva. 'Why didn't you tell us all this?'

'Yes,' added Yudhishtra with a huff. 'What were you thinking, keeping this information to yourself?'

Faced with his elder brothers' outraged glares, Sahadeva folded his hands apologetically.

He spoke to Yudhishtra. 'I'm sorry, brother. I wanted to, but Vijaya suggested I keep it to myself because she knew how distressing the news would be to all of you, especially the sons of Kunti. As she said, it's not like we can do anything about it now.'

There was silence again, this time to avoid pointing out to Sahadeva that he was completely under his wife's thumb. In the forest, when they had lived together with Draupadi in exile, Sahadeva had been the most biddable and easy-going of brothers. Since he'd started living with his wife, however, he'd adopted the irritating propensity of using the words 'Vijaya says' a bit too often.

Finally, Nakula raised a wry eyebrow and muttered, 'Well then, we all must bow to Vijaya's superior judgement.'

Bhima grunted softly in humour, but then looked worried. 'Now that we do know, however, what are we going to do? Anything could happen to them in the mortal world. Surely, they will need protectors.' He turned to Yudhishtra and Arjuna. 'We have to do something.'

'I agree. We cannot sit back, and let our mother and wife fend for themselves, alone in a strange world,' replied Arjuna. After a moment of thought, an idea occurred to him. 'If Krishna allowed them a thirty-day visit to Indraprastha, there's no reason he wouldn't allow us the same privilege. What if we went down there and convinced them to return to heaven?'

Yudhishtra still looked irked, as if Draupadi and Kunti's leaving and Sahadeva's silence on the matter were a personal affront. 'I cannot believe they came up with such a *ridiculous* scheme. It couldn't have been Mother's idea. No, this has

Draupadi written all over it. Ever since we ascended to heaven, she has grown more and more out of hand. I should have kept a tighter rein on her, as I did when we were mortals. This is my fault.'

Arjuna locked eyes with Bhima in a moment of shared understanding. Both of them habitually supressed the urge to rise to Draupadi's defence against Yudhishtra's often unrealistic expectations of her. Both of them had been privy, uncountable times during their mortal lives, to instances when Yudhishtra had treated her as if she were nothing more than a wild mare to be tamed and trained instead of an intelligent, spirited woman. As much as it had bothered them, they had mostly kept silent out of respect for their elder brother, trying to support Draupadi in other ways.

Nakula and Sahadeva, on the other hand, had been so far down the hierarchy of the Pandava brotherhood that their relationship with Draupadi had been more of a formality. She had been the head wife, and they had accorded her the respect, friendship and affection that her position deserved, but neither of them had ever felt any kind of manly love for her. Upon their ascension, when they had reconnected with their birth mother, Madri, their bonds with Kunti and Draupadi had slackened. Of course, their greatest attachment, one that had withstood the ravages of time and was still as indestructible as ever, was to each other.

Arjuna cleared his throat, ever the diplomatic one. 'So, what do you all say? Should we go down and try to bring them back? I say we do it. You heard Sahadeva—Indraprastha is now a great city. I won't deny that I would very much like to see it. A short visit will serve both purposes.'

Yudhishtra frowned. 'What about the impending war of the worlds, between the gods and demons? I have committed us to fighting when the need arises.'

Arjuna looked at his feet so his elder brother wouldn't see the disdain in his eyes. He said in as even a tone as he could manage, 'I think we've been very patient, Brother, waiting and training for that war every day. But it's been millennia after millennia of nothing but posturing from both sides. It's one thing to constantly threaten to attack your enemy and advertise the magical capabilities of your weapons—not that I think most of them really exist—and it's another thing to actually do something. Neither of the worlds has conducted a strike for hundreds of thousands of years. We can, perhaps, safely assume that not much will change in the next thirty days.'

Yudhishtra was adamant. 'But I gave my word!'

Bhima rubbed the dark stubble on his chin. 'What if only one or two of us went down?'

Yudhishtra shook his head. 'No. We have always stayed together.'

Nakula and Sahadeva shuffled their feet and looked at each other in silent support, as they always did when their three elder brothers were arguing over a decision. Neither of them really wanted to go rescue Draupadi and Kunti—Nakula was relatively comfortable in heaven, with his war games and army of nymphs, and Sahadeva was perfectly happy to stay with his beloved wife. But, as usual, they would go along with whatever was decided. Old habits were hard to break.

Arjuna took a deep breath and said in a firm voice, 'I think it's an important mission, one that we owe to the women of our family. It would be dishonourable of us not to come to their aid.' Then, in a conciliatory tone he added, 'Perhaps

Krishna can send word if the war starts while we are on earth. We can return immediately in that case.'

Bhima slapped his thigh in excitement. 'Hah! Splendid idea, little brother. I say we do just that.'

Arjuna smiled and looked at Yudhishtra. He would have the final word. 'What do you say, Brother? Shall we go save them?'

Yudhishtra sighed, his troubled frown deepening. Finally, after a few fraught moments, he relented. 'Very well.'

3

'This isn't the life I expected!'

Overcome, Amba curled into herself while seated on Draupadi's white sectional sofa in her living room. Sobs racked her body in rhythm with her foot, which was mindlessly rocking a baby-chair at her feet.

Draupadi took a deep breath, moments away from reminding Amba to speak softly, lest her newborn daughter wake up and start crying again. One wailing woman at a time, for heaven's sake.

'This happens after a birth sometimes,' she said in a comforting tone. 'I felt sad and overwhelmed after my first-born, Prathivindhya, too.'

'Yes,' said Kunti, who was sitting next to Amba and stroking her back gently. 'I felt it too, and I know many women who also went through this. You'll be better soon. Just remember to get enough sleep and focus on bonding with your baby.'

Amba wiped away her tears, and looked down at her offspring with a mixture of attachment and contempt. 'How can I sleep when she wakes me to feed almost every hour? And then she only drinks a little and leaves my breasts so engorged I feel like they might burst! Zafar is absolutely no help either. He took an assignment in Bhubaneshwar yesterday. Bhubaneshwar! He'll be gone for three weeks! I would never have had a baby if I had known I'd have to take care of it alone!'

Draupadi shook her head. 'Honestly, I can't remember a single time any of my husbands did anything to help with our babies.' She uncrossed her heel-clad feet and smoothed the maroon, body-con dress she'd worn for taping this week's episode of *Us, The Women*, her TV talk show on NPTV, where she discussed women's issues with newsmakers and a live audience. Her feet ached from being strapped into high heels all day, and she still had a heavy pancake of make-up on her face. It would take at least half an hour to remove it and soothe her sensitive skin, but the channel insisted she wear it when appearing on camera.

She sighed. Twelve years she had spent in the forest with nothing but water and air on her face, and not once had she ever had a pimple. Now, unless she maintained a strict make-up removal and moisturising regime, they popped up weekly. God alone knew what was in that wretched foundation.

'That was a different time,' snapped Amba with uncharacteristic irritability. 'We were constantly surrounded by relatives, handmaidens and servants. Now, I'm stuck in a tiny flat with a sick mother-in-law and a screaming baby all day, just waiting for Zafar to come home from work, so I can have a shower, a cup of hot tea, or even just sit and breathe for five minutes without interruption.' Fresh tears welled up in her eyes. 'What a lifetime of rejection, the Great War and months of practicing extreme austerities couldn't do, my own child has done in less than a month—defeated me.' She started sobbing again.

'It gets easier,' crooned Kunti. 'Your body will recover and your daughter will sleep longer, and life will become easier. I promise you, my darling girl, you will look back at this time with a smile one day.' She took a deep breath and looked pointedly at Draupadi. 'Anyway, let's talk about happy things. The orphanage got another large donation a few days ago. I don't have to worry about finances for the next six months!'

Despite herself, Amba blubbered, 'How wonderful! I'm so happy!' and then resumed crying with even more gusto, a twisted smile on her face. 'Happy tears,' she wailed, when Kunti cast her a worried glance.

Biting her lip so she wouldn't grin, Draupadi turned to Kunti. 'It *is* wonderful. Who made the donation?'

Kunti's smile faltered. 'Well, that's the problem. They've opened this Bhartiya Youth of Bharat Mata Centre in the slum recently, and as their first project, they conducted a donation drive for the orphanage.'

'Why is that a problem?' asked Draupadi with a frown. Ever since Shashiben, former warden of the Bal Raksha Orphanage and mortal avatar of the Goddess Saraswati, had died, Kunti, who took over the role of warden, had struggled with funding. She should be jumping with joy.

Kunti hesitated before replying, 'It's not a problem in itself, except that the young men who run the centre are ... Well, they're a bit fervent in their beliefs. Rumour is that they're affiliated to a political party; so, I don't know if it's such a good idea taking favours from them. But then again, it's not like there's a line of donors outside the door. I can't afford to look a gift horse in the mouth.'

'Have they asked you for anything?'

Sighing softly, Kunti shook her head. 'No, not at all. In fact, they've been nothing but kind, enthusiastic and respectful, but ... I don't know. Maybe it's just me.'

There was silence for a moment as Draupadi considered Kunti's words before replying, 'Well, if you ever have a problem, let me know. I've made some connections since I started working at NPTV.'

Her words made Kunti laugh warmly. 'Hardly just that! You've done extraordinarily well in just one short year back on earth. Why, your TV show has taken the country by storm, everyone knows who you are and *such* commendable work you've done for women everywhere.' She smiled at Draupadi warmly. 'I'm proud to call you my daughter, my dear. I'm sure my sons would be proud too, if they could see you now.'

Draupadi returned her smile with equal affection. So much had changed in the last year. She went to work at a job she loved, made decisions and commanded people's respect. She earned enough money to live comfortably. On Zafar's advice, she had recently bought her very own flat, a lovely three-bedroom high up on the fifteenth storey, overlooking the city skyline. Every morning, she had tea on her balcony and marvelled at the fact that she could actually live where previously only birds could fly. She had good friends like Angela, her producer, who was passionate about the same things and enriched her life with new experiences. And, of course, she still had Kunti and Amba, who were her family and closest confidantes.

Not that life didn't have its challenges, of course. With recognition had come an exacting price. Draupadi's movements were constantly monitored, commented upon and criticized. Even though she had adamantly refused to join social media when the NPTV marketing team had asked her to, the internet was constantly trending with unflattering hashtags like #DramaQueenDraupadi and #DraupadiShoutingAgain. Wherever she went, the press asked for her opinion on the politics of the day. If she said nothing, they called her a coward for not speaking up, but if she said something, they'd misquote her and there would be even more backlash. Fame had turned out to be both a blessing and a battle she was constantly fighting yet couldn't win.

And recently, it had brought with it an unwelcome accomplice. A stalker.

When both Amba and Kunti began gazing at her speculatively, Draupadi realized her smile had slipped. She shook her head to clear her thoughts and focused on her former mother-in-law. No point worrying Kunti with problems she couldn't do anything about. 'Speaking of your sons, how is Karan?'

Clutching her forehead, Kunti laughed good-naturedly. 'He's a handful, like all twelve-year-olds! But he's settled well into his school dorm and returns to the orphanage on weekends. I can't thank you enough for putting him through private school, my dear.'

Waving it off, Draupadi replied, 'It's the least I can do. After all, you won't let me pay for anything else.' She looked at Amba's still-hunched, cheerless form. 'Do you think there might be medication for your condition, Amba? After all, they have a pill for everything these days.'

Just then, the baby began to stir. Amba tried rocking the chair more vigorously, but all that did was make the baby cry. 'See? Barely an hour,' said Amba with resignation, as she pulled open her shirt and picked up her daughter to put to a breast. She suckled at Amba's nipple greedily, making all the women in the room smile dotingly. There was just something about a baby ...

Suddenly, there was a thump and crash, and the air around them whooshed dramatically. A male voice shouted something unintelligible in the distance and then a poof! A large cloud of smoke appeared and dissipated, leaving behind six men lying on the floor of Draupadi's living room.

'I can't *believe* I have to do this again,' muttered Narad Muni, the elderly messenger sage, who travelled between worlds, as he stood up and dusted himself off with skinny, wrinkled arms. 'Of all the hare-brained, cockeyed, half-baked schemes the gods have ever come up with ...' He ran his piercing eyes around the room, his gaze falling on a shocked Draupadi, a slack-jawed Kunti and Amba's naked breasts.

He screamed.

Slapping his palms over his eyes, he shrieked hysterically, 'Cover yourself! Cover yourself, you shameless hussy! How dare you try to tempt a sage? This evil world has polluted you, as I knew it would! You will not debauch me, I swear it! *Cover yourself!*' His voice became so high-pitched that Kunti had to shield her ears.

Amba rolled her eyes at Narad Muni and continued feeding without so much as a twitch. 'Not again. What does it take to get rid of you, old man?'

Narad Muni screeched back at her with his hands over his face, 'You think I *want* to be here, brazen female? Your kind are worse than demons, I tell you! And that Saraswati; she is the worst! She complained about me to Krishna. Me! All because of you lot, with your idiotic, extended holidays. If I could, I would smite you all to dust, never mind the consequences!'

Amba snorted. Then she noticed he was dressed in a light brown shirt and trousers instead of his usual sage's habit. 'Why are you dressed like that?'

'Because he's been suspended,' said Arjuna, fidgeting next to his brothers, all of them staring at the floor awkwardly to avoid looking at Amba breastfeeding.

Arjuna's voice snapped Draupadi and Kunti out of their stunned silence. Kunti got up and walked towards them. 'Boys? Can this be true? Are you really here?'

'Mother!' All five of them fell at her feet, their gazes still locked on the ground.

Amba sighed loudly and got up. 'I'll be in the bedroom.'

After she had gone, the Pandava brothers stood up and each one hugged Kunti with a smile. Tears began to flow down her cheeks. 'I never thought I'd see any of you again!' she exclaimed, touching their faces as if to prove to herself they were really standing before her. 'I can't believe it. You're here! In Delhi!'

'Delhi?' asked a puzzled Bhima. 'We were told this was Indraprastha.' He frowned at Narad Muni, who was sulking near the front door.

Kunti nodded. 'Indraprastha is called Delhi now. We've been here for a year.'

Yudhishtra spoke in gentle reprimand, 'We know. We spoke to Krishna and he told us everything. He's allowed us thirty days to—'

'How are you, Mother?' Arjuna interrupted him quickly, earning a puzzled look from his elder brother. Best to get the lay of the land before they sprung the reason behind their visit to earth on their mother. Victory was always easier when you knew what you were fighting.

Kunti smiled. 'I'm well. I've become the warden of a home for orphaned children. It's quite an exciting life.' She didn't mention Karan.

Arjuna smiled down at her, a warm feeling wrapping around him. It was so good to see her face, be reassured that she was safe and well. 'And Draupadi? How is she?'

'Er, hello?' Draupadi stood up and walked towards the Pandavas, a little peeved at being completely ignored so far.

All five brothers turned and stared at her in shock. Then, Arjuna whispered, 'Draupadi? Is that you?'

Bhima stepped closer and bent down to peer into her face, his eyes scrunching up as if he were examining an unknown insect. 'The voice is Draupadi's, but it's difficult to tell from the face. This one is taller.'

Draupadi rolled her eyes. 'It *is* me. I'm wearing face paint. And raised footwear.' She stuck out her heels to show them.

Bhima rubbed her cheek with his thumb, and looked down at the cocktail of colours and shimmers on his finger. Then, he frowned into her face again, mentally check-listing her features against the ones he knew so well. Finally, he grinned and stated, 'Hah! It's her!'

Draupadi's irritated expression turned into an involuntary laugh when he lifted her off her feet and enveloped her in a growly bear hug. Bhima was the only man who could make her feel almost petite.

Arjuna stood back and blinked at her. 'You cut your hair,' he accused softly.

Draupadi huffed at him. 'Is that how you greet me?'

The reproof worked, and he shook his head with a rueful smile. 'No, of course not. I'm sorry.' He stepped forward and hugged her, prompting Nakula and Sahadeva to give her smiling side-hugs too. She returned their affection warmly, and laughed when Arjuna commented that he knew a thing or two about face paint from their thirteenth year in exile.

Only Yudhishtra held back.

Scowling at her, he said in a voice that would have made a nymph feel promiscuous, 'What have you become, my queen?' He pointed to her made-up face, shoulder-length hair, the dress that ended above her knees and clung to her eye-catching curves with a scornful hand. 'You look like a lewd stage performer.'

Draupadi returned his look with a scowl of her own, holding his eyes in a moment fraught with tension. Aeons of resentment and regret poured out of her eyes. Then, she shook her head and laughed, replying in a mocking tone, 'As it happens, I *am* a stage performer now, Yudhishtra. And a good one at that.'

'Nonsense. And don't call me by my name. It isn't becoming for a wife.'

'I'm not your wife anymore.'

Yudhishtra turned to Kunti. 'See? This is exactly the kind of attitude and behaviour I expect from her. What I don't understand, Mother, is why *you* went along with this mad scheme.'

Confused, Kunti asked, 'What mad scheme, son?'

'Coming down here and playing at being mortals!'

Draupadi shook her head. 'Typical.'

Kunti looked from Yudhishtra to Draupadi and back. She spoke in a gentle voice, 'Son, much has changed in the last year. We will explain everything, but first, you must tell us what you're doing here. You mentioned you spoke to Krishna?'

Arjuna interjected again. 'We did, Mother. We were worried about you both and Krishna allowed us to visit for thirty days.' He gave Yudhishtra a pointed look, silently entreating him not to argue their case, for now. Yudhishtra responded with a terse nod.

Kunti beamed. 'That is wonderful news!'

Draupadi looked a little less enthusiastic, but still smiled at Arjuna and said, 'We have much to show you. But first, a few questions.' She inclined her head towards Narad Muni. 'Why is he still here and dressed like a mortal?'

Arjuna cleared his throat. 'Apparently, Goddess Saraswati was displeased by his insubordination towards her avatar. She complained to the gods upon her ascension and they have temporarily suspended him. He has to serve as a mortal for thirty days. And,' he looked at Narad Muni apologetically, 'Krishna mentioned his time might be constructively utilized as the cook and caretaker at Mother's orphanage.'

For a stunned moment, nobody said anything. Then, a choking sound burst forth from the corner of the room. Amba had returned, fully dressed and clutching a sleeping baby. She was giggling hysterically.

Draupadi and Kunti burst out laughing too. The five brothers stood quietly, watching the women expel their mirth and casting sorry glances at a fuming Narad Muni in the corner.

Finally, Kunti relented, wiped the tears from her eyes, and turned to Narad Muni. 'My apologies, O sage. We would be most delighted,' she coughed to cover up another giggle, and Draupadi and Amba burst into another round of laughter, 'to have you contribute to our cause.' She looked at her watch. 'In fact, it is getting late. Will you be returning with me to the orphanage?'

Narad Muni responded sullenly. 'Yes. They've confiscated my usual residence. I'll come with you.' Then, his eyes lit up with a spark of spiteful pleasure. He turned to Draupadi. 'Oh, and Krishna has asked that you host your husbands for the duration of their stay.'

Draupadi stopped laughing immediately. 'What? No! No, no. No.'

'Why not?' Bhima looked hurt.

Draupadi shook her head at him quickly. 'It's not that I don't want *you* to stay, Bhima. Of course I do. It's just that … just that with my work … and the timings …' She looked around desperately. 'There are only three private rooms! And one of them is a study so there are only two beds,' she declared.

Arjuna could have laughed, but said instead, 'I think we'll manage. After all, in the past we've slept on many a forest floor.' He looked at her meaningfully, willing her to remember being with him on said forest floors. He knew she'd remembered when her expression faltered and she looked away.

Yudhishtra nodded. 'We'll be fine. Draupadi and I will take one chamber, and the rest of you can fan out around the house.' He began to walk around the living room, taking in the place. 'It'll be dark soon. We should light some lamps. Where do you normally make your fire, Draupadi?'

'Stop right there!' Draupadi gave him a death glare as she stepped up to him and poked him in the chest with enough force for him to stumble backwards. 'Let's get one thing clear, Yudhishtra. I,' poke, 'am *not*,' poke, 'your wife,' poke, 'anymore. Understood?'

She pointed to a door at the end of the hallway and said in a voice that was sounding more and more shrill by the second, 'That is *my* bedroom. Mine alone. If any of you wish to enter to speak with me, you will knock. Politely. If you are to stay here, you will do so with the clear understanding that you are my guests and nothing more. That part of our existence is *over*!'

Yudhishtra put his hands up in a defensive gesture. 'Calm down, woman. What's gotten into you?'

Clearly distraught, Draupadi shook her head, 'Don't tell me to calm down!' she shouted. 'You will not ... I will not ... *No!*'

'Yudhishtra.'

Kunti's voice was gentle, but no one could mistake the resolve behind it. She walked over to Draupadi and stood next to her in silent support. 'I want you to listen to me, my sons.'

She paused, choosing her words, and then continued, 'Our mortal lives served an important purpose, and we all made sacrifices towards it. I made many decisions I have bitterly regretted over the years. One of them, abandoning my first-born child, was the reason I returned to this mortal world and is the reason I chose to remain here. What has happened already cannot be undone, but I can try to do better going forward.'

Kunti sighed. 'When Arjuna won Draupadi at her swayamwara, we had just escaped a murder attempt and were, rather precariously, hiding in plain sight. You boys were young and susceptible. We needed to band together to face the impending storm. I couldn't have let you three,' she gestured to Yudhishtra, Bhima and Arjuna, 'quarrel with each other over a woman. I saw the way you all looked at her. So I did what I thought I needed to do, to keep you united.'

Turning to Draupadi, she took hold of both her hands and squeezed them. 'My dear, the injustices you suffered from being the common wife of the Pandavas are because of my words. Words that I refused to take back. For that, I am deeply sorry. Let me do better now. From this moment forth, the Pandavas will have no more claim over you. You are free, Draupadi. To belong to yourself or another.'

Yudhishtra's eyes widened in shock. 'Mother,' he whispered.

Unblinking, Kunti looked at each of them, one by one. Her voice had steel in it when she said, 'That is my wish. You are still my sons, aren't you?'

'Of course,' said Arjuna softly. His brothers followed with their own agreement.

She nodded. 'Then, just as you obeyed me without question in the past, you will do so again. Draupadi is no longer your common wife. Is that understood?'

The Pandava brothers looked at each other in confusion.

Kunti frowned and asked again, loudly, 'My sons, is that understood?'

Sahadeva nodded quickly and said, 'Yes.'

Nakula looked from Sahadeva to Draupadi and said, 'Yes.'

After a long moment, Bhima grunted, smiled ruefully at Draupadi, and said, 'Yes.'

Arjuna took a deep breath, emotions running riot within him. In a tight voice, he said, 'Yes.'

They all looked at Yudhishtra. His expression was solemn as he stared at his mother, his angry eyes as unblinking as her own. 'Yes.'

Draupadi turned to face the wall so no one would see the tears sliding out of her eyes. Kunti held her shoulders as they shook soundlessly.

No one said anything. There was nothing more to say.

4

She was different. It wasn't just the way she looked, or even the way she behaved. It was something in her eyes. He couldn't quite put his finger on what that something was. Or decide whether he liked it.

Arjuna blinked as he lounged in the office chair in Draupadi's study. It was a tiny room with a large desk and just enough space for a single man to lie on the floor. Not the most comfortable of arrangements, but he was glad for the privacy. His brothers were sharing the much larger guest room, with the twins taking the floor on either side of the bed. Given that the bed wasn't very wide, he wouldn't want to be the one who had to sleep on Bhima's side.

It was fitting that Arjuna should be in a separate room. Of all the brothers, he had spent the most time alone. Including twelve years in exile, because he had walked in on Yudhishtra and Draupadi in their bedroom once, during their allotted year of marriage.

He sighed. Today, when Draupadi had told Yudhishtra that she wasn't his wife anymore, he'd experienced a momentary bolt of elation before that familiar guilt for feeling disloyal to his brothers had taken over. He'd been the one to win Draupadi as a wife, and he had spent his entire life embittered that she didn't belong to him alone.

Now she belonged to none of them.

On the one hand, he felt cheated. Did their relationship—one they'd shared for thousands of years—not matter any longer? They'd had children together. How could anyone discount their history, sever that connection?

On the other hand, he felt glad that none of his brothers could claim her anymore. He felt, in a small way, freed from the shackles of their previous arrangement. It was obvious Draupadi felt the same way.

He fidgeted; his body as taut as his bow at the ready. He was too big for this room. Standing up, he decided to go find Draupadi. The night had ended abruptly after his mother's words, and Draupadi had disappeared into her bedroom without saying anything.

They needed to talk.

He opened the door slowly, practiced stealth ensuring that no sound disturbed his brothers in their room. Walking across the hallway, he stopped to marvel at the light bulb on the wall. Touching it with his finger, he smiled when he felt a slight burn. At least light still generated heat. The world may have changed much on the surface, but its foundations remained the same.

Knocking softly on Draupadi's door, he listened carefully for a reply. None came. He knocked again, but still no answer. Taking a deep breath, he opened her door quietly and slipped inside.

Her room was unoccupied, lit by a single lamp on the side of her bed. Warm hues of amber, ruby and lemon, along with her signature scent of lotus flowers enveloped him. In heaven, she'd kept live bees, dragonflies and butterflies in her chambers, and now they were painted on her bed sheets and cushions. The dress she'd been wearing earlier lay thrown across her bed. He picked it up and, without thinking, brought it to his nose and breathed her in.

No, that connection was visceral, hard won. It was inseverable.

He dropped the dress back on the bed and looked around, reverting almost too easily to his mortal habit of assessing the safety of his surroundings. He walked to the window and looked out into an unusually well-lit night. Draupadi's house was very high off the ground, almost as if it were situated at the top of a hill. In fact, he would have thought it a hill if not for the similarly tall buildings that stood around, their windows twinkling and flashing with millions of those light bulbs he kept seeing around her apartment. There was no way anyone could climb into this window.

Turning, he walked around the room, pausing to open cupboards full of her clothes and peek inside the bathroom. What an amazing invention the bathroom was, he thought as he remembered his earlier visit to the one off the hallway. Mother had kindly explained the basics of it before she left with Narad Muni. Mortals really had made life very comfortable for themselves.

Resolving to wait for Draupadi to return to the room, he walked over and sat on the bed, absently fiddling with the furniture around it. Beside the bed was a large container of sorts, with two sliding compartments that one could pull out using a brass knob. He pulled the top one open and peered inside. White parchment with writing on it, odd-looking bits and bobs, and small bottles stared back at him. At the back of the compartment was a black, silken bag that was secured with a drawstring. He picked it up and pulled it open, taking out the object inside. His eyes widened in shock.

It was an unnatural replica of a man's phallus. And it was purple!

Disgust washed over Arjuna. His hands tightened on the contraption as he resisted the urge to tear it in half. He felt a small click under his thumb, and suddenly, the phallus started buzzing and shaking in his hand. Vigorously. Incredulous, he stared at it in shock. *This* was what his wife had been doing on earth?

Furious, he flung it across the room. It crashed against a wall and fell on the floor, still shuddering so forcefully that it began to move in slow circles. With a grunt of utter revulsion, Arjuna stood up to go find Draupadi.

He was going to take her back to heaven if it was the last thing he did.

Striding out of the room, and not bothering to be quiet this time, he began to search the house. He found her on a terrace off the sitting area. She was curled into a wooden armchair, her feet tucked into her body, her arms hugging her knees. Staring out at the myriad spots of light in the blackness, her expression was heart-rendingly sad.

Some of his anger immediately dissipated. No good would come of him barging out there and chastising her. He would talk. Calmly. Arjuna pushed and pulled gently at the terrace door but it didn't budge. Draupadi turned her head and saw him.

Sighing, she said, 'You have to slide, not push.'

He slid the glass door to the side, closed it behind him and took a seat next to her, realizing with a small start that this was his first time outside in the mortal world since he'd last been alive. Draupadi's home had been a comfortable temperature, the air cool and constant. Outside, suspended high over the ground as they were, the air felt hotter, heavier and noisier than he remembered. As if he were draped in a blanket of heated dust and there was a battle of out-of-tune instruments taking place nearby.

'You get used to it,' murmured Draupadi absently. 'The pollution, the noisy roads. Not being able to see the blue in the sky. Or stars.'

He glanced up at the sky. There were, indeed, no stars. Just murky blackness.

With a shrug, she continued, 'The mortals make it so that their homes are as insulated from the outside world as possible. Artificially cooled air, soundproof windows and tall fences with armed men to guard them.' She smiled. 'My neighbours, Mr and Mrs Shah, live a mere few paces away from my front door, but I don't know their first names. We've never spoken for more than the few moments it takes for the lift to take us to the ground.'

'Lift?'

She shook her head with a small smile. 'I'll explain tomorrow. Trust me, you're in for quite a ride.'

That statement unwittingly reminded him of the *thing* he had found next to her bed. Arjuna grimaced. Now was not the time.

Draupadi couldn't see his face well in the dark, so she kept going in a soft, husky voice. One would almost think she was talking to herself. 'Imagine living in a massive palace filled with strangers. Always surrounded, yet never seeking them out. That's what it's like living here. Mortals have stopped trusting each other. Instead, they're constantly rushing to do something, be somewhere. Anywhere except where they already are. Why? Because the next place must be better, because they believe it'll make them happier or richer or stronger or safer. Never have I seen such naked, unapologetic ambition in almost everybody. It's exhausting and exhilarating at the same time.'

Arjuna nodded with a small rumble of acknowledgement. 'What about you?'

'What about me?'

'Are you happy?'

She chuckled. 'Compared to what? My previous life or my long years in heaven? Yes, I'm happier than I was before.'

After a moment of silence, Arjuna spoke. 'But?'

Draupadi turned to look at him wistfully. 'What makes you think there's a but?'

He shrugged. 'You look sad.'

She sighed and said softly. 'It's been an emotional day.'

That was an understatement. 'I would think you'd be ecstatic to be free of us, given how much you've complained over the years, especially after we died on the mountain.'

Her eyebrow flew up. '*We* didn't die on the mountain. The five of you left me to die on that mountain. *Alone*.'

A low rumble of exasperation came from his throat. 'We each perished alone on that mountain, Draupadi. Well, all of us except Yudhishtra. It was a different time, and I've apologized on a million occasions since then.'

He really had. Decades after the Great War had ended, and they'd grown old and tired, Yudhishtra had established Arjuna and Subhadra's grandson, Parikshit, on the throne of Indraprastha, and left for the mountains to ascend to heaven with his brothers and Draupadi. On the way, Arjuna had thrown his beloved bow, Gandiva, into the sea, knowing he would never use it again and yet overcome by its loss. He had been so ready for death, so eager to be done with the mortal world, that when Draupadi had fallen to the ground, he'd thought her already dead. It was only later on, in heaven, that he had discovered she'd lain there alone, waiting for her demise in considerable anguish. He had been devastated and tried to make amends. But the damage had been done, with Draupadi refusing to continue her marital arrangement with the Pandavas in heaven. When Subhadra joined Arjuna a few years later, even his platonic conversations with Draupadi had tapered off. Only the guilt remained.

Draupadi acknowledged his words with a nod. 'I suppose so. And you're right, I wanted nothing to do with the five of you after that.' Her cat-like eyes bore into his, the lights in the distance reflected in the black of her irises. 'But just because I wanted to be free of you doesn't mean I didn't care about you. This is ... confusing. Kunti said I belong to myself now, which I *am* ecstatic about.' She chuckled without humour. 'But I went from my father's house straight to my husbands' house and then into heaven, where I was still considered wife to the Pandavas. This last year has passed by in such a rapid frenzy that I've barely given my marital status a second thought. And now, here you all are, in my bloody living room, telling me I'm free to belong to myself? I don't even fully understand what that means!'

Despite himself, he smiled ruefully. 'Neither do I. I've never belonged to myself either. When you figure it out, you must tell me what it feels like.'

Draupadi rolled her eyes, making him grin. God, how many times had he seen her do that. Now she'd say something cutting, send a verbal arrow straight to the centre of her target. She didn't disappoint as she muttered, 'That's rich, coming from a man! You always did exactly as you liked.'

Arjuna shook his head. 'Not true. Perhaps when it came to other women,' he chuckled when she rolled her eyes again, 'but I've been bound by duty more times than I can remember. Some I wish I could forget. You know that better than most, my love.'

She arched a sardonic eyebrow at the endearment. Then, after a moment, said, 'How's Subhadra?'

'She's well.'

'Of course. She always is. Pretty little agreeable Subhadra, who can't live without you. I'm surprised she let you come down here.'

'Stop it.'

'Stop what?'

'You know how important you are, have always been, to me. Just because I love Subhadra doesn't mean I love you less.'

She laughed a small, bitter laugh. 'So you've said many times, Arjuna. But I happen to believe in the kind of love you can't divide. It belongs to one and only one.'

It was his turn to raise his eyebrows. 'Coming from you …'

She glared at him. 'You may have forgotten, given it's been a while, but marrying all five of you was *not* my choice.'

He grumbled, 'Certainly wasn't mine.'

They both sat in silence for a while. Then she sighed and said, 'You can't just wish it all away.'

'No, you can't,' he whispered. Clearing his throat, he spoke in a low voice, 'Anyway, tell me about your life now.'

Draupadi looked away, towards the lights. She smiled to herself. 'I have a profession.'

'I heard. As a performer.'

She laughed. 'It is a performance of sorts, but I don't act or play a character. I speak to people and find out about their problems. Then I try and advocate for those problems to be fixed.'

'Sounds very interesting. Maybe you'll take me along to watch one day.'

She turned towards him with an excited grin that took his breath away. 'Really? I'd love to show you. You know, I'm actually a little famous,' she said, almost coy in her tone.

He grinned back. 'Really?'

She giggled, something he hadn't heard her do for thousands of years. 'Really! People follow me around and ask to take pictures with me.'

'Pictures?'

She waved her hand. 'I'll explain later.'

He nodded, leaning forward. 'Tell me more.'

'Well, almost everyone in the city knows who I am, I get treated with a lot of respect, and people want to give me things for free all the time. It's fun.' Then her expression darkened slightly. 'At least, it was in the beginning. People either love you or they hate you—there's no in-between. Everyone has an opinion and everyone champions that opinion as if their life depends on it, but no one wants to listen to what anyone else has to say. It's become a divided world, and people like me get caught in the middle. I'm just trying to do my best every day. Help those who need help and stay out of trouble.' She paused. 'Although, trouble kind of finds me these days.'

'What do you mean?'

Draupadi hesitated for a moment, but then said, 'There's this man. He's been following me around. Keeps sending messages and pictures to my phone from different numbers, so I can't even block him. I've told the security guards not to allow him into the building, but the other day, he bribed one of them into giving him my apartment number, slipped past the gate and rang my doorbell. Luckily, I saw him through the peephole and called security. Now they don't let him in anymore, but I still see him hanging around outside the gate sometimes.' She sighed. 'I might have to get a bodyguard at some point.'

Arjuna didn't understand many of the things she'd said, but he got the gist of it. She was in danger and had no one to protect her. He wanted to rip that man's limbs out. All the more reason to take her back to heaven, where he and his brothers could keep an eye on her. After all, she'd just admitted that the novelty of mortal life had worn off. It was the right thing to do and he was sure Krishna would agree with him.

He took a deep, calming breath. 'How about, just for the time being, I become your bodyguard?'

Her brow furrowed. 'Don't you want to enjoy your holiday here?'

'I can do both.'

Draupadi gave him a side glance and appeared thoughtful for a few moments before a smile broke through. 'Old habits die hard. All right, for the time being.'

'Good.'

She chuckled. 'I suppose there still are some advantages to having a man around the house.'

He pictured that revolting purple phallus spinning on the floor again. 'Obviously not enough,' he muttered.

'What's that supposed to mean?'

Arjuna couldn't hold back anymore. 'You have a purple *penis* in your bedchambers!'

She looked confused for a moment, but then her eyes widened. 'Oh, that. Angela gave it to me as a gift. I forgot I still had it. Should probably lock that thing in my cupboard—the woman who cleans my house is very nosy.' Then she scowled. 'Why were you looking through my bedroom?' she asked sternly.

He gritted his teeth. 'I'm sorry, I was combing the room from habit. Please tell me you don't ... you know ...' He couldn't bring himself to say it.

She glared at him, her voice rising in anger. 'Why? Does it matter? You and your brothers can cavort with woman after woman, without a second thought, but the minute I get something for myself, I have to answer to you for it?'

'But—'

'No buts!' she snapped, uncurling her legs and standing up. She walked up to him, leaned down and levelled her face with his. 'You have a plethora of nymphs and your precious Subhadra to keep you satisfied. What I do for my own satisfaction is my business!'

He stood up, towering over her, compelling her to take a few steps back. 'If you're unsatisfied, my love, there is plenty I can do about that.'

'Don't call me that!' she shouted.

'I will because it's true!' He was equally incensed now.

'No, it's not!' She pushed away an offending lock of hair that had fallen over her eyes as they locked in a battle of wills. 'If you loved me, Arjuna, you would've fought for me—after the swayamwara, during the dice game, when that villain disrobed me in court, before you abandoned me for twelve years and then again on the mountain. Before you replaced me with Subhadra! Time and time again you showed me that you loved everyone else first, and now you're jealous of a stupid toy?'

'Jealous! Why should I be jealous?' he roared. 'Given all the other men I've had to share you with, believe me, this is nothing new!'

Draupadi's hand struck his cheek with as much force as she could muster. Breathing heavily, they both stared at each other with furious eyes for a long moment.

Then she turned around and walked away.

Before she left the terrace, he said in an aggravated voice, 'This doesn't change the bodyguard thing.'

'Go to hell!' She slammed the door behind her.

Despite his utter exasperation, he raised his gaze heavenwards and laughed. When was the last time a woman had cursed him to hell and stormed off?

He couldn't remember.

5

The gooey, greyish blob of coagulated vegetables slumped off the ladle on to Arjuna's metal plate with a *thwack* that sent bits of it flying everywhere. He blinked at it for a moment before politely enquiring, 'What is it?'

Bhima poked at the blob on his own plate with a spoon, eyeing it with an apprehensive grimace. 'Why is it this colour? Did you mix it with ash?'

'*Just eat it!*' A haggard, dishevelled-looking Narad Muni screeched at them as he scooped up another grey blob and angrily catapulted it on to Sahadeva's plate. His shirt and trousers were wrinkled and smelly from sweat, kitchen fumes and overnight wear. His long hair, usually immaculately styled on the top of his head in a bun, was well on its way to becoming the stringy, matted locks of an Aghori mendicant. 'Hundreds of thousands of years I've served the gods, without a single word of complaint, and *this* is how they reward me? I am *perspiring*! Do you know how disgusting it is to perspire?

And to make me labour like a common servant? Not a *wink* of sleep did I get last night on that flimsy excuse of a charpai! Not an *ounce* of help did I get from any one of those useless brats who were assigned to assist me in the kitchen this morning!'

He whirled around and pointed his ladle at the Pandavas as if it were a sword. 'If you want palace food around here, you'll just have to cook it yourselves!' The last words were punctuated by a welling up of his eyes as he struggled against bursting into hysterical tears.

Kunti put her hands up placatingly. Seated at the head of a table in the orphanage's common room, she gamely began to mix her own vegetable slop with the hard, charred triangle of undercooked rice on her plate. 'This is very nice, O Narad Muni. We are grateful for your tireless efforts to feed the innocent children of our humble home.'

'Inno ... *innocent?*' Narad Muni sputtered, not in the least bit conciliated. 'Demon spawn would be more accurate. Just wait till I get back up there. I'm going to make the gods give all of them lice!' Overcome, he released a distraught whimper before wobbling out of the room, the pot of sludge tipping dangerously to the side under one arm.

Yudhishtra scooped up a small serving of his lunch with a spoon and asked his mother, 'What was that about?' He put the spoonful in his mouth, gagged and promptly spat it out on his plate, his face a study in revulsion.

Kunti put her own spoon down, abandoning any pretence of eating now that Narad Muni was gone. 'The children didn't like the lunch he cooked.' She pointed at their plates. 'They refused to eat it; some made rude comments. A few threw their food at him, and I believe a group of the older ones got together and stuffed their share into his pillow. I'm trying to identify them.'

'I don't blame the children,' said Bhima, who had always been very particular about food. 'This is terrible!' His stomach rumbled loudly and he put a hand on it. 'Not exactly the first meal a man wants to have after not eating for thousands of years.'

Yudhishtra exhaled deeply. 'Well, normally I would say we should be grateful for any sustenance at all and should be detached from the taste, but that was truly inedible.'

Arjuna looked at Kunti. 'If the children didn't eat their food then aren't they still hungry? It's past mealtime.' They'd been in the orphanage since late morning, after Draupadi had given them a short tour of the city in her car, an automated chariot that she drove herself, and then handed them some local currency before leaving for work. The brothers had been amazed to see the sheer size and scale of the city, in the short moments when the car had been stationary and they weren't worrying for their lives. Things grew even more treacherous when Yudhishtra made a comment about women drivers and Draupadi flew into a temper. She'd displayed a dangerous degree of recklessness after that.

Kunti answered his question with worried eyes. 'I ordered in some food and they ate in their rooms to spare his feelings. But I don't know what we're going to do about the evening meal. I already sent the regular cook home for a holiday this morning because I thought Narad Muni would take over. He hadn't visited his village in over a year!'

Bhima shook his head and pushed his chair back. 'This is unacceptable. I cannot sit back and let my mother live like this for the next twenty-nine days! Where is Krishna?'

Kunti frowned. 'Why?'

Bhima began pacing the room. 'He told us to stay with Draupadi, but we need to readdress that plan. We should move here so I can cook for you and the children. Where is he?'

Kunti shook her head. 'I have no way of speaking with Krishna, my son. The gods don't address mortals anymore. But I do have an idol of him in my room. Last year, he addressed us through an idol in a temple, so maybe you could try that?'

Bhima nodded grimly. All of them walked over to Kunti's room. It was a modest space, with a single bed and a small table with a chair in front of it. A face mirror was the only adornment on the wall. Perched on the table was a palm-sized idol of Krishna with a single fresh flower in front of it.

Kunti and four of her sons squeezed into the back of the room, while Bhima bent down and addressed the idol. 'O Krishna, my god and brother, we need to speak with you.' He looked at the idol expectantly.

Nothing happened.

'Krishna, can you hear me? This is an urgent matter requiring your attention. Narad Muni can't cook.' Bhima shook his head with worry. 'I know your instructions were that we reside with Draupadi, but we must ask permission to relocate to Mother's orphanage so I can help with the cooking.' He waited.

The vacant smile on the idol's face stared back at him, unmoving.

Bhima said in a stern voice, 'Krishna, this is no time for fun and games!' He nudged the idol's feet with his finger, pushing it back slightly. 'What's the matter with you? Speak!'

Still nothing.

Annoyed, Bhima straightened up and turned to his brothers. 'It's not working!'

'Maybe we need to do a tapasya,' suggested Sahadeva.

Nakula raised an eyebrow. 'Before dinner?'

Bhima turned around and spoke to the idol again, this time in a voice that had frightened many a demon into hiding, 'All right, enough fooling around. We need to make a decision, Krishna. What do we do?'

The only sounds around them were from the street outside.

'Maybe,' Arjuna said softly, 'he wants us to make the decision ourselves.'

Yudhishtra frowned. 'Or maybe he has delegated authority to me. Bhima,' he turned to his younger brother, 'I think we should stick to our original plan. Perhaps you can come over in the mornings to cook.'

Bhima narrowed his eyes and looked at Arjuna, who frowned back at him. Then, he did something he hadn't done in a very long time. He refused Yudhishtra. 'No. If that old man is the only caretaker this place has, they will need me around the clock. I will move here by myself, Brother.'

Yudhishtra's eyes widened. His brothers always deferred to his judgment. He tried again, 'Bhima, perhaps you didn't understand why I said what I did.'

Bhima squared his shoulders, crossed his bulky arms and looked down at Yudhishtra from his imposing height. 'I understand perfectly. You want us to stick together because of safety concerns. Respectfully, my brother, I think we are no longer in any mortal danger and are each grown men, capable of fending for ourselves. Also,' he looked at Kunti, 'as Mother and Draupadi said last night, that part of our existence is over. I bow to your seniority as my elder, but I must do what I think is right. I will move here by myself.'

Silence screamed inside the room as Yudhishtra stared at Bhima in shock. But, before anyone could think of anything to say to diffuse the situation, there was a soft knock on the door.

A man in his late twenties, small and clean-shaven, with a mop of neatly combed, oiled hair and a striped shirt, leaned inside and smiled at Kunti. With the easy assurance of someone who is used to leading others, he asked, 'Kuntiben, I hope I'm not disturbing you?'

Startled by the interruption, Kunti gave him a flustered half-smile as she looked between the man and her sons for a moment. Then she replied in an awkward voice, 'Not at all, Amitji. Please make yourself comfortable in the common room. We will be there shortly.'

Amit completely disregarded her request. Instead, he leaned in further, examining the five young men standing in her bedroom with intense curiosity. 'Who are these gentlemen?' His body hovered, half-in and half-out of Kunti's door.

Kunti's eyes flashed with irritation, but she quickly smiled again. 'These are my sons. We will be in the common room shortly, Amitji.'

It was obvious that Amit was extremely reluctant to leave, but he replied, 'Of course. I will go there and wait for you. I hope to meet your sons too,' he added in a polite but authoritative voice.

Kunti nodded, waited for him to leave and then sighed, loudly. She turned to the Pandava brothers. 'We'll have to discuss this later. That's Amit Sharma, head of the Bhartiya Youth of Bharat Mata Centre. They've just made a large donation to the orphanage so we need to treat him with respect.'

The brothers nodded and followed her back to the common room, where their forgotten plates and globs of food were being carefully inspected by Amit. He quickly masked his look of distaste as Kunti walked into the room. Gesturing for her to be seated, as if it were his home and not hers, he said, 'I was just wondering what you all were eating for lunch.' He left the statement hanging in the air, making it obvious that he expected a reply.

Kunti sat down and answered in a wry tone, 'Yes, it's a new cook today.'

No one said anything for a while. Then Amit's eyes shifted again towards the food and back to Kunti. He looked perturbed as he asked again, 'What is it? I know there is rice, but the other thing is difficult to make out.'

She shrugged. 'We're trying to figure it out ourselves.'

'Is it vegetarian?'

Confused, Kunti nodded. 'Must be. I haven't tasted it yet so I'm not sure.'

Amit frowned. 'Do you usually serve non-vegetarian food here?'

Kunti looked wry again. 'Amitji, I'm sure you must know that we are on a strict budget and meat is expensive. We try to give the children meals that are as nutritious as possible within our limited funds.'

The clouds cleared from Amit's face, and he smiled again. 'Good, good. Vegetarian food is much healthier for them. As you know, we at the BYBM Centre are ideological warriors, who believe in bringing our glorious, *native* values, like vegetarianism, back to the country. Hundreds of years of invasions have made not only our diet but also our culture weak with dilution. So much so that our traditional way of life, the natural order of things, is in grave danger of being lost forever. All these nightclubs, girls wearing short skirts and jeans, people eating burgers, chow mein and biryani,' he shook his head sadly, 'these are foreign, un-Vedic customs. Best to stick to wholesome, vegetarian fare, like our ancestors did in the Dwaparyug, the age of purity, of spirituality, of order. A pure body leads to a pure mind, no?'

Kunti gritted her teeth and forced herself to nod even as her sons looked at each other in bafflement. What was this man talking about? They had lived during the Dwaparyug, and the only times they'd ever been vegetarian were when they were fasting or conducting religious austerities. The rest of the time, they had enjoyed eating a variety of meats. In fact, some of their best memories of exile in the forest involved hunting deer, fowl and wild pig, and then returning to camp to roast it with spices over an open fire or simmer it in a pot, before ladling it over rice that Draupadi would cook in the Akshaypatra, a magical pot that never ran out of rice. When there was no occasion to hunt, the occasional buffalo or gayal would keep their entire entourage fed for days. Yes, there were small sects of people who didn't eat meat, but the vast majority, from brahmans to mendicants, ate and enjoyed animal flesh. There was nothing native or Vedic about being vegetarian.

Bhima cleared his throat to point this out, but Kunti, pre-empting his words, spoke instead, 'Amitji, what brings you here today?'

Amit waved offhandedly. 'Just a friendly visit, Kuntiben. Now that our centre has been established in the neighbourhood, we consider it our responsibility to watch out for our neighbours. Check if they are having any problems.'

'That's very kind of you. Things are fine here, not to worry.'

Amit turned to the Pandava brothers. 'They must be, now that your sons have joined you. You mentioned your daughters the first time we met, but you never mentioned you had sons as well.'

Flustered, Kunti replied evasively, 'I must have been preoccupied. These are my sons.' She waved in the general direction of the Pandavas, hoping it would satisfy him enough to facilitate his departure.

No such luck. Amit folded his hands and addressed them directly. 'I am Amit Sharma, from Ayodhya. I'm the head sevak at the Bhartiya Youth of Bharat Mata Centre. We are involved in charity works and mobilizing of local youth for the betterment of our nation.' He smiled. 'Your good names?'

There was moment of indecision, during which Kunti considered making up less conspicuous names for her sons. However, Yudhishtra, unable to lie as usual, answered first, 'I am Yudhishtra, and these are my younger brothers—Bhima, Arjuna, Nakula and Sahadeva.'

Kunti groaned softly, but Amit's face lit up with joy. He beamed as he said, 'A pleasure to meet you. To be named after the great Pandavas from the most significant part of our history, the Mahabharata, is an honour of the highest distinction. You even look like them!' He turned to Kunti. 'What impeccable planning! Kudos to you and your husband.' He gave her a little, inappropriate applause.

Yudhishtra smiled and said in a benevolent voice, 'We don't just look like them, my good man.'

Kunti and Arjuna both cleared their throats loudly, but Yudhishtra continued, completely oblivious to their frantic signalling. 'We are indeed the original Pandava brothers, returned from heaven and restored to our mortal bodies. Just yesterday.'

A hearty laugh was Amit's immediate response, followed by surprise that Yudhishtra was frowning disapprovingly at his mirth. 'Oh, you're serious,' he muttered awkwardly. He looked at the tense faces around him for some kind of clarity, but none was forthcoming. Kunti clutched her forehead, and the rest of the brothers were scrutinizing their feet studiously.

Amit Sharma appeared brooding for a moment before a look of calculated reverence crossed his face. He folded his hands and said to Yudhishtra in a voice better suited to a stage, 'In that case, I am truly blessed to welcome you to earth. Sons of gods, truest of warriors and the most revered kings of Bharat Mata!' He bowed deeply and continued, 'Allow me to be your guide. I am an expert on the Mahabharata. I have watched the entire TV serial seven times!'

Arjuna shifted uncomfortably. The man's tone reeked of insincerity, but Yudhishtra couldn't hear it. His elder brother was a wise and principled man, but when it came to the ways of the world, he usually erred on the side of trust rather than suspicion. His unfailing faith in humanity had shaped all of their mortal lives, and not always in a good way.

Amit then fell at Yudhishtra's feet. 'O great emperor Yudhishtra, Dharmaputra, bravest of the brave, wisest of the wise, allow me to introduce you to the youth at my centre, so you can awe and inspire them with your insight and advice.'

Yudhishtra's chest expanded, and he stood a little taller, never happier than when someone acknowledged his position and prominence. It was something he had missed sorely in heaven, where former mortals were nearer the bottom than the top of the social hierarchy. He looked down at Amit and blessed him by putting a hand on his head. 'Stand, Amit Sharma. You may do so.'

Amit smiled almost triumphantly and stood up, smoothing a lock of his carefully combed hair back into place. 'Excellent! Actually, we're having a talk in about an hour. An MP from Bihar is visiting the centre and speaking to the members. I'm sure he would be happy to give up his place to you.'

Yudhishtra bent his head politely. 'I wouldn't want to inconvenience him.'

Amit chuckled and waved his hand with a small sneer. 'Don't worry about that. He's a hopper from the Opposition who still hasn't managed to get an appointment with the party president. He'll be in town for a while, so there's no hurry. We can leave together now. I have a car parked outside.'

Yudhishtra had no idea what most of those words meant but he nodded. 'Very well. I—'

'Son!' Kunti's voice was agitated but firm. 'We still need to have that discussion, remember?'

She turned to Amit and said with an uncomfortable smile, 'Family matters. Perhaps he can visit your centre another time.'

Yudhishtra gave Bhima an annoyed look before saying, 'Yes, but I thought our *discussion* was already concluded.'

'Still, I would like to spend a few more minutes on it.' Kunti refused to be put off. 'Perhaps Amitji can wait in his car for a short while?'

Amit bowed to Kunti, the reverence on his face decidedly less emphatic than it had been for Yudhishtra. 'Of course, Kunti Ma. Your word is always final, as we know. I will wait in the car.' He walked out slowly and shut the door behind him.

Arjuna held up his hand to ensure no one spoke. After a few moments, he instructed Nakula and Sahadeva to shut all the windows and walked to the door to check that the hallway outside was empty. Finally, when he was certain their conversation couldn't be overheard, he turned to the others and said softly, 'I don't trust that man.'

Nakula scratched his chin, frowning. 'I agree. There's something off about him.'

Kunti nodded. 'Yudhishtra, I don't think you should go with him.'

Sahadeva said quietly, 'Me neither.'

Unused to his actions being challenged, especially by everyone collectively, Yudhishtra got a mulish look on his face. He said through gritted teeth, 'Well, that's a surprise. I thought since we decided to disown our wife, go our separate ways and completely disregard each other's sentiments, that I was free to do as I liked.'

Bhima, still defensive about his decision to stay at the orphanage against his brother's advice, replied in an angry voice, 'Letting Draupadi go was not our choice, and I'm moving here because Mother needs me!'

Arjuna put a steadying hand on Bhima's shoulder to stay his quick temper. He spoke to Yudhishtra, 'The three situations are different, Brother. We don't know anything about this man. He was too quick to believe that we are the real Pandavas, and his manner seemed suspicious. Besides, Krishna told us not to get involved in the mortals' lives, remember?'

Lifting his brow, Yudhishtra said in a voice that held all the hauteur of a king, 'Krishna also told us to stay together, but we're already disregarding his instructions on our first day here. It is *Bhima* who has decided to get involved in mortal lives, not me. Besides, a simple talk with a few mortals hardly constitutes involvement, or mortal danger. This man, Amit Sharma, seems to be the only one in this room who values my opinion. So he shall have it!'

Arjuna grimaced and put an apologetic hand on his chest. 'Brother, I'm sorry. The last thing I want to do is offend or hurt your sentiments. We value your opinion more than any other. Please, let's just spend time with Mother and Draupadi, and focus on the reason we came here.'

After a moment of thought, Yudhishtra looked at Bhima. 'Does that mean you will reconsider your decision?'

Bhima crossed his muscular arms over his chest, his jaw clenched. 'No.'

Yudhishtra set his jaw too. 'Fine. Then neither will I. Excuse me, Mother.'

He bowed to Kunti, turned and left the room.

6

It was early evening before they finally arrived at Draupadi's place of work. Kunti had been distraught after Yudhishtra left, but after some reasoning and persuasion, she had accompanied Bhima to the kitchens to help him get organized before the evening meal. Then, she'd taken Arjuna, Nakula and Sahadeva to a nearby shop and used the currency Draupadi had provided to buy them all more suitable, up-to-date clothing. Walking around in oversized, outdated clothes would only make them more conspicuous.

Arjuna shifted uncomfortably in the tight, dark blue garment that hugged his lower body unforgivingly. His hand crept to its front for the hundredth time to try and discreetly adjust himself in a way that didn't press or chafe against the stiff fabric. No such luck. His private parts were firmly incarcerated in an unyielding, airless, blistering prison of dense cloth that the man in the shop had called 'slim-fit jeans'. Arjuna shook his head with a frustrated grunt. It was a wonder that mortal men could still impregnate their women.

Nakula obviously felt the same way. He shimmied his hips a little and said, 'They must have balls of brass these days.'

'How on earth do they keep from sweating profusely?' asked Sahadeva, looking equally discomfited.

None of them had an answer to that.

The three brothers walked stoically down the road towards the building that housed Draupadi's place of work. The road itself was a grim canal of stone, metal, flesh, fumes and assorted debris. A mass of both human and animal bodies weaved around on its sides while a mass of vehicles, emitting a mind-numbing cacophony of sound, weaved precariously around each other at its centre. Heat and dust completed the setting to present a potent picture of the Kalyug in action.

Arjuna looked at the tall buildings surrounding him as they walked. While there were a lot of them, they all looked the same. Giant, box-shaped beehives in assorted mud colours. Once in a while, they'd walk by a metal monstrosity, but for the most part, none of these modern buildings displayed any of the colour, lightness or passion that the people of his own time had poured into their structures. He remembered the palace they built when Yudhishtra had ruled Indraprastha. It had been covered in adornment and was a veritable rainbow of hues. Its striking façade transformed with the movements of the sun and moon, and its playful interior told a different story in each of its chambers. An inanimate edifice of elements that felt alive.

He stopped at a street vendor and showed him a piece of parchment that had Draupadi's office address written on it. 'Do you know where this building is?'

The vendor, standing behind a large pot that looked like it was filled with pond water that had been stagnant for a few years, barely glanced at the parchment before waving them further down the road. 'Go straight.'

'For how long?'

He scratched his crotch and replied irritably, 'Do I look like a map to you? Just keep walking.'

Normally, Arjuna would have been put off by such rudeness. He might even have tried to give the impertinent young man a piece of his mind. But, glancing down at the man scraping the fabric of his jeans with his fingernails, he felt a strong affinity for the vendor's predicament. Arjuna felt itchy down there too!

After meandering through the streets and regularly stopping to ask for directions, most of which were completely contradictory, they finally arrived at the correct address. It was one of the tallest and newest-looking buildings in the area, and Arjuna felt a slight rush of anticipation. They could probably get a bird's-eye view of Indraprastha from the top.

Pressing the button for the twenty-fifth floor on the lift, Arjuna marvelled at the glass container that lifted them with such precise and constant changes of speed that they barely felt its movement. No wonder Draupadi liked living and working so far up from the ground. She got to ride in these every day.

He thought about their conversation last night. He shouldn't have lost his temper. God knows she'd suffered enough because of his anger and guilt over their marital arrangement. It was one of his biggest regrets and also the reason he had kept her at a distance in heaven.

Arjuna sighed. No more discussions about the past, he resolved. No questioning her choices either. He would be supportive and give her all the space she needed.

Before he convinced her to come back to heaven.

They walked into a brightly coloured hall where dozens of people were hurrying around as if there were a fire somewhere. Arjuna walked up to one of them, a woman who was rushing past with a harried look on her face. She was wearing slim-fit jeans too.

'Where can I find Draupadi?' he asked, in a voice loud enough to stop the woman in her tracks.

The woman looked at him with a grimace of confusion, as if she had just stepped out of a trance. Then she mumbled, 'Reception,' pointed at a large counter with the letters 'NPTV' carved on it and hurried away.

Arjuna walked up to the counter. Behind it were two people, a woman and a man, with some sort of apparatus attached to their heads. They were both talking to themselves.

'Where can I find Draupadi?' Arjuna asked the man.

The man put a wiry finger up in front of his thin, bearded face, indicating that Arjuna should wait for him to finish. Then he continued talking into the air. Arjuna turned to exchange a look with his younger brothers, both of whom were staring at the man and his outstretched finger as if he were insane.

Finally, after a few tense moments, the man looked up and spoke in a bored voice with an irritated look on his face, 'Can I help you?'

After the morning fiasco at the orphanage and the run around he'd been given by people on the streets, who really shouldn't have given him directions when they didn't know any better, Arjuna was rapidly losing his patience with the mortals. 'Where can I find Draupadi?' he asked in the commanding voice he used with his soldiers.

The man behind the counter was unfazed. He looked at Arjuna with barely disguised contempt, as if to question his right to be told where Draupadi was. 'Who are you?'

'Her husband.'

Everyone in the hall froze, turned around and stared at him, their eyes wide with shock. Arjuna groaned inwardly. He probably shouldn't have said that, but the man's impudence had gotten to him. Draupadi would be spitting mad with him. Even more than she already was.

He looked around at the dozens of eyes that were gaping at him from around the hall and said, 'I meant, I'm a friend,' knowing it would be completely pointless. The damage had been done.

A young woman stepped up to him and asked softly, 'Are you really Draupadi's husband?'

Arjuna shrugged. 'I used to be. Not anymore.'

'Wow,' she said. 'I can't imagine Draupadi being married. Anyway, she's shooting promos right now. I'll take you to her.'

They followed her through hallways and even more busy, rushing people, until they got to a darkened room with metallic contraptions lying everywhere. All the light in the room was focused on one spot. And in the centre of that spot stood Draupadi. She was dressed in a tight-fitting, bright red dress that skimmed the tops of her breasts, and showcased her long legs and flawless curves. Her lips were the same colour as her dress, and her hair was lightly moving with the wind caused by a small contraption on the floor in front of her. Arjuna inhaled sharply as he watched her speak to a group of people whose faces were obscured by the dark. Last night, when he had first beheld her with all the face-paint on, he'd been distracted and confused. But now, under all this light, with her hair and her dress and her lips ... She was breathtaking.

'Watch me on *Us, The Women* at 9.30 p.m. every Friday on NPTV. Let's forge a better future for everyone.' Draupadi smiled confidently into the darkness.

Someone shouted, 'Cut,' and she dropped her smile immediately, replacing it with a scowl. She shook her head and said, 'I can do better.'

A female voice spoke out of the darkness, 'Try it with less angry and sexier.'

Draupadi's scowl deepened as she snapped at the voice. 'I'm a talk show host, Angela, not a film actress. My job is not to be sexy, but to talk about the issues.'

Angela's reply rang with sarcasm, 'Your job is to make people listen to you. I don't make the prime-time ratings rules, babe. In an ideal world, the way you look shouldn't matter, but if men in this country need to get off on your pretty package while you educate them about serious stuff, then that's what we'll give them. Okay?'

Draupadi set her jaw and muttered, 'Fine.'

Angela's voice turned softer, 'Hey, babe, remember why we do this. It's about the women out there.'

Draupadi nodded, twin looks of resignation and resolution on her face.

'Let's go for another take. Rolling ... action!'

Draupadi smiled and tilted her head. 'Watch me on *Us, The Women* at 9.30 p.m. every Friday on NPTV. Let's forge a better future for everyone.' She lowered her chin and smouldered into the darkness.

'Cut! Perfect. Break for twenty everyone!'

The young woman who had led them in leaned back and whispered, 'You can go talk to her now.' She gestured Arjuna towards Draupadi with a hungry look of anticipation.

Arjuna didn't really want an audience for his conversation with Draupadi, especially after the husband debacle, but he stepped forward and said, 'Draupadi,' in a low voice.

Draupadi started and looked towards him. For the tiniest moment, she hesitated, but then she pulled a black string-like contraption out of her dress and walked towards Arjuna. She glared at him briefly, as if to inform him that she was still angry but was going to let it go temporarily for the sake of propriety. He hadn't expected any differently.

She smiled at all three of them. 'I'm glad you all could visit. Come, let me introduce you to my producer.'

'I'm right here,' said a small woman as she walked up to them. Dressed in jeans that were far tighter than 'slim fit' and an even tighter tube of pink cloth across her breasts, she looked like she was in her thirties, and was very pretty. She looked up at the three men, and her expression became a mix between amused and flirtatious. 'Well, well, what do we have here?'

Draupadi shook her head in amusement. 'This,' she pointed at Angela, 'is my producer and friend, Angela. A year ago, she convinced me to stay in Delhi and join NPTV.'

Angela was considerably shorter than Draupadi, but she gazed up at her in an almost maternal way, with a blend of affection and pride. 'Ah, yes, I discovered our girl here when she stumbled into my studio. She's one of a kind.' Smiling roguishly up at the three men, she gushed, 'You have *no* idea how happy I am to meet you. I didn't think she even knew men existed before today.'

Rolling her eyes, Draupadi said, 'These are my friends—Arjuna, Nakula and Sahadeva. From the ashram.' She shot a pointed stare at her husbands, verifying whether Kunti had explained the ashram story to them before they left the orphanage.

Arjuna nodded. This morning, Kunti had told them to tell mortals they had grown up in a forest ashram near a small town called Indrapur, where modern amenities weren't available. It was easier than telling them about heaven and wouldn't lead to doubts about their mental stability. Her explanation had, unfortunately, come *after* Yudhishtra had revealed all to Amit Sharma and then stormed off. Not that Yudhishtra would've adopted the story anyway—his brother's ideas about truth were set in stone, and lying, of any kind, was unthinkable.

Now it was Angela's turn to roll her eyes. 'Seriously, this ashram of yours, was it like a Mahabharata-themed place or something?'

Draupadi cleared her throat tersely. 'Something like that.'

Angela got that mischievous look again. 'So what, are you married to these guys? Mahabharata-style.'

'No, no, nothing like that,' replied Draupadi, shifting uncomfortably. 'They're just friends, visiting Delhi.'

'He said he's your husband!'

The eager declaration came from the woman who had escorted them from the entrance hall. She'd been standing behind them all this while.

Draupadi turned to her. 'What?' she asked in an ominously low voice.

The woman visibly shrank, but squeaked, 'At the reception. He,' she pointed at Arjuna as if he were a criminal, 'told Ravi that he was your husband. Everyone there heard it.'

Arjuna brought his hands up defensively and said to Draupadi, 'I only said that because the man wasn't going to let us in to see you.'

Draupadi's eyes blazed at him, but to his utter astonishment, she took a deep breath and looked away, towards Angela, with a small, wry smile. 'Remind me to tell Ravi not to let in every guy who says he's married to me,' she quipped.

To say that Arjuna was surprised would be the understatement of the century. In the past, Draupadi would have exploded in a fit of temper and probably charged at him. 'My mistake,' he added with a smile. To Angela, he said, 'We're just family friends from the ashram. So, what is your show about?'

Angela was gazing up at Nakula, who had been unable to keep his eyes off her from the moment she'd walked up to them. She didn't look at Arjuna when she answered. 'I'll let Draupadi tell you about it. You,' she held out a flirtatious hand to Nakula, 'are very handsome.'

He was. Well-built, with chiselled features and generously-lashed eyes, Nakula was easily the most handsome of the brothers, and he regularly used that to his advantage with women. He took Angela's hand, holding it lightly in his own as he smiled back at her and replied, 'And you are very beautiful.'

Angela grinned. 'It's a pity I have to get back to work because I would've loved to see where that conversation goes over a cup of coffee. In fact, if our girl Draupadi is anything to go by, I'll bet you've never even tasted coffee before. But alas, not now. Tell me, are you free this Saturday?'

Draupadi groaned.

Angela put up her other hand, the one that wasn't holding Nakula's, to silence Draupadi before she could say a word. If Arjuna was astonished before, he was completely flabbergasted when, instead of swatting Angela's bossy hand away and telling her off, Draupadi actually kept quiet. This past year had obviously mellowed her.

Angela asked Nakula again, 'Are you free this Saturday?'

It said something about how taken Nakula was with her that he didn't look at his brothers before he said, 'I am.'

Sahadeva frowned at him. 'Actually—'

'Great!' Angela bounced briefly on her toes in a girlish show of eagerness. She turned to Draupadi. 'There's a music festival at the race track this weekend, and Indus Ocean is performing on Saturday night. I have an unlimited number of VIP tickets, of course.'

Draupadi shook her head with a pained look. 'Of course.'

'You will come, as my guests. All of you, including you, Miss Kuru. We will keep the paparazzi at bay, don't worry.' She reached up and affectionately pulled a lock of Draupadi's hair. 'Say yes, babe.'

'Angela …'

'Say yes.'

'Fine, yes,' mumbled Draupadi with a huff.

Angela turned to Arjuna, who'd been gaping, slack-jawed, at Draupadi, and smiled a sly smile. 'Perfect.'

7

It had been perfect until they started asking questions.

Yudhishtra had gotten into the car with Amit Sharma and driven the short distance to the BYBM Centre, a new building that featured a field with chalk drawings on the ground, classrooms, a shop of sorts, an indoor sports area, canteen and a large hall. Portraits of elderly men, and colourful depictions of gods and their avatars hung in the sparse hallways. Milling around were an inordinate number of young men with seemingly no other objective than to lounge on every available surface, talking to each other and giggling.

Yudhishtra pursed his lips as he ran a disapproving eye over the youths of the centre. In his day, if you were old enough to grow a beard, you had an occupation and a family to keep you busy. At no point in his own mortal life had he been without some purpose, or just sat around doing nothing but gossiping in the middle of the day.

Which was why, when Amit Sharma introduced him to a gathering of the same young men in the large hall as the avatar of the great Pandava Yudhishtra, from the Mahabharata, he decided to talk about the importance of finding a purpose in life.

'Every man has a path that he must follow for collective destiny to be realized,' he'd said to the gathering. 'The ideal path, the most dharmic path, for men of your age is one of grihastha. Work for the betterment of your society in your prescribed profession. If your father was a farmer, till the land. If your father was a soldier, fight for your motherland. Take a wife and beget sons who will carry on your good name. Earn a living that will provide enough for your family, but will leave enough for everyone else. Be sure to give alms to the poor, conduct religious ceremonies for the gods and, most importantly, care for your aged parents. These are the tenets of our great scriptures.'

He'd gone on to talk more about the scriptures, and the principles of dharma in great detail and for a lengthy amount of time, slowly drawing in not only more young men but also the occupants of the nearby street and neighbouring buildings, until the large hall was crowded with people of all ages, listening carefully to his soul-stirring voice.

Yudhishtra had never been a natural orator, but time and practice had taught him how to deliver a speech that inspired a crowded marketplace or impassioned a fretful army. In heaven, where he had been reduced to a subject instead of a monarch, there had been no opportunity for him to mesmerize people with his carefully modulated words, to have people looking up at him as if he was their saviour, to feel worthy. Now, gazing down at the rapt expressions on the faces of his audience, he felt powerful in a way he hadn't felt for millennia.

It was like coming home.

Amit Sharma stood behind him the entire time, carefully watching the scene unfold. Had Yudhishtra looked back at him, he would have probably noticed the shrewd look of a man who was busy making plans, but he didn't.

After a while, his throat began to feel a bit parched, a sensation that Yudhishtra hadn't felt since he was last a mortal. He stopped talking, turned to Amit and signalled for some water, but in the moment it took for him to do that, a hand went up in the audience. Seeing it, other audience members also started putting their hands up in the air. Yudhishtra thought it was some kind of new way to show one's support until Amit spoke from behind him. Folding his hands and bowing dramatically, he said, 'O great Yudhishtra, your disciples would like you to do a question and answer session.'

Yudhishtra frowned. No one had ever dared to ask him questions before. 'What kind of questions?'

'Oh, just about dharma and how to lead a good life. To ask for your guidance.'

Joy washed over Yudhishtra. Modern mortals wanted his counsel, his tutelage. He turned to the audience benevolently and raised his arms. 'I have been told you wish to seek answers. Ask me anything.'

A gaggle of voices started speaking all at once.

'Why did you insist on marrying Draupadi when she was won by Arjuna?'

'Why did you agree to the dice game?'

'Why did you agree to the second dice game when you knew you would lose again?'

'Why did you stake your kingdom, brothers and Draupadi?
'Why did you allow Draupadi to be disrobed in court?'
'Why did you keep cursing your family members in anger?'
'Why did you love a dog more than your own brothers and wife at the end of your life?'

Stunned, Yudhishtra blinked and looked at Amit, his expression confused. Amit frowned back at him but said nothing.

A wave of anger pounded him in the chest. Were these the kinds of questions mortals wanted to ask about his life? What about his belief system, what about all his virtues, what about truth and dharma? Had his life, the complex decisions he'd had to make, counted for nothing? Yes, he had insisted on marrying Draupadi. It was a well-known fact that she was destined to have five husbands. Who was he to stand in the path of her destiny? Yes, he had agreed to the dice games, and yes, he had staked his kingdom of Indraprastha, his brothers and his wife, and lost them to his cousins, the Kauravas, whom he knew to be dishonest and scheming. He was the first to acknowledge that these corrupted games had led to their thirteen-year exile and the Great War, which had caused the death of many of his beloved family members, including his own children. But, as much as everyone liked to point out his penchant for gambling, the truth was that he couldn't have refused the invitations to play dice even if he'd wanted to. As a warrior king, it went against moral code to refuse a challenge. Any kind of challenge. It had torn him apart to watch Draupadi's many humiliations during her life, but she was his wife, and it was her duty to share his destiny, ease his suffering and suffer alongside him. Just like it was the duty of his younger brothers to support him. Why couldn't people see that?

Yudhishtra raised his arms to quieten the audience, his expression furious. 'Silence! Is this the kind of society that inhabits the world today? Where are your priorities? Silence!'

The crowd fell quiet, their faces full of apprehension.

Yudhishtra looked around the gathering sternly. 'Life, whether mortal or heavenly, is not lived in isolation. Each of us is a part of something larger, a shared destiny that is as inevitable as the rise and fall of the sun every single day. We are, individually, but a wave that makes up a tiny part of a vast, mighty ocean. That is not to say we are not important. We each have a role to play.'

He took a deep breath and repeated what he had told himself during countless moments of anguish and regret, both during his mortal life and afterwards. 'I knew, had been told by the great sage Vyasa himself, that disaster would strike us. I knew that we would lose everything and spend years in exile. It was a future that was set in stone, and I was merely a cog in the wheel, playing my part and bearing my burden.'

He looked around, pausing to let that sink in. 'A shoemaker is virtuous if he diligently makes shoes of good quality. That's all it takes. How is an emperor of the world, one who has performed the Rajasuya sacrifice and has millions under his dominion, to be virtuous? It is infinitely more complicated. I did what I had to do, knowing fully well that many would suffer. At every stage of my existence, I have questioned the righteousness of my actions and every time I have come to the same conclusion. Dharma is not about any one person or society. Dharma is truth, and truth bears no judgement from man. Truth is conscienceless; it is absolute. Truth is unforgiving. Only the enlightened, those who have truly detached themselves from the humanity of existence, can aspire to it. As I did. And while I did not always succeed, I tried my best.'

For an endless moment, there was silence in the hall. Then, after taking a quick, assessing look around, Amit started clapping enthusiastically from behind Yudhishtra. Seeing the head of their centre clapping, many of the members started applauding too. Soon, the rest of the hall joined in, their combined applause resounding off the walls and echoing through the streets outside.

Slightly mollified, the man of the moment nodded to his audience. A small surge of pride went through Yudhishtra. He still had it. The ability to enthral a crowd. He shook his head immediately, ashamed of the self-congratulatory thought. He should be above such shallow pleasures, he chided himself. But a small part of him rejoiced at the crowd's collective approval. At their validation. Their love.

A man, middle-aged and overweight with coloured stone rings generously distributed on his fingers, walked up to Yudhishtra with folded hands. He bowed and touched Yudhishtra's feet reverently. Looking up, he said, 'My name is P.S. Aggarwal and I own the chemist shop on this road. I am blessed to be able to witness the miracle of Dharmaraj's rebirth on earth!' He took a small wad of money out of his fist and held it up to Yudhishtra over his bent head. 'Guruji, please accept this small donation as a gift from your humble devotee.'

As a gesture, it was one Yudhishtra had seen many times. It had been a common occurrence for people to offer gifts to him as their king. He had usually accepted whatever small trinket it was and given them a generous gift in return, such as gold

The Misters Kuru

or land. Even when the Pandavas were in hiding and soliciting people for alms as brahmans, Yudhishtra had only been gifted food and living essentials. Pots, plates, cloth and the like.

No one had ever tried to give him money before. As if he were selling something.

He was about to politely decline when Amit stepped up, his hand stretched out to receive the money. 'Guruji thanks you for your support,' he said to the man as he pocketed the money with a smile. 'This donation will go towards spreading Guruji's teachings and also towards the charities that he is helping.'

'What charities?' asked Yudhishtra.

Amit cleared his throat and muttered, 'I will tell you later,' under his breath. Then he proceeded to take money from a few others who stepped up to touch 'Guruji's' feet and take his blessings.

Yudhishtra touched the heads of all the people who stepped forward, as directed by Amit, but it was with a deep sense of discomfort. This didn't feel right, but he couldn't identify what exactly was wrong with it either. Was he overthinking things? Perhaps mortal rituals had changed and money played a greater part in the world now. He had never pictured himself as a guru before, but Yudhishtra found he liked the feeling of being recognized and valued for his opinions. The gods knew there had been precious little of that in the last few thousand years. Besides, he was only here for thirty days—what harm could a little jaunt into the public eye do?

He would think of it as one last act of service. For a mortal world entrenched in a terrible Kalyug.

'Guruji, please come with me,' Amit said after a while, gesturing for him to leave the hall.

Yudhishtra followed him to the other side of the building, where Amit unlocked the door to a conference room. There, he was served a tray of food and drink while four other men entered the room and shut the door.

Amit stood up and walked to the head of the table. 'It has been an enlightening day. While I knew that our members would like to hear Guruji speak, I was surprised when the entire community came out. This is the kind of spirit we want to support at our centre. So, I suggest we take this forward, to a wider base of people who will benefit from his wisdom.'

He paused and looked around questioningly. The other men in the room murmured their agreement, so Amit nodded and continued, 'Today's talk has heralded Guruji's re-entrance into the world in a small but good way. Now we must think about next steps. Guruji,' he turned to Yudhishtra and folded his hands for the hundredth time that day, 'we should start shaping your brand.'

'My brand?' Yudhishtra was confused.

'Yes,' said Amit. 'Let's start with your image. These clothes you are wearing,' he pointed to the oversized trousers and shirt given to him by Narad Muni in heaven, 'are fine for a normal man, but you must look like the enlightened soul that you are. A kurta–pyjama ... No, perhaps a dhoti with draped shawls, so we can show off your arms and shoulders. In saffron. It's a classic look.'

One of the seated men interjected, 'I think it'll be better to dress him as his character from the Mahabharata. With a gold crown and some costume jewellery. And a bigger moustache.'

Yudhishtra's hand instinctively went to his face and fingered the modest scruff on his upper lip. 'What's wrong with my moustache?'

The man shook his head with an apologetic look. 'Nothing, Guruji! It's just that big, handlebar moustaches are in fashion these days. Ever since Bollywood started making historical films.'

Amit took a sip of his drink, a focused look on his face. 'We don't want him to be too Bollywood, but we should definitely highlight his youth and high-caste status. How about a saffron dhoti with thick gold hoop earrings and matching wristbands? With a small, saffron stole draped across his shoulders. Also, leather sandals and a sword.'

'Yudhishtra's weapon was a spear,' said one of the men as he scribbled furiously on a piece of parchment.

Amit nodded. 'Good. Find me a picture of the spear from the TV serial—I know someone who does props. Also, contact the wardrobe department at party headquarters and see if they have the rest. Measure his foot size. We'll need to organize a photo shoot ASAP, and arrange a promo strategy meeting with the marketing company.'

He began to pace the room, snapping out instructions and frowning in concentration, 'Write a bio. Let's start his social media profiles with the photos we took today and contact IT for the first 50,000 followers, with likes and comments. Buy another 75,000 followers. We'll start boosting posts the minute we have publicity shots. Oh, and start an events diary and accounts book, and incorporate a subsidiary company. I've already given today's proceeds to Shailesh. Make sure we have receipts for everything.'

All the other men nodded and busily took notes as Amit was speaking.

Yudhishtra frowned. 'What is all this talk about accounts? Are you asking me to dress up and hold a spear?'

Amit smiled. 'Not dress up, Guruji, but dress appropriately. You see, these days we have a particular image in our minds when we think about Yudhishtra ... I mean, you. If they see you in a shirt and pants, they will think you are just like them. We need to make you stand out. Dress you in a way that they will recognize you and your greatness.'

He pointed to all the other men in the room and said, 'We at the BYBM Centre are honoured that you have trusted us to be your helpers. Let us handle trivial matters. Soon, you will be inundated with requests for speeches. Plan your words and actions carefully. Focus on your message, your mission, your devotees. The world needs you and your wisdom right now, O great Yudhishtra. Desperately.'

That much was true, thought Yudhishtra. Besides, gurus had subsisted on the generosity of others in his day too, albeit in a different way. They had either roamed from home to home collecting alms, or they had set up an ashram to teach disciples who collected alms on their behalf. Sometimes, they visited wealthy patrons and stayed in their homes, meeting the local communities and doling out advice. Either way, they had bartered their wisdom and knowledge for food and shelter. This was no different. The currency and protocols may have changed, but the ideals remained the same. Best not to overthink it.

'Very well,' he said to Amit. 'Let us proceed.'

8

This is ridiculous, thought Arjuna as he ran aimlessly through the streets, his long legs effortlessly keeping up with many of the vehicles that moved on the congested road next to him. Draupadi had told him, early this morning, that running was a popular form of exercise these days.

'Where do they run to?' he'd asked her. 'Is it a race?'

'No, they just run around on the roads, for fun. Try it,' she'd suggested. 'Might make you less jumpy.'

Arjuna huffed. This wasn't fun at all. In the old days, grown men only ran if something was chasing them.

Still, this was a good way to have a look around the neighbourhood as well as get some much-needed exercise. One of the downsides of returning to the mortal world was having to cater to the demands of the human body. In heaven, you were restored to the prime of youth, and no matter what you did, your form remained unchanged. Your stomach stayed satiated without the need to eat and your muscles remained firm despite lack of training. Desire could be summoned and dismissed with a single thought, completely under your control.

Down here, Arjuna's body seemed to have a mind of its own. He was hungry and restless all the time, constantly pacing around the confines of Draupadi's apartment like a caged animal. Not to mention his involuntary physical reaction every time he looked at her in one of those tight dresses. Given that the last time he'd had to practice any kind of sexual restraint was thousands of years ago, he felt like a clumsy adolescent every time it happened. He hoped Draupadi hadn't noticed.

After about an hour of running in the noise and dust, Arjuna was sweating profusely from the heat but still as keyed up as before. He'd scoured the neighbourhood, made a mental list of things he wanted to ask Draupadi about later, counted the number of people he saw staring at their phones while they walked and generally gotten bored with his lack of purpose or direction.

He stopped next to a large, muddy field, which was being utilized by a group of young men playing a sport he couldn't identify. Two men stood at either end of a long rectangle with wooden planks in their hands. Another man ran up to the rectangle from one side and threw a ball, which one of the planks-men hit into the field. The ball was then caught and thrown back in a hurry by one of many men standing around the field and watching. Meanwhile, the two planks-men ran back and forth from one end of the rectangle to the other. Once in a while, all the men shouted and jumped around for no apparent reason.

It made no sense.

He walked up to an elderly man leaning against a large, white car that was parked on the side of the field. He was dressed in a white uniform with a matching cap.

'Are you familiar with this sport?'

The elderly man's eyes widened as he looked up at Arjuna. 'Are you crazy, or have you just been living under a rock for the last hundred years?' His tone was good-humoured rather than offensive.

Arjuna lifted a wry brow and replied, 'The second one. I'm Arjuna. Can you tell me about the game?'

The elderly man considered him idly for a moment and then nodded. 'I'm Hariram. This is cricket.' He waved at the field almost reverently.

'How is it played?'

Hariram took a deep breath and said with a brusque rumble, 'There are two teams. The bowler—that's the boy holding the ball—he has to bowl towards the three wooden sticks in the middle. They're called stumps. He's supported by the ten boys out in the field called fielders and one wicketkeeper. Protecting the stumps is the batsman—that's the boy holding the bat. He has to defend the stumps from being hit by the ball. While doing so, he has to try to hit the ball and score runs. He can do that in two ways—he hits the ball and runs to the other side, while the other batsman does the same in reverse. Each time they do this, they get one run. Or, he can hit the ball hard enough to reach the boundary for either four or six runs, depending on whether the ball touches the ground within the boundary before reaching it.'

Taking another deep breath, he continued, 'There are different ways the batsman can get out. He can get bowled, which means the ball hits the stumps. Or he can hit the ball into the air and it's caught by a fielder before touching the ground; or the ball can hit his leg instead of the bat, and if the leg is directly in front of the wicket, it's an LBW. Leg before wicket, which is an out. Or, he can be in the middle of a run and a fielder or the wicketkeeper—that's the boy with the glove—can hit the stumps before he's crossed the line, in which case it's called a run out. Anyway, the two batsmen keep going like this, trying to stay safe and score as many runs as possible for their team within the allotted overs. One over is six deliveries from the bowler. The number of overs depends on the game. Twenty-over games are becoming more popular now. Anyway, every time a batsman gets out, he's replaced by another batsman from his team. Each team is eleven players, by the way. So, the innings for each team are over either when the allotted number of overs are over, or all ten of your batsmen get out. Not eleven, because there must be two batsmen in the game at all times. So, once the first team has gotten their total score, the opposing team switches places with them and tries to beat their score while trying not to get all their batsmen out.'

Hariram paused for a moment, slightly out of breath. He pointed at the young men playing on the field. 'Look here. The bowler just bowled an out-swinging, full-pitched delivery, slightly outside the off-stump. He's trying to get the batsman to go for a cover drive, so that the ball can clip the bat and get caught by the second slip fieldsman. Now, the next time he won't do that because the batsman will be expecting it. Ah, you see that? He bowled another full-pitched delivery on middle and leg stumps. The batsman stepped forward and flicked it along the ground to the square leg fielder, who threw it back to the wicketkeeper. He'll be happy with a single for that one.' He looked up at Arjuna and announced. 'That's cricket.'

Arjuna blinked and stared back at him, stumped.

Hariram shook his head and spat out a stream of coloured spittle on the ground. 'The bowler tries to hit the stumps. The batsmen try to score runs. The fielders try to get the batsmen out. The team with the highest score wins.'

'Ah, I see.' Turning his head to observe the game, Arjuna asked, 'And do many people play cricket these days?'

Hariram chuckled. 'In this country, it's more like a religion than a sport. People are crazy about it. The players in the Indian cricket team are like gods. Indians follow them around the world to cheer them on during their matches.'

Arjuna raised his brow as he observed the game intently. 'Fascinating.' He turned back to Hariram. 'Do you play?'

The elderly man made a sound somewhere in between a laugh and a cough. 'In my younger days, I used to be a very good all-rounder.'

'Will you teach me how to play?'

Hariram thought about it carefully for a minute. Then, he looked around and said, 'I could. As long as I keep an eye on the car. My employer has crashed it twice when he was drunk, but if I so much as get a scratch on it, he cuts half my salary.'

They stepped on to the sports field, Arjuna waiting on the side while Hariram went to borrow a bat and a ball from the young men playing in the centre. Then he proceeded to show Arjuna how to hold the bat and swing. Walking a short distance away, he threw some practice balls at Arjuna, and taught him the different types of shots he could try and how to position his bat, so the ball went in the direction he wanted.

Arjuna gently tapped the ball with his bat in response, easily picking up its essence, and becoming attuned to how it felt in his hands, how it responded to him and the ball. Like a weapon, the bat had a personality and language of its own. Its strength, form and bulk, the way it steadied and shifted in his hands in different positions, the way it reacted every time it swung or made contact with the ball. He quickly learned, through holding, moving, listening and feeling, exactly what the bat was trying to tell him, and soon, they were working in perfect tandem with each other.

He felt bad that he was making Hariram run around to catch the ball, so he suggested he bowl instead. After learning the basics of how to grip the ball, do a run up and all the different ways he could throw it, Arjuna installed an out-of-breath Hariram as the batsman and gently bowled to him.

After a few half-hearted lobs that barely traversed the distance, Hariram grumbled, 'Stop trying to make allowances for me, boy. I've been a cricketer all my life. Bowl harder!'

'Are you sure? I don't want to hurt you.'

Hariram cough-laughed again. 'This is your first time playing. I think I'll be fine.' He drew a line behind him in the mud and stuck a thin, upright stick into it. 'This is the stump. Hit it!'

'All right.' Arjuna took a few steps further back and did a run up before he bowled, properly this time. The ball swung with enough force to make the old man step back and cover his face with his hands, dropping the bat for fear of being struck. After a fraught moment, Hariram lowered his hands and looked at the stick behind him with wide eyes.

It was lying flat on the ground, neatly broken in two.

Shocked, Hariram turned to Arjuna. 'What the hell?'

Arjuna shrugged. 'You asked me to hit the stick; so I did.'

The young men who'd been playing in the centre of the field ran over to them, their faces flushed with excitement over what they'd just witnessed. One of them ran up to Arjuna and thumped him on the shoulder. 'That was a bloody fast ball!'

Hariram mumbled, still in shock, 'Hit the stump too.' He pointed to the broken stick on the ground.

The young man's eyes widened in much the same way Hariram's had when he first saw the stick. 'No way!' He turned to Arjuna. 'Hi, I'm Arjun. What's your name?'

Arjuna smiled, pleasantly surprised to find out that mortal men were named after him. 'I'm Arjuna too.'

'Cool.' Mortal Arjun didn't seem to think that was unusual, which obviously meant that his was a common name here on earth. Arjuna grinned as mortal Arjun said in a voice that burst with enthusiasm, 'Come, join our game. We really need a fast bowler.'

That sounded like fun. Arjuna looked at Hariram for permission to leave. The elderly man grinned at him for the first time, displaying his rotting, orange-stained teeth before declaring, 'You have real talent, boy. Go play with people your own age. I have to stay with the car anyway.'

Thanking him for the cricket lesson by folding his hands and bowing low, Arjuna then walked to the centre of the field with mortal Arjun and the rest of his friends. They gave him a ball and asked him to bowl to the batsman. He did, without holding back. Again, and again.

Not only did the ball whiz past the batsman at dangerous speeds, it knocked the middle stump out of the ground every time.

By the end of an over, all of the men on the field were standing and staring at Arjuna with open mouths.

'Are you a professional?' Mortal Arjun asked Arjuna.

He shook his head. 'I've never played before.' Then, when they all squinted in disbelief, he added, 'I've done some archery and ... er, played war games. This is not that different.' He shrugged. It was true. Training for sports was much like training for battle. It was about strength, endurance, speed, flexibility, focus and coordination. And natural athletic instinct, which you were either born with or not.

'Wow,' said mortal Arjun. 'You *should* be playing professionally. I mean, I've seen bowlers on TV who aren't as good as you.'

Arjuna shrugged again. He wouldn't be around long enough to play professionally, but they didn't need to know that.

'No, seriously.' Mortal Arjun scratched his chin for a moment, and then his eyes lit up with an idea. 'I've got it! We'll make a BouTube video!'

'A what?'

Mortal Arjun grinned in excitement. 'It's an internet video-sharing platform. There are tons of cricket players who post their own videos. All the scouts use BouTube to find players nowadays. It's a genius idea!'

While Arjuna wasn't used to people declaring themselves geniuses, he had to smile at mortal Arjun's compelling enthusiasm. Not that he understood even half the words that had just spilled out of the young man's mouth. He decided to play along. 'What do I have to do?'

Mortal Arjun was on a roll. Whipping out what Arjuna recognized as a smartphone, similar to Draupadi's, from his pocket, he held it up. 'We'll make you bowl in different ways and I'll record it on my phone. Then, we'll upload the video and wait!'

'For what?'

Mortal Arjun slapped Arjuna on the back. 'For destiny, my friend! Now come, let's get you started.'

Over the next hour, the young men made Arjuna bowl all kinds of balls repeatedly at a batsman, using the same terminology that Hariram had used. Bouncers, in-swingers, out-swingers, reverse swingers, yorkers and many other names that he couldn't remember. They taught him how to adjust his line and length to make deliveries trickier for the batsman. Not that the batsman in question needed any kind of trickery. The poor boy wasn't able to hit a single one of Arjuna's deliveries.

At the end of their recording session, mortal Arjun brought his smartphone to Arjuna's face and showed him moving images of himself bowling the ball. Despite the fact that he'd learnt about the concept of recording moving images, called videos, when Draupadi had given him a tour around her workplace, Arjuna was amazed to see himself in them. Was that what he looked like? It felt like the first time he was truly seeing his face and body in all its detail. All too soon, Mortal Arjun removed the smartphone from in front of him and gushed, 'You were fabulous!'

He smiled down at his namesake. 'So, what will you do with those videos?'

'Well, first we create a BouTube channel for you. Let's call it "SuperFastBowler" and your age. How old are you?'

How old did he look? Arjuna thought about himself in the videos and figured he appeared anywhere between nineteen and twenty-six years in age. Older was probably better. He replied, 'Twenty-six.'

'Okay, so SuperFastBowler26. What's your phone number?'

Arjuna recited the number that Draupadi had given him in case he ever needed to speak to her on her phone. Mortal Arjun peered into his own phone busily for the next few minutes before declaring, 'Done! You're online, brother. Remember me when you become famous, okay?'

Arjuna smiled dryly. One famous person in the family was quite enough. Still, he pocketed the small piece of parchment that mortal Arjun handed him with his 'password' details and phone number, thanked them all profusely for teaching him a new skill and started walking home.

As he roamed the streets, retracing his steps, he felt his body unwind for the first time since his descent from heaven. Despite the fact that he hadn't put much strain on himself during the game physically, he felt stretched and emptied in the same way he did after a training session. Probably because cricket was, in fact, a little like training for battle. He'd used his mind as much as his body, used skill and thought and strategy, more like a warrior than an athlete.

It had been fun.

Arjuna began to hum softly to himself. Maybe he could put together a team in heaven when he got back.

9

'What the *hell* is going on?'

Draupadi pointed her phone at Arjuna, brandishing it like a weapon. She'd just walked into the apartment after a gruelling day at work. A day made infinitely worse by the constant pinging and ringing of her phone. Given that this had happened mere hours after she'd given her five ex-husbands her phone number, she was certain they had everything to do with it.

'I gave you my number for an emergency! Not to be handed out like pamphlets! And who the hell is SuperFastBowler26?'

Arjuna, who unfortunately was the only ex-husband currently at home, lounged back on her sofa, snacking on chocolate-covered biscuits. He held one up with a slight grimace. 'These are ridiculously sweet. What's a pamphlet?'

Draupadi picked up a cushion from an armchair and threw it at him.

Arjuna laughed as he caught the cushion and set his plate of biscuits down. 'So, Angela gets the calm and reasonable Draupadi, and I get things thrown at me? How do I get the other Draupadi's number?'

She rolled her eyes. He wasn't going to charm his way out of this one. 'My phone went crazy today,' she snapped. 'I had to turn it off in the afternoon because it wouldn't stop ringing. When I switched it back on after a few hours, I had a thousand new messages, all addressed to SuperFastBowler26. Would you happen to know anything about this or do I have to strangle one of the other four to death?'

Arjuna lifted an eyebrow. 'Really? A thousand messages? What did they say?'

Draupadi threw up her hands. 'I don't know because I had to work! Why does the entire world think my phone number belongs to SuperFastBowler26?'

Taking a deep breath, Arjuna raised his hands in a defensive gesture. 'I'll tell you, but you have to promise you won't get angry.'

Too late. 'Start talking!'

He stood up, automatically making the generously sized living room feel smaller. With his imposing height and broad shoulders, he was one of the few men Draupadi knew who was proportionately sized to her own tall, voluptuous figure. And ever since he'd started wearing jeans that clung to his also-well-proportioned lower half, he made her feel other things too. Things she hadn't felt in a very, very long time. Things that had made her life very complicated back when she'd been married to him. Damned jeans. She should buy him some pyjamas to wear around the house. Baggy ones, with rainbows on them.

Completely oblivious to her thoughts, Arjuna smiled down at her in the apprehensive-yet-gloating manner of a precocious child who's stolen a treat just before mealtime. 'It's me. I'm SuperFastBowler26.'

Draupadi frowned, temporarily forgetting her anger in her confusion. 'You? How?'

'Well, I played cricket today.'

'With whom?'

'Just some boys I met when I went out running. By the way, your neighbourhood is on low ground. Doesn't it get flooded during the monsoon season?'

'I'm on the fifteenth floor! What happened when you played cricket?'

Arjuna shrugged. 'They thought I was good.'

Draupadi grunted in frustration. He always did this. As sharp and diligent as he was in every other area of his life, when it came to their conversations, it was impossible to get a complete answer out of him. He was constantly trying to manage her, as if she were a child. And then he wondered why she was always angry with him. She took a deep breath, said a quick prayer for patience and prodded him. 'And?'

He shrugged again and continued, 'They recorded videos and images of me bowling the ball, and put them on this thing called Bluetood or something.'

'BouTube?'

'That's the one. Arjun, he's the boy who recorded me ... By the way, is Arjun a fairly common name nowadays?' he asked with a smirk.

'Focus!'

He sighed. 'He recorded me, put the images on BouTube and asked me for a phone number, so I gave him yours. I'm sorry; I didn't expect this to happen to you. Obviously, I would never bring you any trouble on purpose.'

No, never on purpose. But unintentionally? That was a whole other can of worms that Draupadi didn't have the time to address right now. There were billions of videos on BouTube and millions of new ones added every day. The fact that she'd gotten so many messages and missed calls meant that Arjuna's video was getting attention. A *lot* of it. Why?

She looked down at her laptop bag. 'I think we need to get on BouTube. Did this Arjun chap give you a username and password?'

Arjuna gave her the piece of paper that had the necessary details. Opening her laptop on the coffee table, Draupadi quickly signed into BouTube and found Arjuna's video. It had been uploaded ten hours ago.

And viewed over a million times.

Draupadi hissed out an astonished breath. No wonder her phone had gone ballistic. Quickly, she pressed 'play' to see what all the fuss was about. Arjuna was shown bowling a cricket ball to a batsman and repeatedly knocking out the stumps from behind him. The ball was moving so fast, it was difficult to follow it with the eyes.

'Wow,' she whispered. 'You're really good.'

Arjuna let out a chuckle from behind her. 'Not the first time you've said that.'

Despite herself, Draupadi smiled. 'Shut up and wait while I delete the phone number from your write-up.' She scrolled down and saw that Arjuna's BouTube channel already had hundreds of thousands of subscribers and hundreds of comments. She quickly deleted her phone number and opened some of them.

'What did people say?' Behind her, Arjuna leaned over to read them, his face just a couple of inches above her shoulder, next to hers. She held her breath as a frisson of awareness shot through her. Not now, she scolded herself as she read some of the comments.

'Omg! He's toooo amazing!'

'So fast. Need a player like him for Team India.'

'Are these special effects? Can someone confirm?'

'He's yummy. #hottie ♥♥♥'

'Solid action bro. Keep it up!'

'Somebody hire him yaar. Our boys in blue urgently need a fast bowler.'

'He can bowl me over anytime ☺'

'Indian Shoaib!'

'SPECIAL RATES to boost your subscriber count …'

Arjuna chuckled softly as he looked at her face without moving away. 'I guess I am pretty good.' His breath brushed against her cheeks.

Draupadi couldn't breathe, her insides curling up with heat. She cleared her throat to force a breath in and said in a husky voice, 'Don't flatter yourself. I get much nicer ones on my social media profiles.'

'I have no doubt you do,' he murmured. He gazed at her for a long moment. Then, he sighed and stood back up. 'So, what do you want to do about this?'

Draupadi felt her body slowly uncoiling and realized that she'd inadvertently stiffened when Arjuna had leaned close. He'd probably felt her tension and moved back. Guilt washed over her, and she bit her lip angrily. She'd been pushing him away ever since he'd gotten here, as if they meant nothing to each other. There had been many good times, brief but memorable moments of shared pleasure and camaraderie during their marriage. Physically, they had been perfectly matched in a way that she hadn't been with any of the other Pandavas. Arjuna had been a skilled, generous lover and a good friend. Yes, they'd had their ups and downs, and things hadn't gone the way either of them would have liked, but that still didn't discount the good times. They may no longer be husband and wife, but they were still each other's family. And could still be friends.

As long as she didn't become a molten puddle of lust every time he was in the room.

'Draupadi?'

'Hmm?'

His expression a bit concerned, Arjuna asked again, 'What do you want to do about these videos?'

Oh, right. 'I'm not sure. Let's decide later.' Closing her laptop, she sat back on the sofa and patted the space next to her. When Arjuna sat down, she said in a soft voice, 'Look, I'm sorry I yelled at you. You weren't to know what would happen. I'll just have my number changed. It's not a big deal. Here,' she turned on her phone and handed it to him, 'use it for the time being.'

Arjuna nodded and took the phone from her, setting it down on the sofa between them. 'I'm sorry too. It just happened, and I actually had fun doing it.' He looked down, his jaw a little tight, and then back up at her. 'If I were to be completely truthful, it's been a while since I've had fun. Done something that truly made me happy.'

Draupadi gave him a teasing look. 'I thought that's what nymphs were for?'

He smiled. 'That was fun in the beginning, yes. But the novelty wears off; and once it does, you realize there's not much else to do up there. Except maybe train for a war that probably won't ever happen.'

'What about court life? And Subhadra.'

He sighed. 'Court life doesn't suit me. That's more Yudhishtra's thing. And Subhadra ...,' he paused, seemingly unsure how to continue. 'She's been busy.'

'With what?'

Arjuna shook his head and exhaled ruefully. 'Never mind. I shouldn't have said anything.' He turned to her, angling his body so they faced each other. 'I need to ask you something.'

Draupadi really wanted him to tell her more about Subhadra, but she held back her questions. Not the right time. 'Ask away.'

He focused on her eyes, his own wary and a little wounded. 'Why didn't you come back to heaven?'

The question threw her off, but she recovered quickly. After a pensive moment, she replied, 'I could sit here all evening and give you reason after reason. Because I wanted to be my own person, because I wanted to help other women, because the world has become infinitely more interesting, or because I finally found a purpose to my life that didn't involve the men I was married to. But I think the real reason I didn't come back to heaven was that I was having fun too.' She tilted her head coquettishly. 'Why? Did you miss me?'

'Yes, I did.'

She raised an eyebrow at his heartfelt tone. 'Really? We barely saw each other by the end of it. In fact, you tried to avoid me as much as possible. Bhima was the only one of the five of you whom I saw regularly.' Draupadi knew

Arjuna wouldn't like to hear that. If there was anything he'd begrudged even more than Yudhishtra's constant demands of her during their mortal lives, it was her relationship with Bhima. Yes, she was close to Bhima, but her love for him was more familial than the kind of love a wife feels for her husband. Arjuna had never understood that.

As expected, his jaw tightened upon hearing Bhima's name from her lips. After a few fraught moments though, he sighed resignedly. 'You know what? I did avoid you, and I regret that now. I've spent too much of my existence holding on to resentment. In a way, I'm happy Mother freed you from our marriage. Even if you aren't mine any longer, at least you aren't theirs either. So, in a sense, now I can be free too. And, as for the other thing ...'

He smiled, absently lifting a lock of her long hair and playing with it, his eyes boring into hers. 'You should know that I've always missed you. Every second, from the moment we met. Even when you were right there, in front of me.'

There were many times in the future when Draupadi wondered what exactly it was about that moment that made her do what she did, but she could never quite put her finger on it.

Putting her hand on his cheek, she whispered, 'I missed you too,' and leaned in and kissed him.

Arjuna expelled a breath of potent relief before his hand circled around the back of her neck and gently pulled her in even closer, deepening their connection. Their mouths tangled in a rhythm that was at once familiar yet new. It had been so long, Draupadi had forgotten how good, how exhilarating, how *right* this passion they'd always shared felt. Like soaring off a cliff.

Like coming home.

RIIING!

They jumped apart with a gasp, struggling to catch their breath as they stared at the screaming, vibrating phone that lay on the sofa between them.

Draupadi moved away quickly, muttering in a hoarse voice, 'Press the green circle on the screen.'

Arjuna cleared his throat and nodded, picking up the phone and following her instructions.

'Hello? *Hello?*' a man's distorted voice on the other end said loudly.

Draupadi leaned over and pressed another circle on the screen, which amplified the man's voice so they could both hear it. Then she stepped away from the sofa.

'Hello? Can you hear me?'

Arjuna frowned. 'Who is this?'

The voice replied, 'Finally! I've been calling you all day. Are you SuperFastBowler26?'

'Yes.'

'Good. Now listen to me carefully, son. My name is Rizwan Hussain, and I'm a franchise scout for YPL cricket, representing the Delhi Captains. I saw your video, and I'm interested in meeting you.'

Looking confused, Arjuna asked, 'For what?'

'What do you mean "for what"? Didn't you hear what I said? I represent the Delhi Captains!'

He looked at Draupadi, who said softly, 'It's a cricket team.'

The man's voice continued, 'This can be a huge opportunity for you, son. What is your name?'

'Arjuna.'

'Arjuna. What is your surname?'

He looked at Draupadi again. She sighed and said, 'Kuru.'

He spoke to the phone, 'My surname is Kuru.'

'Arjuna Kuru. Okay, listen. I want you to meet me on the centre field at New Delhi Cricket Club tomorrow. Ten a.m. sharp. Wear something comfortable, with running shoes. I'll leave your name at the entrance. Okay?'

For the third time during this conversation, Arjuna looked at Draupadi with questioning eyes. She stayed silent. This was something he needed to figure out on his own.

'Okay? Will you come, Arjuna?'

He continued to stare at her, his face giving nothing away. Finally, he said, 'Yes.'

'Okay, good. See you tomorrow. Don't be late.' The phone beeped and then went silent.

Draupadi felt tingles crawl up her back. 'What are you doing?'

'Having fun,' he replied lightly.

She bit her lip, confusion and frustration churning her insides. 'You do realize that your wife is waiting for you in heaven, right? The one for whom you made all those fancy vows?'

That made his jaw tighten again. 'I know.'

'She won't be happy about this. Any of it.'

'I know.' He stood up and ran a hand through his hair, flustered.

She didn't understand. 'Then why are you doing it?'

He shook his head and took a deep breath, looking into the distance. 'I don't know.'

Then he walked into the study and shut the door.

10

'It's not like I'm asking *you* to kill it.'

'No, no, absolutely not!' shrieked Narad Muni.

Bhima grunted, a squawking chicken in his hand and a scowl on his face. 'So, you'll eat it, but you won't let me prepare it?'

An irate Narad Muni folded his arms over his chest and turned away. 'If I allow you to cook that bird, who'll have to clean all the blood and guts and feathers after you've butchered it? Me, that's who! I refuse. Not if you ended this hellish experience right now. Not even if you promoted me to a god. I'm not touching that thing!'

Bhima shook his head, his quick temper rising. Narad Muni had been more hindrance than help ever since he'd taken over the kitchen. A noisy one at that. Not only did the old man refuse to help with the chopping, washing up and serving, which was significant given there were over a hundred mouths to feed every day, he'd also made a fuss about household chores. Bhima couldn't do everything himself, and he certainly didn't want his mother breaking her back doing housework when she was already up to her ears taking care of so many children. Kunti had asked him to be patient with the recalcitrant sage, but he'd had enough.

Grabbing Narad Muni by the collar of his shirt, Bhima hauled him up until his toes were barely touching the floor. 'Listen, old man. I'm sick and tired of your whining and rudeness. Instead of accepting Krishna's command with honour, you make more noise than this chicken. Neither my mother nor I are obliged to take care of you until you return to heaven. So, you can either work for your keep or you can get out and fend for yourself. Which one do you choose?'

Narad Muni's eyes went so wide his eyelids were in danger of disappearing into his reedy face. Bhima was known to have a slack handle on his temper, but there was usually someone from his family around to mitigate it. Alone and unchecked, this Pandava could kill him if he wasn't careful. Narad Muni wanted nothing more than to leave the orphanage, but he wanted to starve and beg on the streets even less.

'I will stay and help. Forgive me.' He folded his hands and quickly scampered towards the door once the hold on his shirt was released.

Bhima nodded. 'Good. Now go clean the rooms and send the clothes to the dhobi. We've got two hours until lunchtime, and the children are looking forward to eating chicken, some of them for the first time. I'll cook and clean the mess here. Send one of the older children to help me.' He turned away.

Narad Muni made a face at his back and slunk out of the room.

The Misters Kuru

Bhima grumbled softly to himself as he tied the chicken's foot to the yard door. He would need to find a suitable butchering knife and sharpen the blade before he killed it. Not to mention one bird wasn't nearly enough to feed all the children, he thought in frustration. This morning, at the butcher's shop, he'd been shocked to find out the price of meat. There was no way the orphanage could afford it. In fact, this chicken had been a gift from the butcher after Bhima had shown him a technique of carving goat flesh such that the cuts looked eye-catching and plump. Bhima would have loved to buy a few more birds and maybe roast them with spices over a fire in the orphanage's yard, but he didn't have enough money in the lunch budget. Instead, he would have to make a watery curry with miserly portions of dal and vegetables, and cut the chicken pieces really small. That way, at least each child could have a small taste when they mixed it with their rice. It wasn't even close to meeting the nutritional needs of the children, and it was a complete and utter waste of Bhima's exceptional culinary skills.

They needed to source more money. But how?

Before he could come up with any solutions, however, the door to the kitchen swung open. A boy of about twelve, tall and gangly with face spots that usually signalled transition into manhood, walked in with a noticeable swagger. He stopped just inside the door and looked at Bhima with a sour expression.

'Narad Muni sent me,' the boy said in a tight voice.

Bhima nodded and started searching for a knife. 'I need help with lunch. There are onions inside the bags in the corner. Start by chopping them. As small as possible.'

The boy didn't move. Instead, he kept staring at Bhima. 'Are you really Kuntiben's son?'

Bhima wasn't in the mood to make conversation, so he uttered a short, 'Yes,' while rummaging in a rickety cupboard.

'Are you going to take her away?'

Startled, Bhima turned and looked, really looked, at the boy for the first time. His foot was twitching ferociously, and there was uncertainty written in his intelligent eyes. 'What's your name?'

The boy's back straightened. 'I'm Karan. Her adopted son.'

Uh-oh. Bhima knew he would have to come face to face with the reincarnation of his former half-brother, Karna, at some point, but he'd hoped that Kunti would be around when it happened. Karna and Bhima had shared a bitter enmity in the old days, fighting each other in many battles and eventually killing each other's offspring during the Great War. Karna had killed Bhima's eldest son, Ghatotkacha, and in revenge, Bhima had slain Karna's son, Banasena. The only reason he hadn't killed Karna himself was because Arjuna had vowed to do it, and so Bhima had held back, allowing his younger brother to fulfil his oath.

Twelve-year-old Karan, Karna's present reincarnation, had no idea who he'd been in his previous lives, so he obviously wouldn't remember Bhima or their history of antipathy.

But Bhima remembered.

He eyed Karan awkwardly, trying to figure out what his mother would want him to say. At the end of the day, he was here to help her, not create problems with her mortal family. Not to mention he could hardly start fighting with a pubescent boy. Finally, he muttered, 'I am her son. And so are you.'

That didn't appease the boy. He folded his arms across his chest and asked again in an aggressive voice, 'Are you going to take her away?'

Bhima almost laughed. New Karna liked him as little as old Karna had. Some things never changed. 'I'm here to help her. Are you going to help me help her?' He nodded towards the bags that held the onions.

Karan appeared to consider that for a moment, even while continuing to give Bhima an unfriendly, appraising look with eyes that shone with a maturity far beyond their years. Then, he turned, walked over to the bags and began to fish out the onions.

Bhima found two knives and started rubbing one against the other to sharpen it, all while keeping an eye on Karan. When he was satisfied his blade would do the job, he walked over to the chicken and held it upside down, petting and crooning to it in a deep, soft voice that was the antithesis of the one he used to address most humans. From the corner of his eye, he saw that Karan was watching him closely instead of chopping onions, but he held his peace for the moment. His palms felt the bird relax as blood rushed to its head from the rest of its body. With a swift movement, he gripped the chicken's neck in his hand and broke it with a clean snap.

Karan's eyes widened. 'Wow, you're strong. Is it dead?'

Bhima nodded. 'Now comes the dirty part. I have to bleed, gut and defeather it. Without making a mess; otherwise, the old man will tear my ears apart for the rest of the day.'

Karan gave him a reluctant smile. 'He does complain a lot. Kuntiben says it's because he's not used to housework, but I know men like him. My school principal is the same. They think the world owes them respect just because they're old. Even if they behave like idiotic pricks.'

Since Bhima was a few thousand years older than Karan's school principal, he decided not to prove the boy's point by asking him idiotic questions like the meaning of the word 'prick'. Instead, he said, 'Why aren't you in school today?'

'It's a holiday, so I got to come home.'

'You still chopping those onions?'

Karan looked down at his large pile of onions with a sigh. He then gestured towards the dead chicken with a hopeful expression. 'Can I help with that instead?'

Shrugging, Bhima said, 'You can, but it'll get messy.'

'I don't mind. I've seen plenty of blood and guts before.'

Bhima regarded him with a thoughtful expression. That was an unusual statement coming from a child. He knew Karan had been an orphan until Kunti came along, but hadn't really thought about what that entailed. He'd obviously had a difficult life. 'Fine. But you do as I tell you.'

Karan nodded.

'Take off your shirt and cover your pants.'

For the next half an hour, they prepared the chicken for cooking. Bhima taught Karan his skills, relishing his role as a teacher as well as the boy's enthusiasm for the job. He was a sharp learner and didn't have a queasy bone in his body—something Bhima appreciated more than most.

Together, they butchered, cleaned, cooked and served the afternoon meal with an uneasy but successful camaraderie, driven by a shared love for Kunti and a fervent desire to unburden her to the best of their abilities. The meal, while not extravagant, was delicious.

'This is the best meal the children have ever eaten,' said Kunti effusively as she sat down to eat with Bhima and Karan in the common room after the children had finished. 'They were licking their plates!'

'It's really good.' Karan was licking his own fingers as he wolfed down his portion. 'This is better than a restaurant.'

Bhima was less satisfied. 'We can do better with better ingredients. I'm wondering how we can increase the food budget without taking the money out of the running expenses.'

Kunti shook her head. 'That'll be a challenge, Bhima. We need to make the donation money last for a few more months.'

'Can't we earn money somehow?'

Chewing a mouthful with some gusto, Karan said, 'We could sell this food. It doesn't have to be fancy or expensive. Just one main dish, some chilli or cucumber, and rice or roti. Maybe puris or stuffed parathas once in a while. Simple, clean, home-style food at a good price. The people employed nearby would happily buy it for their lunch.'

Shaking her head, Kunti said, 'We'd need a licence, son.'

Karan shrugged, in the way adolescents did. 'Not if you're a home vendor. The home science teacher at school does catering on weekends. She said she just needed to register on the government website.' He turned to Bhima. 'We could operate out of a window in the building. I can spread the word through my street contacts, so we don't even need a banner or anything. As long as there are no kids cooking the food, no one can say anything.'

Bhima thought about that. 'Would it be profitable?'

Karan shrugged again. 'The man who runs the food cart down the street just bought his wife a gold chain.'

Kunti frowned at him. 'How do you know that?'

Grinning, Karan replied, 'Just because I don't live on the streets anymore doesn't mean I don't know what's going on.'

'Karan …'

'I'm not doing anything wrong, don't worry. I promise.'

Before Kunti became the orphanage warden, Karan had been involved with a gang that peddled drugs through street children, and Bhima knew that she constantly worried about him getting involved in illegal activities again. He quickly changed the subject, 'We'd need an initial investment, wouldn't we?'

Giving Kunti a mischievous look, Karan said, 'Luckily, Kuntiben has a rich and famous daughter.'

Kunti sighed. 'We already take a lot of money from Draupadi for your education and expenses, Karan.'

'It would be a loan, Kuntiben. We can pay her back with profits. I haven't told you yet, but that BYBM Centre is doing some pretty shady stuff in the slum. Don't take anymore money from them. Let's do this instead.'

She looked undecided. Bhima leaned towards her and said, 'Draupadi will be happy to give the money, Mother.'

'Of course. It's not that.' Kunti looked at the two of them. 'The idea is good, and we could use a source of income. I just don't want to stir up any trouble.'

Bhima shook his head. What trouble could a harmless lunch business stir up? 'Don't worry, Mother. I'll take care of everything. Trust me.'

Turning to Karan, he said with a new-found liking for this quick-witted and enterprising boy, 'Now, I need to speak to Draupadi.'

'Easy.' Karan picked up Kunti's phone and tapped it a few times.

A ringing sound echoed around the room from the phone and then Draupadi's voice rang through it. 'Hello, Mother. Everything okay?'

Kunti smiled. 'Everything is fine, my dear. Bhima will speak to you.'

'Draupadi.' Bhima's voice dropped to a smooth rumble as it always did when he spoke to her. 'I need some of your money to start a food business here at the orphanage.'

'Of course, just tell me the amount and I'll bring it. Got to run, so let's talk later. Love you.'

He knew she'd come through. Draupadi may not be his wife anymore, but she would always be his soulmate. Bhima cleared his throat and replied in an embarrassed voice, 'You too.'

Then, he smiled at Karan. 'Spread the word. We start in two days.'

11

'Sir, where do I put the diya stand?'

Amit Sharma looked harassed enough as it was, but this question was the straw that broke the camel's back. He glared at the man holding a shoulder-high, carved brass lamp that featured six holders for diyas and snapped in a scathing voice, 'Where do you *think*? On my head? Put it on the stage, fool! And don't forget to put the diyas in it like last time.'

The man scurried away to the stage as Amit mumbled, 'Stupid idiots, every one of them,' under his breath.

Yudhishtra frowned. This version of Amit was far removed from the solicitous, cheerful, enthusiastic character that he'd been privy to until now. He shifted on his feet, briefly slipping them out of the leather sandals that were cutting into his flesh. He'd have blisters before the day was through. Not to mention that he was dressed like an exaggerated version of a sage, in an unnaturally bright orange dhoti, with a smaller cloth of the same colour draped across his shoulders. The material was so stiff, the dhoti billowed out like a cloud around his hips and legs, making his lower half look like a giant orange.

Then there was the jewellery. His thick earrings and wristbands certainly looked like gold, but they were actually made from a flimsy, almost weightless substance that made his skin itch. The spear in his hand looked and felt like a child's toy instead of an actual weapon. All of this he'd pointed out to Amit and his friends earlier, but they had folded their hands again and insisted the get-up complemented his 'brand', whatever that meant.

Now, as he stared at his surrounds, he wondered if listening to them had been a good idea. They were standing inside a very large cloth tent that was being held up by wooden poles dug into the ground. Covering that ground was a dusty red carpet that was worn so thin it had holes everywhere, making it a bit of a hazard, because you never knew when you might trip on one of the holes. Especially if you couldn't see your feet because of your fruit-dhoti. Placed all around were rows and rows of metal chairs, all facing a large stage on one side of the tent's interior. On the stage was a large throne, the likes of which he'd never seen or even imagined. It was made from wood that had been painted to look like gold and was elaborately carved with bunches of flowers, hearts and some sort of odd-shaped crest with the profile of a lion on it. The seat and the centre of the back of the throne were upholstered with a garish, bright-red cloth and were shaped like enormous hearts.

It was the ugliest thing he'd ever seen in his life.

A niggling dread began to simmer in Yudhishtra's chest. In theory, spreading the word of dharma amongst the people of the Kalyug sounded noble and altruistic. In practice, it was turning out to be quite different from what he'd envisioned. Still, at least it gave him something to do while he was down here. From the moment they had landed on earth, his brothers had disregarded his wishes and dispersed to pursue individual undertakings. Bhima was helping Kunti at the orphanage, Arjuna was handling Draupadi's personal security needs, and the twins were out and about soaking in the sights. Yudhishtra had barely even spoken to Draupadi after he'd been unexpectedly uncoupled from her by his mother, but he knew she was busy with her new life. It wasn't appropriate for him to be intervening in her affairs anymore. No, it was best he kept busy doing something worthwhile until their time here ran out. Then they could go back home and everything would be normal again.

Amit interrupted Yudhishtra's thoughts by shouting out to one of the men standing in the distance, 'Where are the film crew and photographers?'

'They're having tea at the back!' the man shouted back.

Amit nodded tersely at one of his associates who had accompanied them from the BYBM Centre to this place. 'Get him ready. The buses have arrived.'

'Come, Guruji,' said the BYBM associate, with a smile that belied his tense exchange with Amit.

They were treating him like a child! 'Where?' asked Yudhishtra in an equally terse tone.

The man folded his hands immediately. 'The audience will start coming in now. Maybe you could go on stage and think about your talk. We will start soon.'

'Now? Shouldn't I come on stage once the people are already seated?' asked Yudhishtra.

The man nodded. 'Yes, normally that's what would happen, but this is a promotional shoot, so it doesn't matter. Once you're on stage, we can set the lighting and maybe do some portraits of you. Once the audience comes in, we'll shoot you entering the stage separately. Don't worry, Amit will explain it as you go.'

'Shoot me?'

The man looked confused for a moment, and then he laughed. 'No, no! We'll shoot you with a camera, Guruji, not a gun. Those we use for other things,' he said with a wink. 'Follow me.'

Despite his reservations and utter confusion, Yudhishtra followed the man to the stage where he reluctantly sat on the hideous throne. He had already committed to doing this, and it was his duty to see it through, he told the part of himself that wanted to abandon this enterprise and leave. He was Emperor Yudhishtra, and he had given his word. It was as good as set in stone.

Amit soon followed him up on stage as people began to stream in through giant slits in the tent to take their seats. A few sleepy-looking men ambled inside from the back and began to set up black contraptions all around the stage, shining blinding lights into his eyes repeatedly. Amit gave them non-stop instructions in a rapid monologue interspersed with words like 'skin-tone', 'filter' and 'glow', none of which he understood.

One of the men came up and whispered into Amit's ear, causing him to turn his head and shout into the distance, 'Make-up!'

A young man scampered up on to the stage and put a large box on the floor in front of Yudhishtra. Then, he whipped out a small brush, dipped it in a light-coloured liquid and started painting on Yudhishtra's face with it.

He batted the man's hands away, wiping the liquid off in disgust. 'What are you doing?'

'Just some light contouring, Guruji. Don't worry; it won't show on camera.'

Yudhishtra scowled. 'No. Take it away.' He pointed at the brush.

Amit hurried up to them and bent down to speak in Yudhishtra's ear. 'Guruji, the strong lights are making your skin look pale and washed out. Abhijit here is our make-up boy. He'll just put a little bit on your face, so it looks normal under the light. You won't even feel it once it dries.'

'Why can't you just turn the lights off?'

Amit smiled. 'Because then you'll look dark and blurry on camera. Trust us, we've done this a million times.'

'A million?'

Folding his hands for the hundredth time since the morning, Amit laughed. 'No, no. I just meant a lot of times. I promise you will look better like this, and the people will respond to you better. This is how it's normally done.'

Once again, Yudhishtra capitulated against his better judgement. 'Fine.'

'Good, good. Please excuse me, Guruji.' Glancing critically at the sparse, distinctly un-warrior-like sprinkling of hair on Yudhishtra's torso and his boyish abdomen, he turned to Abhijit-the-make-up-boy and said quickly, 'Paint some abs too.'

Abhijit nodded, blew on his brush, and asked Yudhishtra to close his eyes while he drew shapes on his face, neck and shoulders, rubbing the liquid into the skin with his fingers.

It was an unwelcome and uncomfortable experience, but Yudhishtra stoically kept his eyes closed and sat still through it. However, when Abhijit asked him to stand up and started painting on his stomach, he jumped back and finally put his foot down. 'No. I don't care if my stomach looks dark and blurry on camera. Don't touch it!'

'But your abs!'

'No!'

Abhijit put his brush away in surrender. But then he rummaged through his box and tentatively held up a bushy tuft of black hair for Yudhishtra to examine. 'Moustache?'

That was it. They had insulted his moustache for the last time. '*Enough!* Begone, you scoundrel, before I send you back to your maker!'

Abhijit retreated a few steps and cowered. 'Sorry, sorry.'

Amit ran up to the stage and shouted at Abhijit in an outraged voice, 'How dare you disobey Guruji? Get off the stage!'

Abhijit blinked at Amit. 'But you said—'

'Get out!'

Abhijit left in a huff, a wounded expression on his face. Amit turned back to Yudhishtra with his hands folded. As usual. 'Guruji, forgive me. You will not see him again.'

Yudhishtra's face, covered in layers of pastes and powders, was pinched with irritation. 'Let's just get this over with.'

'Of course, Guruji.' Amit hurriedly started shepherding people to their seats and organizers to their various posts. When all the chairs were full of people, noisily talking and ignoring Yudhishtra completely, Amit went to the centre of the stage and tapped on a black stand with a rounded limb. His voice suddenly became amplified and resounded across the tent. Yudhishtra stared at him, stunned. That small, black contraption had just made Amit's ordinary timbre sound like the voice of god.

'Everyone, please be quiet. *Quiet!*' The audience stopped talking amongst themselves and stared at Amit, unimpressed by the booming command. 'We're shooting Guruji today. It will take about two hours. Drinks are on the side and toilets are outside. Only ten minutes are allowed for a bathroom break, otherwise no payment. Men are getting 500, women 300 and 100 per child. Look interested when he speaks, and when my colleague lifts the sign,' he pointed to a man holding a large sign that said 'CLAP', 'you have to clap loudly and smile. No whistling or shouting. At the end of the talk, Guruji will light the lamp, and I will present him with the BYBM Spiritual Leader of the Year Award. The photographers and film crew will keep taking shots, so just look happy and interested when the cameras are pointed at you. Okay, let's do a quick rehearsal and then start.'

The man with the CLAP sign lifted it in the air and the crowd started clapping enthusiastically. He set it down and the crowd looked at Yudhishtra, happy and interested. He lifted the sign again, and the audience broke into applause. He then set it down, and they were happy and interested again. Like trained dogs.

Amit nodded and raised a fist with his thumb pointing upwards. He came up to Yudhishtra and said in a low voice, 'Guruji, you just walk to the front, wave to the crowd for a few minutes and smile. When you see me give you a thumbs-up,' he held out his fist again to demonstrate, 'you start giving your talk. Speak into the mic so the people in the back can hear your voice. No need to shout.'

He didn't have to tell Yudhishtra twice. In the past, he had needed to do vocal exercises to enable his voice to carry over a large crowd. But this device would eliminate the need to shout. He couldn't wait to try it.

He walked up to the front and waved. The man raised the CLAP sign and everyone began to applaud, as rehearsed. Observing the crowd's enthusiastic response, Yudhishtra felt a twinge of displeasure that they were being paid to do this, but he quickly tamped that down. Waving, smiling and nodding to the audience, he waited until Amit gave him the signal and then started talking. His voice resounded majestically, a fact that thrilled him no end. Staying on the theme of dharma, truth and duty, he expanded on it by using instances from the lives of his family members and the people he had known during his time. And his enemies, of course. Truth and duty didn't only count when they were applied to those one loved. A truly dharmic person, he explained, not only treated everyone, beloved and despised, equally, but also treated every twist of fate, whether good or bad, with the same equanimity and respect.

By the end of his talk, many of the audience members were genuinely attentive, and a few of them looked positively enraptured. Pleased with his success, he generously lit the diyas on the lamp and graciously received a metal trophy, amid much clapping and cheering. Yudhishtra didn't even let the constant flashing of lights in his face ruin his moment.

In the car, on the way back to the centre with Amit, a thought occurred to him. 'You mentioned that the audience members would be getting paid. Where is the money coming from?'

Amit seemed uncomfortable with the question. 'From the donations, Guruji.'

'But we only received one donation.'

'Er, there were a few others also, made directly to the centre in your name.'

Yudhishtra frowned. 'Weren't they supposed to be used for charitable causes?'

Now Amit looked positively jittery as he replied, 'There are always some start-up costs. However, they will lead to more donations, which we will then donate to charities.'

Yudhishtra was dismayed. 'But that's lying! It goes against everything I've been talking about!'

A hard edge coming into his voice, Amit retorted, 'It's not lying, it's business. You worry about your talks. Let me handle the rest. Guruji.'

12

Too bad women didn't drive battle chariots during his time, thought Arjuna. The way Draupadi was hurtling her car this way and that on the road, narrowly avoiding collisions with people and other vehicles, she would've made an excellent charioteer.

Provided the occupants of the chariot didn't die of fright first.

'I still think this is a bad idea. You're leaving in a few weeks. What's the point of raising his hopes?' uttered Draupadi, tyres screeching as she made a sharp right turn.

Arjuna held on to the sides of the front passenger seat, not trusting his seat belt to prevent his large frame from colliding with the door. 'We've already discussed this. Fun, remember?'

Her eyes narrowed suspiciously. 'You're not getting competitive with the mortals, are you?'

'Technically, I'm a mortal right now too; so I have no unfair advantage.' Arjuna couldn't help a smug grin. 'Besides, it's hardly a competition. There's a reason they name their boys after me.'

Yes, it was an obnoxious thing to say, but he wasn't going to apologize for being competitive. That was part of who he was. As a middle-born child, his choices had been to either stand out or be ignored. He had chosen the former, carving out an illustrious career for himself as a warrior and athlete. It felt good to stoke that fire again.

'It would be interesting to find out if they also name boys after the rest of us. Do you know, Draupadi?' asked Nakula from the back seat, where he was sitting with Sahadeva. Upon hearing about Arjuna's cricket adventure that morning, they'd decided to come along and watch him play. Well, actually Nakula wanted to watch. Sahadeva had voiced the same concerns as Draupadi and pointed out that they would be leaving soon. Still, he'd humoured his elder brothers and tagged along.

'I've met many Arjuns, a few Nakuls, but not many of the rest of us,' said Draupadi, still looking at the road. 'Names these days are just about what's fashionable. Arjun is currently popular, but I'm sure that'll change soon. I'm working on it.' She gave Arjuna a quick roguish glance, to which he replied with an even wider grin than before.

They arrived at the New Delhi Cricket Club and Draupadi parked her small car in between crowded rows of much larger cars. Walking up to the entrance, she turned quite a few heads, many of them recognizing her and asking to take a photo, or just greeting her with a shy smile and a compliment. Draupadi smiled and chatted with grace and an easy confidence. Walking alongside her, Arjuna felt a surge of pride. Her new success was something she had accomplished all on her own, without any assistance from him or his brothers. No wonder she hadn't gone back to heaven.

Arjuna sighed as they made their way through the club. The more time he spent with his runaway ex-wife, the less certain he was that she would agree to return with him. The scary thing though was that he was beginning to appreciate why.

Who would leave all this to return to being an immortal sidekick?

A portly man of about fifty stood on the side of the centre field, impatiently tapping his foot and checking his wrist. When he saw them, he smiled and walked over, stretching his hand out and taking Arjuna's in a firm handshake. 'Good to see you, son, good to see you. Call me Rizwan. You're taller than I expected, but that's better. Come, meet one of the club's senior coaches. Your friends can wait in the stands.'

He waved to a man dressed in white clothing, who ran down to the field, while Draupadi gave Arjuna a pointed glance before reluctantly making her way to the seats in the stands with Nakula and Sahadeva. She clearly didn't want him committing to anything without her.

'Nice to meet you, Arjuna. I'm Coach Vasu,' said the coach with a toothy smile. He was younger than Rizwan, but had the same paternal vibe. 'Rizwan Sir has told me all about you. Who's your coach right now?'

Arjuna shook his head. 'No one. I'd never played cricket before yesterday. That video was my first time.'

The other two guffawed in that forced manner with which men often greet bad jokes. Rizwan slapped Arjuna's back good-naturedly. 'Come, tell us. How long have you played?'

'I'm telling the truth,' said Arjuna with a slight shrug. 'I've never played before. Whether you believe or disbelieve me is your choice.'

An uncomfortable silence hung in the air, none of the men sure how to proceed. Finally, Coach Vasu nodded and patted Arjuna on his shoulder. 'Never mind. Come, let's see what you can do, okay?'

Arjuna nodded and followed the coach to the side of the field, where a series of long lanes were fenced by walls of loose green nets. Handing Arjuna a cricket ball, Coach Vasu said, 'Why don't you do a few warm-up tosses first and get the feel of the ball. We'll start when you're ready.'

'I'm ready,' replied Arjuna, throwing the ball in the air and catching it. 'Where do I bowl this?'

The coach looked at him sceptically and pointed to the lanes. 'In the nets.'

Arjuna walked over, and realized that each net-encased lane was about the size of the rectangle in the middle of a cricket ground and featured a set of three stumps at the end. 'Here?' He pointed inside one of them.

Coach Vasu nodded, stepping back with Rizwan to observe.

Arjuna quickly stretched his legs and did a couple of squats to loosen them. Then he went some distance from the nets, did a run-up and bowled the ball into one of them. It sliced through the air and, as expected, knocked the middle stump out of the ground. Arjuna turned to the two men.

Coach Vasu was staring at him with his mouth open and Rizwan had an intensely focused look on his face. 'Again, please,' said Rizwan.

Arjuna bowled a few more balls, and each one had the desired result. Finally, Rizwan held his hand up in the air and turned to the coach. 'Let's see how he fares with a batsman?'

Coach Vasu nodded with barely concealed excitement and grabbed a bat from the ground, hurrying over to the nets when he was stopped by Rizwan, who said, 'I think you should pad up, coach.'

Arjuna could tell that the coach wanted to argue with Rizwan, but he nodded and disappeared into the stands. He walked up to Arjuna and said in a light voice, as if they were talking about the weather, 'Your action will need work. Remember, when you're playing against a batsman, the game is as much about the mind as it is about skill. Make the batsman afraid of the ball, of getting hurt, and he'll try to deflect it instead of hitting it. If you can make the batsman nervous enough to deflect the ball into the air for a catch, it's as good as hitting the stumps.'

Arjuna's eyes lit up as he nodded. He didn't need to know the rules and terminology of cricket to understand how to play mind games. He'd played them throughout his mortal life, on and off the battlefield. This just got a lot more interesting, he thought as he stretched his neck, arms and shoulders.

Coach Vasu came out, bundled up in padded armour, complete with a helmet, picked up his bat again and went to the stumps-end of the nets. Rizwan stepped back and signalled for Arjuna to start.

Sending Coach Vasu a glare that was somewhere between angry and condescending, Arjuna strode back and began his run up. Keeping his action so rapid that it would've been difficult for the batsman to see the ball, he flung it to the ground in a vicious bouncer, sending it flying perilously close to the batsman's face, causing him to jerk away to avoid being hit.

Arjuna smirked. Even if Coach Vasu hadn't moved, the ball wouldn't have hit him. But it was close enough that he didn't realize that.

Again and again, Arjuna made the ball fly dangerously close to the batsman without actually putting him in any danger, shifting angles and styles so that it was impossible to predict where his next ball would go. Coach Vasu only managed to deflect a couple of them. Finally, once he was sure that the coach would be fairly demoralized and nervous, Arjuna swayed the ball at a high speed, causing it to deflect off the bat into the air and straight into his waiting hands.

Arjuna looked at Rizwan for a reaction. The scout was grinning from ear-to-ear and clapping his hands.

'Excuse me!'

A man, dressed in jeans and a T-shirt, with a cap sitting low on his forehead, and dark glasses, was running towards them. Rizwan squinted at him and his eyes widened.

The man, who looked about the same age as Arjuna, stopped in front of him with a smile. 'Hi, I'm Rohit.'

'I'm Arjuna.'

Rizwan hurried up to them, grinning at Rohit. 'Rohitji, how nice to see you here.' He turned to Arjuna and said with a good deal of reverence in his voice, 'This is Rohit Jadeja. He plays international cricket for India. One of our country's top batsmen.'

Rohit Jadeja brushed him off with a polite shake of the head and spoke to Arjuna instead, 'I was meeting some people in the coffee shop and noticed your deliveries. Fantastic stuff, bro.'

'Thanks.'

'Who do you play for?'

'Right now, myself.'

Rohit Jadeja looked at him in an assessing way. 'I've never seen anything like it. Want to bowl a few balls to me?'

'It would be my pleasure.' If this was one of the country's best batsmen, thought Arjuna, it'd be interesting to see how their skills compared. The competitive fire in him flared in excitement.

Rohit Jadeja took the pads and bat from Coach Vasu, and went up to the stumps. Arjuna smiled to himself. Who would have thought that within days of his landing on earth, he'd be testing his mettle against the best the mortals had to offer? So much for staying incognito. He ran up and threw the ball as hard as he could, bouncing it towards the batsman in the same aggressive manner he'd used with Coach Vasu.

To his credit, Rohit Jadeja didn't jerk away to avoid being hit. Instead, he raised his bat high to defend his body and blocked the ball, deflecting it to the ground. It rolled close to Arjuna's feet uselessly.

'Arjuna,' Rizwan said quietly, walking up to him. 'That was good. You got him to play on his back foot. Now, don't throw anymore bouncers. A batsman of his calibre will quickly adjust to your speed, swing and play them. You have to be unpredictable going forward. Vary your deliveries. Change your line and length, play with the seam and try different speeds. Show us what you can do with the ball.'

Grinning, Arjuna nodded, wiping a thin sheen of sweat off his forehead with the back of his hand. His body felt like a taut bow, radiating with anticipation and unspent energy. His mind felt focused and still, all the cares and worries of the world filtered out until nothing remained but him, the ball and what they had to do next. God, it felt good to feel alive like this again. He'd forgotten just how good.

For the next hour, Arjuna and Rohit Jadeja played so scintillatingly well that most of the clubhouse gathered around to watch them. Over a hundred people crowded around the nets, peeking over each other's shoulders to get a glimpse of two stellar players battle it out one-on-one. Fans of the Indian cricket team said that Rohit Jadeja was equally matched in talent by the unknown bowler, but Rizwan Hussain knew better. Arjuna's action, his movements were brilliant, but completely untrained. If he was this good without any kind of formal coaching, he would be unstoppable with it. Far, far better than the opponent he was currently up against.

Arjuna Kuru was a huge, flawless raw diamond. The kind that was unearthed only once in a generation.

13

He loved his twin, he really did.

Nakula, fourth of the Pandava brothers, sighed. Sahadeva was the closest person in the world to him. When their mother, Madri, had committed Sati, the twins had been adopted by Kunti, who already had three sons of her own. While she had loved them and never treated them any differently, they had never quite felt as close to her as her birth sons did. So, they banded together as children, being for each other what no one else could be. For Nakula, Sahadeva had come before his wives and even his children, and the same was true for Sahadeva.

Until they died and went to heaven.

In the realm of the gods, there had been no battles to fight, no challenges to overcome. There had been no emperor to report to, no kingdom to oversee or court to manage. They had reconnected with their mother, and worked to establish that blood connection they'd missed during their mortal lives.

They became their own masters for the first time in their lives. In the absence of any purpose, Nakula had taken full advantage of the legion of beautiful and willing nymphs available in heaven and applied himself to hedonism full-time. Sahadeva, however, being the more reticent twin, started spending more time with his wife, Vijaya.

As a result, thousands of years later, they were still as loyal to each other as they'd always been, but didn't really have much to talk about anymore.

'Why does every conversation with you turn into a lecture, Brother?' he asked Sahadeva with a humourless chuckle.

Sahadeva's lips turned prim with disapproval, as they did so frequently these days. 'It's not a lecture if I ask a simple question.'

'No, but it's usually the beginning of one.'

Sahadeva glanced down briefly at Draupadi, sitting lower in the stands and staring at Arjuna playing with rapt attention. Ensuring that his voice was out of her hearing range, he murmured, 'I was just surprised that you accepted that lady's invitation for tonight without consulting me. Or that you would encourage Arjuna to come here, when you know Krishna specifically told us not to get involved with the affairs of mortals.'

Nakula shrugged. 'I didn't think it was that serious a matter.'

'How can you say that? Our actions may change the course of destiny for the mortals we come into contact with. It's a very serious matter. Our time here will pass, but our actions might have consequences. What happens if you leave that woman with child?'

Nakula smiled as he pictured pretty, petite Angela. 'That'll be one good-looking child.'

'Be serious.'

'I don't know, Brother,' retorted Nakula. 'I don't know what will happen tonight, or what'll happen with Arjuna, or with mortals. I'm just trying to have a good time before we need to go back.'

'Then let's keep sightseeing, trying the food and drink, and having new experiences like we've been doing so far. Forget tonight. I've already requested Draupadi to speak to Arjuna. He might actually listen if it comes from her. Yudhishtra cannot be guided by any of us, as we've seen many times in the past. But you I care about the most. I don't want anything untoward to happen to you.' Sahadeva put his hand on Nakula's shoulder.

The gesture should've felt comforting, as it always did. But today, Nakula felt the weight of Sahadeva's hand instead of its support. 'It's just a night out with some friendly mortals, Brother. Don't read too much into it. We'll have some harmless fun, and then you can go back to your family in heaven, safe and sound.'

Sahadeva's eyes widened in surprise. 'How can you say that? *You* are my family. The closest one I have!'

Nakula gave a small snort. 'Am I? Have you heard yourself speak lately? I feel like I'm having a conversation with your wife every time we talk.'

'That's unfair!'

Nakula kept staring straight ahead at the field, a sardonic look on his face. 'I would've understood if it was Draupadi who held a crop to your hide, but Vijaya? Who knew timid little Princess Vijaya had it in her?'

Sahadeva scowled. 'Sarcasm doesn't suit you, Brother.'

'Humourlessness suits you even less.'

They were quiet for a while. Disagreements weren't uncommon between them, but they tended to be about trivial, easily resolved things. Never had either of them disparaged the other's wife before. There were some lines you just didn't cross, and this was one of them. Especially with Sahadeva. While Nakula had never neglected his husbandly duties, he'd never been particularly devoted to his own wife, Karenumati, and neither of the twins had been close to Draupadi. Sahadeva, on the other hand, had always been deeply in love with Vijaya. Right from the very beginning. It was the kind of love that made everyone else's feel inadequate in comparison. The kind of love that had only grown stronger as the millennia went by.

Unfortunately, it had also grown into the kind of love that held itself so far above others, it had become judgemental and sanctimonious to an annoying degree. Vijaya and Sahadeva seemed to think they were qualified to offer unsolicited advice to all and sundry about their lives and relationships, completely unaware that it was unwelcome.

Nakula was tired of stepping around his brother's self-righteousness to maintain the peace. He had a short window of opportunity to make the most of this earthly trip, and he wasn't going to pass that up. He kept silent.

It was Sahadeva who apologized first. 'I'm sorry. I didn't realize you felt that way. The truth is, I didn't really want to come down here in the first place. I only came because of you, to support you as I have always done. And now, I just feel like this situation is getting out of control, and I don't want to jeopardize our plans.' He cleared his throat and said in a stilted voice, 'I will try not to mention Vijaya so much if it bothers you. I understand that your marital relations with Karenumati are over, and it must hurt you to see me in my relationship.'

Nakula had begun to feel equally apologetic at the start of Sahadeva's speech, but by the end of it, he was angry again. 'I don't miss my marriage, Brother, nor do I want yours. Try to step off that pedestal of yours and see my point of view. I like change. I like risk and unpredictability. I don't want to feel safe and comfortable all the time. I don't want someone who simply loves and accepts me the way I am. I want someone who pushes me, challenges me, calls me out. Someone who excites my mind as well as my body. Someone fearless and fiery.' He smiled, thinking about the bold, openly sensual way Angela had flirted with him. 'If tonight is all I get with Angela, I'm taking it.'

'Fine.' Sahadeva gave a soft sigh.

His anger dissipating as quickly as it had risen, Nakula looked at Sahadeva and gave him a wry grin. 'Besides, if I fall, I have you to catch me, right?'

Sahadeva laughed and shook his head. 'Always.'

Nakula nodded. 'I'm sorry for my harsh words about your wife. They were undeserved. Now, why is Draupadi getting up?'

Looking over at the field, he saw that Arjuna had stopped playing, and was now standing and talking to the batsman with a crowd around them. Draupadi was hurriedly making her way towards him.

With a quick look at each other, the twins jumped out of their seats and caught up with her. Elbowing their way through the crowd so she didn't have to, they stopped next to a grinning, sweat-soaked Arjuna, whose bowling was being generously complimented by the equally sweaty batsman.

'Seriously amazing, bro. Look, I know the team and our coaches would love to meet you. Why don't you come to one of our practice sessions at the cricket stadium? I'll message you the details. Okay?'

Before Arjuna could answer, Draupadi stepped forward and said, 'Hi, sorry to interrupt. Arjuna, can I speak to you for a second?'

Arjuna turned to grin at her before seeing the strained, polite smile on her face that belied her angry eyes. He nodded with a wary, 'Yes, of course.'

'Hey, you're Draupadi Kuru, aren't you?' Rohit Jadeja beamed at Draupadi. 'I've seen you on TV.'

Draupadi smiled back. 'I've seen you on TV too.'

The look on Rohit's face became questioning as he pointed between Draupadi and Arjuna. 'Do you two know each other?'

Draupadi replied, 'We're friends.'

'Oh, great. Then you should come to the practice session too.' Rohit's eyes took on a distinctly keen spark.

'I don't think so.'

'No, you should totally come. I'd love to find out more about your talk show.'

Nakula watched Arjuna's eyes narrow as Rohit and Draupadi's conversation progressed. Trepidation filled his heart as Arjuna turned to Rohit and said in a firm, gruff voice, 'I will be happy to attend the practice session. My *friend* Draupadi is usually very busy at work, so she won't be able to make it.'

That made Draupadi's eyes widen. 'You're going?'

Noticeably irritated, Arjuna nodded. 'I am.'

'But what about the ... ashram?'

Arjuna mumbled, 'We'll discuss that later.' He turned to Rohit. 'I have to go now, but please message me the details of the session. I will meet you then.'

To Rizwan, he said, 'Thank you for today. This was very enjoyable. I'll consider your offer.'

Amid a few more backslaps and compliments on his playing, the group dispersed, and Arjuna was able to walk away with Draupadi, Nakula and Sahadeva. No one said anything until they were all seated in Draupadi's car. When the last door slammed shut, Draupadi couldn't hold back any longer.

'Are you *mad*?'

Arjuna's jaw clenched. 'Can we have this conversation later?'

'You're leaving in a few weeks! This isn't child's play, Arjuna. Rizwan wants you to sign up with him. You can't just make commitments and disappear!'

'It's a game, Draupadi. One that I'm good at. I won't sign with him or make any commitments; don't worry.'

'You just made a commitment to Rohit Jadeja!'

'It's just one day of playing cricket!'

Draupadi glowered at him for a moment, breathing heavily, her eyes seemingly tormented by a thought she couldn't voice.

Nakula cleared his throat loudly from the back seat. Both Draupadi and Arjuna started, as if they'd forgotten the twins were in the car.

Draupadi turned to face the front and muttered, 'Why couldn't the five of you have just stayed up there? From the moment you entered my life, it's turned into a bloody mess.'

Arjuna laughed. 'Some things don't change, do they?'

Draupadi throttled the steering wheel and let out a growl of frustration. It made Arjuna laugh harder.

14

'Welcome, my ashram friends!' shouted Angela.

Nakula barely heard her, busy as he was trying to take his eyes off her legs in the barely there dress she was wearing. She looked like a fantasy come to life as she laughed at Yudhishtra holding his hands over his ears and looking around as if he'd just walked into the demon world.

Moments earlier, they'd entered a large ground that Draupadi explained was normally used to race cars. Now it was covered in tents of all sizes—massive ones that flashed with lights and boomed with deafening music, medium-sized tents with crowds spilling out of them, and an assortment of smaller tents featuring everything from food to drinks to shopping to medical care. A large Ferris wheel, lit up with twinkling lights of every conceivable colour, stood as the centrepiece of it all. Thousands of people milled around.

As fairs went, it was the largest and noisiest Nakula had ever been to in his life.

'Did you get in okay?' Angela asked Draupadi with a saucy glance thrown Nakula's way for good measure.

Nakula grinned back, glad he'd stayed firm on coming tonight. Yudhishtra had made a token effort to dissuade them when he'd come home from the BYBM Centre earlier to find that they were going to a music festival, but Nakula told him that they had already made a commitment to attend. Yudhishtra couldn't argue with that, so he decided he would come along, to ensure their safety.

Now, Yudhishtra was looking at Arjuna, Draupadi, Sahadeva and him like he was on the verge of insisting they leave.

Draupadi nodded to Angela. 'I showed them our VIP passes at the fast-track lane, as you instructed. This is ridiculous, by the way.' She pointed to the cap and sunglasses she was wearing, despite the fact that the sun had already set.

Angela winked. 'That was just to ensure that you weren't delayed by the crowd at the gate. You can take them off now. Lots of celebrities will be walking about, so people are used to it. They might take pictures of you though, so make sure you're always camera-ready.' Then, she turned to Arjuna and said, 'Draupadi tells me you're on bodyguard duty from now on. I'm sure you'll be staying *really* close to her at all times, so I won't worry about her safety.' She wagged her eyebrows and smirked at him.

Draupadi rolled her eyes. Yudhishtra narrowed his.

Angela grinned and waved a hand, sweeping the entire grounds. 'Okay, so we've got four stages, plus a bunch of other stuff apparently. Indus Ocean's performance starts at 8.30 on the main stage, so let's go there first? They have a special VIP box to view the show. Later on, we can walk around. Come!' She sidled up to Nakula, folded an arm into his and tugged.

Nakula leaned down and whispered into her ear as they walked, 'You look beautiful.'

Angela smiled up at him, her eyes twinkling. 'So do you.'

He felt his stomach flutter nervously, something it hadn't done since he was an adolescent. This woman was unlike any he'd ever met before. There was confidence and charisma, but not one iota of guile in her eyes. They showed no desire to play power games, or bring him to heel. Every woman he'd ever been with, apart from nymphs because they didn't count, had seen him as a challenge. A shallow, vain, desirable, promiscuous man who needed to be reformed and tamed by a woman. Even his own wife, Karenumati, had started their marital life with a purposeful glint in her eye. That glint had slowly faded, and worn into despair and then bitterness. In reality, Nakula was anything but shallow, despite being well aware of the effect his appearance had on people. He didn't want to be tamed or enslaved by a woman. He wanted something real, somebody to see him for who he was, not what he looked like.

This tiny woman, who had her arm circled around his, whose blatant flirting and twinkling glances were lighting a fire in his belly, had an openness about her, a candid, honest charm that promised Nakula he would get exactly what he saw.

And what he saw looked pretty damn good.

As they got closer to the main stage tent, the booming music got even louder. Yudhishtra peered at the flashing lights with a grimace. 'Are they trying to break down a giant door with a battering ram in there?'

A burst of laughter erupted from Angela. 'It does kind of sound like that! You've got a great imagination, Nakula's brother.'

Well, that was a first. Everyone in the group looked away, either at the ground, the sky or people milling about. Anywhere except at Yudhishtra's expression of utter astonishment. Draupadi was trying her very best not to laugh.

They walked into the tent and saw a spectacular sight. An arena, covered in bright, sparkling and roaming lights of every colour, with an uncountable number of people all facing a grand stage. A group of men were performing on stage with instruments the Pandavas had never seen before. Earth-shatteringly loud music engulfed the arena. Everyone seemed to be enjoying it thoroughly, Nakula observed as he looked around. The audience was screaming and chanting along with the singers on stage as they swayed together, like a shoal of fish, with their phones over their heads.

Angela pointed them to the side, and they went up a walkway that was guarded heavily at various points by groups of bulky men and women. They climbed up into a box-like structure that was suspended over the heads of the audience. The wall on one side of the box was made entirely of glass, with a large balcony outside that looked on to the stage. Inside was a darkened lounge with cooled air, and a long counter, behind which uniformed staff served drinks. People milled about, all holding drinks in their hands, either chatting animatedly in groups, watching the performance or sucking on stick-like contraptions and blowing smoke out of their mouths. A large table laden with food sat on one side of the lounge, but no one was eating.

'This is just the opening act,' Angela murmured into Nakula's ear as they stepped out on to the balcony. It was much noisier out here than inside the lounge. 'Indus Ocean will be coming on soon. Let's get drinks.'

She took them all to the bar and handed them each a glass with an alcoholic beverage that Draupadi called whisky. Arjuna took the first tentative sip and his eyes lit up. Turning to his brothers, he held up his glass. 'To our first drink in ... a *very* long time.'

The others followed, sipping their whisky with an almost reverent enthusiasm, each of them letting out a small sigh of relief and pleasure after taking that first taste.

Angela looked bemused by their expressions. 'It's been that long, huh?'

'You have no idea,' replied Nakula, breathing in the earthy, spicy scent of the liquid before feeling its sting on his tongue as he rolled it around before swallowing.

'What else haven't you done in a really long time?' Angela wiggled her eyebrows suggestively.

He shook his head with a chuckle. 'Not what you're thinking. The, er, ashram is alcohol-free, but everything else is fine.'

She rolled her eyes. 'I *really* have to visit this ashram someday. It sounds unreal.' Then she smiled. 'So, anything else you haven't done in a while, Nakula?'

'Truthfully?' Nakula smiled back. 'I haven't been this attracted to a woman in ages.'

Angela inclined her head to one side. 'Was that because there were no women around or because you were attracted to men?'

He laughed. 'No, not men. There was simply no one like you around.'

'There rarely is,' she said in a theatrical voice as she winked. 'Although, you should know that I'm a handful.'

'I like having my hands full.'

Angela grinned. 'Good answer.'

'Well, well, look who's arrived! The show can start!'

A short, lean man, dressed in a multicoloured, patterned jacket, with the kind of cheekbones that turned heads, sauntered up to them and kissed the air next to Angela's cheeks, punctuating each kiss with a 'muah' for dramatic effect. Then he turned to her companions and smirked. 'I see you've brought an entourage as always. Hmmm, I already know you,' he pointed in Draupadi's direction. 'Don't want to know you, you and you,' he said as he waved dismissively towards Yudhishtra, Arjuna and Sahadeva. Narrowing in on Nakula's face, the man fluttered his lashes and exclaimed, 'But *you*, yes. I must know you. Angela, darling, where are your manners? Chop, chop!'

Angela shook her head and sighed, obviously used to the man's behaviour. 'Be nice, GT. Everybody, this is Gautam Thakur, fashion designer and my personal tormentor. GT, these are Draupadi's friends—Arjuna, Yudhishtra, Nakula and Sahadeva.'

'Oh god,' GT said to Draupadi. 'What is it with the names? You'd think they picked you lot straight out of the forest. But still, I applaud your TV show, darling, and ever since you wore my Kaira dress, they've been selling like hot cakes. So, all's forgiven!'

Draupadi looked bemused as he blew her a dismissive kiss and turned back to Angela.

'There, see? I've been nice,' GT stated. 'Now, what's the hottie's name and when's he visiting my place to, ahem, bounce some ideas around?' He gestured towards Nakula.

Angela laughed. 'Back off, sister, this one's mine.'

She tightened her hold on Nakula's arm and curled her body into his. He liked her playfulness. A lot.

"He is my date tonight.' She looked up at Nakula, her big eyes dilating as they met his searing gaze. 'Right?'

Nakula felt an untimely surge of desire, which he quickly masked with a wicked smile. 'I'll be anything you want me to be.'

Fanning himself with one hand, GT declared, 'Such hotness is totally wasted on a straight guy. Fine, I'll back off. On one condition.' He looked at Nakula and said in a serious voice with a lot less drama, 'Model my fall line for me. With your shoulders and that face, you'll be an overnight sensation. Trust me, Bollywood will come knocking in days.'

Nakula had no idea what he was talking about, but before he could say anything, Angela said in an excited voice, 'You *would* make a great model, Nakula!' At his confused expression, she slapped her forehead, 'Right. I forgot you came here straight from the same ashram as Draupadi. I'm guessing you don't know what modelling is, do you?'

Nakula shook his head.

'Never mind.' Angela waved it off. 'I'll explain after the show. GT, if he's interested I'll get back to you.'

After giving Nakula an assessing stare, GT finally nodded reluctantly. 'Think about it, darling. It'll be the opportunity of—'

'*GT!*'

GT started, cast a quick glance over his shoulder and seemed to visibly shrink. 'Oh god no, no, no …'

'Breathe,' Angela ground out through the fake smile pasted on her lips. 'She's headed this way.'

Draupadi frowned in the direction of a tall, thin, middle-aged woman whose face looked like it had been painted on by a child. 'Isn't that Romila Balani, the actress?'

GT huffed loudly. 'Oh, please. The only acting she's done lately has been at political rallies.'

He turned as the woman reached him. 'Romila, darling! Looking as young as ever. Is that a new haircut?'

Romila preened, cut a sharp glance through the group, decided no one was worth her attention and smiled coquettishly at GT. 'No, still the same. It's so crowded here! Isn't this supposed to be the VIP deck?'

GT nodded with a casual wave of his hand. 'Everyone's a VIP nowadays.' Then, with a sly glance her way, he added, 'You should know about that.'

Romila Balani gave no indication that she had understood the sentiment behind his statement. Instead, she pouted some more and played with her hair. 'I just thought it would be more exclusive than this. Took me ages to get here in traffic. These anti-government protests are so pointless. Can't even use the roads in our own country because of those academic types and their students. Don't they have jobs?'

A terse silence greeted her tirade. Completely oblivious to it, Romila carried on, 'You know what, I'm sure this *is* their job. They're totally being paid to sit there by foreign governments. Anyway,' she smiled again at GT, 'I heard your fall line is coming out soon. When am I getting my outfits?'

GT feigned surprise with the practiced look of someone who answers that question daily. 'What? You mean my team hasn't sent them already? A complete oversight! They'll be on your doorstep tomorrow.'

Now Romila Balani's eyes narrowed suspiciously in GT's direction. 'You know that I have over a million followers. People are paying me good money for visibility.'

'I have no doubt, darling,' responded GT. 'You don't get that kind of vitriol for free.'

Once again, Romila's face was entirely free of comprehension. Reassured that he understood just how influential her platform was, she air-kissed GT and disappeared into the crowd. GT, Angela and Draupadi visibly exhaled.

Draupadi asked Angela, 'Do you think people really pay her for visibility?'

Angela shrugged, contempt in her eyes. 'I doubt it. Most of her followers are fake. She's just posturing, trying to stay relevant. And selling her soul and dignity in the process. Best to ignore people like that. They just want attention, negative or positive is not a consideration.'

A loud announcement, along with the blinking of gigantic lights and a fireworks display around the stage below, signalled the start of the Indus Ocean performance. The crowd roared in collective anticipation. Angela quickly got everyone a fresh round of drinks and shepherded them on to the balcony to watch. All except Yudhishtra, who sat inside the lounge with a tortured look on his face. He clearly regretted coming tonight, thought Nakula.

Next to Nakula, Angela was swaying, dancing and singing along with the group of men that had started performing on stage. She knew the words to all their songs. Even Draupadi was dancing along and clearly enjoying herself. Meanwhile, Arjuna stood back, sipping his drink and watching Draupadi with a contemplative expression.

Sahadeva shouted into Nakula's ear, 'Should we leave? Yudhishtra doesn't look happy.'

For once, that didn't make him feel in the least guilty. Bhima and Arjuna were doing exactly what they wanted on this trip; why shouldn't he? Nakula shook his head. 'I'm staying.'

15

'So, wearing clothes and walking up and down a stage is a real job?'

Angela nodded. 'A real and well-paying job,' she answered, tucking her legs to the side as they sat on a road divider at the edge of a food tent.

Nakula was baffled. To think that clothing was so important to mortals these days that they bought clothes just because they were worn by attractive and famous people, who were paid to wear them in the first place. In his day, clothing had featured very little variation and depended largely on one's status and standing in the community. Most men and women wore draped cloth that covered their legs, and some women, especially those of a higher caste, wore a breast cloth and perhaps a scarf, if they were particularly modest. Materials, colours and designs varied a little, but the basic composition was the same for everyone.

He took a bite out of the roll in his hands. Inside a fried roti wrapping was a combination of egg, meat, raw vegetables and some kind of spiced sauce. The combination of flavours burst in his mouth, and he sighed in contentment. Tonight was turning out to be even better than he'd hoped. After the show, everyone had dispersed. Arjuna, Yudhishtra and Draupadi had gone off in one direction, and Angela, Sahadeva and him had come to a food tent to eat.

Sahadeva was looking a little sullen as he ate his own roll quietly, and Nakula immediately felt guilty about their discussion earlier in the day. He'd been angry, and his words had been unnecessarily harsh. After all, despite all his objections and warnings, his twin was still sitting here dutifully, looking out for him.

'It's good, isn't it, Brother?' Nakula pointed to the roll.

Sahadeva gave him a small smile and said, 'It is good. I wish Vijaya could taste it.'

'Who's Vijaya?' Angela asked though a mouthful of food.

Sahadeva, who hadn't warmed up to Angela, said in a tight voice, 'My wife.'

'Why didn't you bring her with you on this holiday?'

Sahadeva shrugged. 'It was supposed to be just my brothers and I, but now ... I wish I had.'

Angela took another bite before saying, 'Next time, you should. Maybe if I can convince Nakula here to stay in Delhi and do a bit of modelling, you both will have a reason to visit.'

Sahadeva looked at her warily. 'Nakula won't be staying, or doing any modelling.'

Angela raised an eyebrow. 'Isn't that for him to decide?'

'We're twins. You won't understand.'

Nakula felt his temper rising. Yes, he may have said some disparaging words about Vijaya earlier, but he had apologized, and they'd both moved on. Sahadeva had no right to be rude to Angela. 'She's right, Brother. I'm a grown man, and I can answer for myself.'

Sahadeva's eyes widened. 'You're not seriously considering it, are you?'

Nakula shrugged. If Yudhishtra could go give speeches to mortals, Bhima could cook for a building full of mortal children and Arjuna could play sports with mortals, what was stopping him from strutting around in some clothing? It was harmless fun, and it would make Angela happy. 'Why not?'

Sahadeva's eyes lit up with anger and frustration. 'Brother, we've talked about this already.'

'We haven't decided on anything.'

They glowered at each for a moment in an unspoken argument. Sahadeva said in a low rumble, 'You said it was just tonight.'

Nakula exhaled in frustration. 'Maybe I changed my mind. Don't make this into a battle, Brother.'

Sahadeva got up abruptly, mumbled, 'I knew it,' and, without saying another word, strode away.

'Wow, he feels strongly about your decisions,' said Angela with a low whistle.

Staring at the ground for a few silent moments, Nakula finally looked up. 'He does.'

'Why?'

He shrugged. 'We've always done everything together. And now ... things have changed.'

Shrugging as well, Angela said, 'You're both fully grown men. You can't stick to each other your entire lives.'

Smiling, Nakula thought about how that was exactly what they'd always done, even as grown men. Stuck together and done their duty as the youngest of the Pandava brothers. Their afterlife had seen Sahadeva find himself and Nakula lose himself, but still, the ghost of their mortal dependence remained. Or at least the pretence of it.

'We were orphaned at a young age, so we only had each other for a long time. Sahadeva's the more sensible twin,' Nakula said with a smile. 'So he feels like it's his responsibility to protect me, prevent me from making mistakes. I understand that, and I appreciate it. But I also feel trapped by it sometimes.'

Angela nodded. 'I get that. Everyone deserves the freedom to make their own choices, even if they're the wrong ones. At least that way you're not stuck in a prison of other people's expectations. When I first told my parents that I wanted to be a news producer, they thought I'd do it for a few years, get married, get pregnant and settle down into family life. For years, every visit home was about trying to find me a man to marry. From their point of view, they just wanted me to be happy, live in a safe and stable environment. And for good reason. Life in news is hard; the timings are terrible and pretty much everyone hates you if you're a successful woman. But I genuinely believe I'm happier than I would've been had I listened to them. And even in the moments when I'm not happy, I still know I'm doing the right thing. For me.'

'What about your parents? Aren't they angry with you for not listening to them?'

A wry look flashed in her bewitching eyes. 'They were, in the beginning. Now, not so much. They've gotten used to it over the years. That's not to say I won't ever get married.

Maybe I will, if I meet someone special, or maybe I won't. I'm fine either way, both emotionally and financially.'

Before he could stop himself, he ran his thumb over the back of her hand, gently grazing her knuckles. 'I think that's very admirable of you. I've never been able to go against my family.' He sighed. 'Truthfully, I know I'm not living the life I want. Sahadeva thinks I'm envious of him because he has a good marriage and a contented family life. But the fact is, while I'm not envious of his relationship or his life, I *am* envious of his happiness. He's moved on, found his peace, and I still have no idea where to find mine.'

'Maybe you're looking in the wrong places.'

Nakula smiled, and moved his hand to her face and traced her jaw. 'Where should I be looking?'

Angela smiled back. 'Are you trying to distract me so you don't have to talk about your feelings anymore?'

Nakula shook his head and whispered. 'No. I'm trying to distract *me* so I don't have to feel anymore.'

'Is it working?'

'It could. Give it a minute.'

She laughed. Sliding closer, she cupped his face with her palms. 'Do you want to know what I think?'

'What?'

'I think you should give GT's offer a shot. You'll never know what you want if you never try anything new.'

Nakula brought his face closer, teasing her nose with his own. 'Will you come with me?'

Her breathing changed, becoming uneven. She brushed her lips against his, a tiny whisper of softness against his. 'Wild horses couldn't stop me.'

'Why would wild horses try and stop you?'

She chuckled lightly. 'It's a saying. Will you do it?'

'Yes.' He slid his arm around her waist, pulling her even closer. 'Keep kissing me like that and I'll do anything you want.'

She kissed him gently again. 'Good. Now that we've eaten, where do you want to go next?'

'Anywhere I can be alone with you.'

Laughing, she eyed him seductively from under her lashes. 'I know just the place.'

She stood up, grabbed his hand and started running.

16

The dance floor throbbed, its thumping beat travelling from the soles of her shoes into her body. Wild rays of multicoloured lights flared and leapt over the heads of a few hundred people who writhed, jumped and moved together to the music.

Draupadi hadn't gotten the chance to dance much in heaven. Only nymphs danced, to entertain gods and men. So, she'd rediscovered her love of dancing in this new life. Nowadays, Angela took her out regularly to dance clubs. For the few hours she lost herself on the dance floor, Draupadi felt uncoiled and free in ways she couldn't explain.

She turned to Arjuna and Yudhishtra. 'Come on, let's dance.'

Both men looked at the moving bodies in utter shock.

After a moment, Arjuna looked at Draupadi incredulously, and seeing the slightly defiant look on her face, tried valiantly not to laugh.

She ignored his shaking shoulders and twitching lips, and asked, 'Are you coming or not?'

Yudhishtra burst out, 'To do *that*?'

This time, Arjuna did laugh. Draupadi narrowed her eyes at Yudhishtra. 'Yes, this is how mortals dance these days.'

Yudhishtra eyed Draupadi with no small amount of disapproval and trepidation. It was obvious there was an internal debate raging inside him. She knew, from the years she'd spent with him, that he was trying to decide whether he had any authority over her anymore or not.

Since their marital connection had been severed, Yudhishtra had said little to her, treating her as if she were a polite acquaintance in whose house he was obliged to stay. It was ridiculous really, given how much they had shared, but Draupadi wasn't surprised. Yudhishtra was rigid in his beliefs and would never offer an unsolicited opinion to a woman who wasn't his wife, sister, daughter or mother. No, he would consider that to be an imposition on whichever man was in charge of the woman in question. Still, for all his foibles, he was a good man at heart. She had tried her best to remember that during the years they'd spent together.

Finally, Yudhishtra took a deep breath and said in a cautious voice, 'Draupadi, while we may not be married anymore, I still consider you a member of my family. As such, it is my duty to point out that you are a former queen of this realm. Queens do not dance and they *definitely* do not dance like that.'

Draupadi should have been angry, but instead she laughed. 'Don't be silly. Queens in our day danced all the time in the privacy of their palaces and gardens. Anyway, I'm not a queen anymore, Yudhishtra. So I don't have to act like one.'

'Still, this is highly inappropriate, Draupadi. I cannot allow it.'

Arjuna groaned and hung his head even as Draupadi straightened to her full height and glared at him. 'Allow it? *Allow* it?'

Arjuna cleared his throat. 'Draupadi ...'

'You stay out of this,' she snapped at him. Turning to Yudhishtra, she pointed a finger in his face. 'You have no right, no right whatsoever, to tell me what to do. If I want to dance, I will. Irrespective of whether it's inappropriate or obscene or even if I have to strip naked to do it; that will be *my* decision, not yours!'

Yudhishtra looked horror-struck by the idea that she might dance naked in front of hundreds of people. 'I don't see where all this animosity is coming from, Draupadi. Our entire lives, I did nothing but take care of you, respect you. You were my queen, my empress. I put you before all the other women in my life. Everything I have ever asked of you has been for your own good. Still, you have done nothing but disrespect me from the moment we arrived at your house. Why?'

It was Draupadi's turn to look incredulous now. 'You still don't see it, do you? How can anyone be so wrapped up in themselves that they're completely oblivious to how everyone around them feels? The other night, when you arrived, when Kunti ended our marriage, she said she was responsible for me being common wife to the Pandavas. That it was her fault because she refused to take back her words. But the truth is that she *did* take back her words. In that hut, on the day of my swayamwara, when she told you all to divide up equally what you had obtained, she immediately took her words back when she saw me. It was you, Yudhishtra, who decided that I would be your common wife. Not Kunti, *you*.

'You say you've always respected me?' She laughed derisively. 'Were you respecting me during the dice game, when you decided to gamble me off and then watch as your cousins humiliated me in court? What about when you sat back and did nothing as Kichaka attacked me during the thirteenth year of our exile? Was that you trying to improve me for my own good? If I've disrespected you lately, Yudhishtra, it's only because you've disrespected me time and time and time again. I know you never meant to, but you did. And you don't get to do it anymore.' Her eyes shone with unshed tears.

Yudhishtra glared back at her. 'You knew all of that was predestined, as Vyasa told me! I wanted none of it!'

'Oh, please!' Draupadi retorted. 'Destiny is an excuse, a crutch people use when they're too weak, too lazy or too stubborn. When they're selfish or have too much pride. You had choices, Yudhishtra, but you chose not to make them. You allowed others to make them for you. Maintained your precious virtuousness by playing the bloody victim!'

Yudhishtra stepped towards her, eyes bulging and teeth clenched in rage. Draupadi shrank back instinctively, a natural reaction from having been assaulted by men in the past. However, before he could reach her, Arjuna stepped in the way and put a gentle but firm hand on his brother's chest. Yudhishtra pushed against it briefly, but Arjuna didn't budge.

Breathing heavily, Yudhishtra met Arjuna's eyes. 'You'll take her side?'

Arjuna's hand tightened a little. 'Leave it, Brother.'

'Very well,' replied Yudhishtra, taking a step back, his anger directed at his younger brother now. 'I will leave.' He swivelled around and stalked off.

For a few tense moments, both Arjuna and Draupadi watched him walk away. Then, Draupadi said, 'Let him go. He'll sulk for a while, but will come around after you apologize to him.'

Arjuna frowned at Yudhishtra's departing back. 'I'm not going to apologize this time. That was inexcusable.' He turned burning eyes towards Draupadi. 'Did he ever hit you?'

She shook her head quickly. 'No. I've said much worse to him when we were together, but he would just walk away. This was the first time he's ever reacted like that.' She added in a disappointed voice, 'So much for staying friends.'

'I don't understand what's happened to him on this trip,' muttered Arjuna. 'He's become oppressive, questioning us at every turn, trying to lash out. He's never been like this before. Not with us.'

'He's never needed to. We followed him blindly,' replied Draupadi bitterly. She looked at Arjuna. 'Thank you for standing up for me. I know how difficult it must have been to go against him.'

He nodded wordlessly, staring into the distance for a long moment. Then, he turned to Draupadi with a half-hearted smile, a valiant effort to change the mood. 'So, where should we go next?'

She smiled back, determined to move on too. 'I suppose dancing is out of the question?'

Arjuna smiled ruefully. 'Maybe another time.'

She nodded. 'I don't think I would enjoy it after that scene anyway.'

They walked to the large Ferris wheel at the centre of the ground, showed their VIP passes at the gate and climbed in. Draupadi laughed at Arjuna's expression when he finally managed to squeeze his long legs into the snug, two-seater cart. Soaring into the air, the ride gave them a fine view of the festival grounds, all lit up and electric with excitement and activity.

Still, as they sat there enjoying the view, the exhilaration of the ride's motion and the wind in their hair, it was obvious they hadn't gotten over their altercation with Yudhishtra.

Finally, Draupadi spoke as she pushed flyaway locks of hair behind her ears. 'To be fair, Yudhishtra has had a pretty crappy week. I've broken up with him, Kunti's preoccupied with her kids, Bhima's gone off to the orphanage to start a food business, you're busy being a cricket prodigy, and Nakula's dragging him to noisy festivals and talking about modelling. To top it all off, he was called "Nakula's brother" today! Things are changing, and he's having a hard time with it.'

'That's no excuse,' replied Arjuna. 'I'm sick of being held back just because he's older than me. I couldn't live how I wanted the last time on earth, and heaven didn't turn out that much better either. But now, I have a chance to finally do something for myself that doesn't involve him or anyone else. Even if it's only for a little while, I plan to do it.'

Draupadi stared at him. 'This is the second time you've mentioned you weren't happy in heaven. Why?'

'Can we please discuss this later?'

She didn't want to fight tonight, she really didn't. It was a lovely, cool evening, they'd had fun at the concert, and just sitting here with him on this ride, looking out at the lights and people, felt so good. It had been a long time since she'd sat this close to a man, cuddled up in a confined space with his warmth, solidness and scent filling her senses. Even longer since she'd done this with Arjuna. She chuckled under her breath. Intimacy was one of those things you didn't usually miss in the usual hum of daily life. Until you experienced it. Then you wondered how you ever lived without it.

Draupadi hooked her arm through Arjuna's and rested her head on his shoulder. He sidled closer and placed his chin on top of her head lightly, his hand finding hers and entwining their fingers. She sighed softly and closed her eyes, a warm swell of contentment making its way through her. When the ride was over, she would go back to not needing a man, and he would go back to being in love with Subhadra. But they could have this, right now.

Soon, they came to a stop with a jerk. Draupadi opened her eyes and looked up at Arjuna, only to find his eyes already on her. For a few endless moments, they kept sitting there, gazing at each other, neither wanting it to end just yet.

'*Oy, hero!*'

They jumped apart.

Standing in front of them was the man who operated the ride. He was holding their cart-gate open and grinning down at them. 'Ride is over, Devdas. Take her somewhere else.'

Embarrassed and flustered, Draupadi climbed out and glared at the ride operator. He sniggered and put his hands up defensively, saying to Arjuna, 'No happy ending for you tonight, hero.'

Arjuna gave the man a look that made him step back and almost fall off the platform.

When they'd walked some distance in silence, Draupadi could no longer stop herself from asking. 'Why aren't you happy in heaven? Did something happen with Subhadra?'

Arjuna huffed and looked up at the night sky as if someone up there could help him get out of this conversation. Finally, he relented. 'Why are you and Subhadra so obsessed with each other?'

Draupadi tried to stifle a smile, unsure why that piece of information gave her a small trill of satisfaction. 'She talks about me too?'

'Draupadi.' His tone didn't warrant further discussion.

'Arjuna.' He should know her better than that.

He clutched his forehead and grunted softly. 'Fine. Yes, she thinks I favour you over her, and you always thought I favoured her over you. Obviously, I couldn't keep either of you happy.' He laughed without humour.

Draupadi shook her head with a rueful smile. 'We were young. I was so very jealous of her.' She looked up at him, her eyes large and forlorn. 'I lost you so many times before, but I always knew you'd come back to me. After her ... you never came back. Not in the same way.'

Arjuna looked like he wanted to argue, but then exhaled in resignation. He turned and pushed a lock of her hair off her face gently. 'I was jealous too, my love. When I first met Subhadra, I was angry. I had walked in on you with my brother, and had that unbearable image of you two embedded in my mind. So unbearable that I had already married two other women to try and get rid of it.' He shook his head, as if trying to dislodge that image, even now. 'I needed to lash out. At fate, and if I'm being truthful, at you. Subhadra was Krishna's sister, sweet, simple and unsullied by life. Our relationship healed me, allowed me to love you again, kept me united with my brothers. I needed that.' He looked into Draupadi's eyes, silently apologetic. 'I needed to love someone who belonged to me alone.'

Draupadi nodded, the old hurt bubbling to the surface after so long. She'd always known in her heart that Arjuna marrying Subhadra and bringing her home was the direct result of him walking in on her and Yudhishtra in bed together. It was the final straw, permanently severing an already precarious connection. A connection with that rare combination of passion and friendship that few married couples shared. For a short time, they'd had something special.

She smiled sadly. 'I wished constantly that things had been different between us. More times than I can remember. Had I been allowed to marry you alone, we could have avoided all the turmoil, the unhappiness, perhaps even the Great War. We could've been happy together.'

Arjuna gaped at her. 'You never told me you felt that way before.'

Shaking her head, she said, 'No, I never said it out loud. It didn't seem fair to the others. But I'm sure they knew anyway. Everyone knew how I felt about you. Except you.'

He said nothing. Probably because there was nothing more that could be said after all this time.

Draupadi cleared her throat and asked again, 'So what happened? I thought you and Subhadra were happy.'

Arjuna smiled. 'We were. But then we got to heaven, and the years went by, and before I knew it, things had changed. I wish I could be more specific, pinpoint a moment when it changed, when we stopped being us, but I can't. We went from sharing a chamber and spending all our time together to living separately and not feeling the need to talk for centuries.'

'Maybe you've grown apart. It's been thousands of years after all.'

He shrugged. 'Probably. I just never thought it would happen to Subhadra and me.'

'Have you spoken to her about it?'

'I've tried, but she seems to find reasons not to talk to me these days.'

Draupadi looked at the ground. Subhadra was a fool. 'I'm sorry to hear that.'

Arjuna shook his head. 'Don't be. The fact that we've grown apart isn't the problem. It's that I don't feel sad about it. I know our relationship went wrong, and I don't want to fight for it. I don't think she does either. We worked really well together in a world where I was busy either trying to retain our kingdoms, or fighting to get them back. Where she was busy raising our children and being a queen. But when it's just the two of us with nothing else going on …' He chuckled ruefully. 'We have nothing to say to each other.'

'You don't have me around to fight about either.'

He threw his head back and laughed. 'No, we don't. Maybe that's the problem.' He looked down at her, humour sparking in his eyes. 'Life with you around is never boring.'

Grinning back, Draupadi squashed the rush of heat she felt when he'd laughed. She was secretly pleased to hear that Arjuna and Subhadra weren't as perfect a couple as she had always believed, even though she knew that all marriages went through ups and downs. Oftentimes in a coupling, people changed as they grew older. She couldn't even count the number of palace women she had known who reached middle age and realized they didn't love or want their husbands anymore. Of course, divorce hadn't been an option back then. That was one thing modern mortals had gotten right.

Spotting a tent with the words 'VR Gaming' and 'Swordfighter Challenge' on its banner, Draupadi turned to Arjuna and said, 'Let's forget the past for now and have some fun. I've got a surprise for you.'

She pushed him into the tent, said hi to a few people who recognized her and then told the VR game operator that Arjuna would be playing the game.

'What game?' asked Arjuna.

'The virtual reality game, sir,' said a bearded young man who was wearing a T-shirt with a cartoon drawing on it and shoes that glowed in the semi-darkness of the tent's interior. 'It's the brand-new Swordfighter Challenge! Currently, the world's most advanced VR sword-fighting game, complete with detailed, real-time battle simulation and the most advanced graphics yet.'

'Sword fighting in a battle?' Arjuna asked.

'Yes, sir.'

Arjuna looked at Draupadi with a raised brow, as if to say 'I'm in a dark tent with nothing but contraptions and an overgrown boy. I don't even see a sword, let alone a battle.'

She leaned in and whispered into his ear, 'It's a make-believe game. You put the headset around your head, and you'll feel like you're in a different world, but it's not real. You'll be fighting images in front of your eyes; so you can go ahead and kill them. You'll understand once it starts.'

She stepped away and smiled at Arjuna, who was staring back at her with a baffled expression. 'Trust me, you're going to love it.' She winked.

17

Arjuna grinned, the memories of many shared adventures that started with a wink from Draupadi returning to his mind.

He turned to the game operator, who introduced himself as Nik, and was led into a cordoned-off area with a large screen on one end. Handing him a small, white rod that weighed no more than a child's toy, Nik said, 'This is the sword. You hold it from the handle and move it like a real weapon. Try not to walk around too much, and stop when you see a wall. The characters will come to you to fight, so don't worry.'

Moving with practiced efficiency, he strapped a small box to Arjuna's head and covered his eyes with it. Like a hard, heavy blindfold.

'I can't see anything except flashing letters. Am I supposed to fight blind?' Arjuna asked the air in front of him.

He heard Nik's voice, laced with irritation and superiority, reply to him, 'Sir, you have to wait till I switch the game on. You'll be able to see the characters then.'

Arjuna nodded. He turned his head in Draupadi's direction. 'Draupadi?'

'Yes?'

He shook his head. 'Nothing. I just wanted to check how far you are, so I don't hit you by accident.'

'Sir, like I said, please try not to move around too much and stay within the virtual walls. Ma'am and I will stand outside the fighting ring and watch your fight on the big screen,' said Nik as his voice shifted further away.

Arjuna turned his head in Nik's direction. 'If you think it's possible to fight without moving around, you've obviously never fought before. Don't worry; I won't hit you. Unless you move.'

As Nik turned on the game, the words that Arjuna was seeing through the virtual reality box became images that looked lifelike, but with a slight other-worldly quality to them. Arjuna's virtual reality arm didn't look like his own, even though it moved exactly like his. It was an armoured arm with a large, ornate sword that looked much deadlier than the toy rod that he was holding in his hand. He was walking through a maze-like structure that looked freakishly ancient in its setting, with fire lamps on the side and stone walls. Suddenly, a soldier ran towards Arjuna and attacked with his own sword.

Instinctively, Arjuna ducked to avoid the blow and proceeded to swiftly fight with his sword arm as if he was in actual battle. While he wasn't as adept with a sword as either Nakula or Sahadeva, Arjuna could hold his own when required. Within seconds, he had beheaded the other soldier, a splash of blood spurting out of his headless neck with gruesome accuracy and detail.

A rush of excitement enveloped him as he finally understood the point of this game. Smiling widely, Arjuna straightened and rolled his shoulders in preparation. He half-turned his head in Draupadi's direction and murmured, 'You were right, Draupadi. It's a bit slow, but I love it!'

Over the next few minutes, Arjuna's body came alive, circling the sword over his head threateningly, lashing out and manoeuvring his body to evade or deflect his opponent's sword, thrusting, sparring, parrying and striking with the kind of precision he would need if he were fighting real men. He quickly advanced through maze after maze, his blood stirring every time he cut down an adversary.

The game got progressively harder and faster, challenging his skill and training. Arjuna fought soldiers, monsters, magical creatures and even groups of fighters with apparent ease.

Finally, he was undisputed at the end of the game, the screen declaring him the winner of the swordfighter challenge. That was when he registered a collective roar go up in the tent, followed by applause. He removed his headset to find a massive crowd of people encircling the fighting ring, all furiously clapping for him with awe on their faces.

Draupadi was clapping too, her eyes beaming at him with pride and warmth. He winked at her before nodding to the crowd in acknowledgement of their applause.

An ecstatic-looking Nik scurried over to Arjuna and gushed effusively as he took the VR equipment back from him, shaking his hand and asking him if he was a professional swordfighter. Arjuna shook his head, thanked him and walked over to Draupadi, a happy grin on his face.

'That was amazing,' he raved as they walked out of the tent. 'It's not exactly accurate and is obviously much slower than real life, but they've taken all the risk out of it. One of our biggest problems during training was that we could never replicate battle conditions without seriously hurting or even killing each other. If only we'd had something like this!' His blood was still bubbling with excitement.

Draupadi chuckled. 'Wait till I introduce you to guns.'

'What's a gun?'

'You shoot an arrowhead that is this small,' she held her thumb and index finger an inch apart, 'but deadlier than a full-size arrow, and you shoot it out of a metal case as big as your palm and lighter than a bowl of rice. At the press of a button.'

Arjuna's eyes widened. 'I love this world! When can I try a gun?'

Laughing, Draupadi shot him a glance that was half-affectionate, half-flirtatious. 'All in good time, my love.'

He stopped in his tracks and stared at her. 'What did you say?'

She immediately stopped laughing. 'Nothing. Don't make too much out of it, please.'

'You called me "my love". You haven't done that since ...'

'I *said* don't make too much out of it!'

He stared at her intensely for a few seconds, conflicted. Draupadi hadn't called him 'my love' since he had married Subhadra. Despite him saying it to her all the time. Arjuna wanted to interrogate her, find out what she meant by it. But that would only push her away.

After a moment, he dropped his gaze and sighed. Draupadi exhaled with relief, obviously glad he'd decided not to pursue the subject. But then his eyes locked with hers again, full of purpose. 'Fine, I'll drop it. But let me ask you another question. Why did you kiss me that night?'

Draupadi rolled her eyes. 'I don't know. Don't—'

'Make too much out of it?'

She growled, a sound she made whenever she had no befitting retort. Which wasn't often. He smiled. Tilting his head to one side, he asked in a careful voice, 'You know what I think?'

'What?'

Leaning down, his lips to her ear, he brushed them against her and whispered, 'I think the reason you're so angry with me all the time is because you're still in love with me.'

'Nonsense! I've never been *in love* with anybody. I mean, I love you like a family member and friend, of course. No more or less than Bhima.'

'What are you so afraid of, Draupadi?'

Flustered and angry, she glowered up at him. 'The question shouldn't be what *I'm* afraid of, the question should be why you're acting this way. Playing cricket with professionals, meeting scouts, flirting with me as if we've got all the time in the world. You're going back to heaven in a few days, Arjuna!'

He drew back, closing his eyes briefly, his mind a tumultuous pit. Then he opened them, and breathing heavily, speared her with his gaze.

'What if I didn't?'

18

It was a mutton curry, simmered overnight in a large pot with spices until its gravy was thick and full-bodied, and chunks of meat melted on the tongue.

A deep sense of satisfaction infused Bhima's insides as he tasted it before marvelling at his new cooking tools. The gas-powered burner was a dream come true, eliminating the need to nurse a fire through the night. The pots were new too, along with a plethora of kitchen accessories and utensils that Draupadi's money had purchased for the orphanage. The best part, though, were the spices. Bhima had spent the better part of yesterday walking through the spice lanes of Old Delhi, studying the seemingly infinite variety available these days. It had been an assault on his senses, in the best possible way.

Of course, he'd had no idea what to do with most of the condiments he encountered, which was why he had taken the time to speak to shopkeepers about recipes in which he could use their flavours. One of the shopkeepers, an old man with a long beard and a cap on his head, had invited him to sit inside his shop, taking out a handwritten book of recipes penned by his grandmother. Bhima hadn't understood the script, but the patchwork of coloured stains on the worn parchment revealed how generations of the old man's family had enjoyed the recipes within. That was where he'd gotten the mutton curry recipe.

Of course, the butcher, who'd become a good friend by now, had shared his own recipe. He had also imparted some very useful, cost-saving tips that involved freezing meat. The orphanage didn't have a fridge yet, but Bhima was convinced that profits from the lunch business would not only provide better quality meals for the children but also finance a fridge and the cost of keeping it running.

One step at a time, resolved Bhima as he ladled a spoonful of mutton curry over a bed of rice on a plate and passed it to Narad Muni. He watched as Narad Muni added some pickled vegetables on the side of the plate along with a couple of fried chillies and handed it over to a customer. Grumbling the entire time, of course. Narad Muni had been a lot more helpful since Bhima had threatened to throw him out, but no threat was big enough to get him to stop grousing.

'Oh my god! This is delicious,' said the customer, one of three rather dishevelled young men dressed in vests, boxer shorts and slippers, who apparently shared rented rooms nearby. 'I didn't believe your online reviews at first, but this is the best meat curry I've ever tasted. Better than my mom's back home.'

The other two agreed, nodding with their mouths full of food.

Bhima thanked them. So far, they'd only had a handful of customers, but it was still early. Karan and his friends were out there, spreading the word. Karan had even put some images of Draupadi on their 'web page' and 'posted fake reviews online', not that Bhima knew what any of that meant. He guessed it was what had brought the current customers.

'Bring your friends next time,' he said to the three men with a smile.

'Definitely,' they replied, leaning back against the wall of the orphanage. Bhima had set up a table and chair for Narad Muni outside the common room window, where he took payments from customers, added accompaniments to the food, and generally complained about the heat and the dust. Inside the common room, along one of its walls, Bhima had set up the burner to keep the curry warm and a table with food, banana-leaf plates and cutlery. It was a haphazard arrangement and deprived the children of their common room for two hours over lunchtime, but everyone agreed this was in the best interests of the orphanage. The older children had even offered to help, but Bhima had put them to work serving lunch to the younger children with Kunti instead. There were laws against making children work for money, and besides, Bhima wanted to oversee this enterprise himself.

'Smells wonderful in here.'

Bhima turned around to see Draupadi walking into the common room, wearing one of her usual tight dresses with her long, wavy hair falling around her shoulders. She really was a very beautiful woman. Shame she wasn't his wife anymore, Bhima thought distractedly. As much as he was enjoying his time here on earth, he did miss the regular supply of nymphs to take care of his needs. He wasn't a fussy man though. He would take care of himself until he found a willing woman. Someone whose appetite matched his own.

'There you are. It's mutton curry with rice. Come, sit.' He gestured to the dining table, which he'd pushed up against the opposite wall.

Draupadi sat just as Bhima walked up and put a plateful of food in front of her. She smiled and said in a teasing voice, 'Well, this is a first. I was always the one to serve you in the old days.'

'Hah!' he chuckled, before instructing Narad Muni to call him if there were new customers and sitting down with her. 'This time, my love, you're a guest. Besides, I'm a better cook than you.'

She laughed and took a bite of the food. Closing her eyes, she hummed in delight. 'This is delicious.'

'I discovered a lot of spices yesterday, so this is a new recipe. You really like it?'

'I do. If all the food you make is this good, you'll do very well.'

Bhima shrugged. 'Not just me, all of us. You, me, Mother and the kids. We just have to each do our part and hope for the best.'

They sat in comfortable silence for a while as Draupadi ate. Finally, swallowing the last bite, she spoke. 'I need to ask you something.'

He nodded.

She inhaled slowly, as if preparing herself for an argument. 'You're going back to heaven in a few days, Bhima. Who's going to cook the food and run this business when you're gone?'

He looked at her with a steady, unconcerned gaze.

She continued, 'I'm busy with my job. Kunti has her hands full with the children. I keep telling her I'll pay for a caregiver, but she refuses to take the money. The old caretaker isn't a good enough cook, and Karan is busy in school, besides being a child. Once you and Narad Muni are gone, there will be no one left. Why give them false hope?'

Bhima leaned forward and said matter-of-factly, 'I'm not going back.'

'*What?*'

He shrugged again. 'You shouldn't be surprised. You think I would leave you and Mother here to fend for yourselves? Yes, I know you're doing very well, and I'm proud of you, Draupadi. But Mother is struggling and she needs me. So, that's that.'

'But what about eternity? If you stay here, Bhima, you'll grow old, die and re-enter the cycle of rebirth. You'll never go back to heaven. Immortality, comfort, eternal youth, nymphs! All that will be lost to you forever. Are you willing to go through life's hardships—old age, sickness, strife, heartache—all over again?'

Nothing she said was anything he hadn't already thought about, late at night while he shifted uncomfortably on his too-small bed in his too-small, sweltering room. It wouldn't be an easy life, trying to support not only himself and Kunti, but a building full of destitute children. This time around, he wasn't a prince and would have no resources at his disposal. It would be a lot harder to have a good life under these circumstances. But Bhima was a simple man, and, in the end, his mother mattered more to him than his afterlife. If she wouldn't come back with him, then he would stay with her. She'd do the same for him.

Besides, there was that one other thing he had come to discover about himself.

'Draupadi,' he said, sitting back in his chair. 'I'm better off now than I have been in a very long time. Life on earth isn't easy, but it's useful. Here, I have purpose, a mission. I'm a man who needs to *do* things. In heaven, I used to move boulders from one end of my chambers to the other every time I was bored. Or do those battle re-enactments, just to while away the years. Down here, I have no time to be bored. I'm busier than I've ever been, and I like it. So, yes, I've thought about it, and I'm staying.'

'You're sure?'

'I'm sure.'

She looked like she was going to argue, but then her eyes lit up. 'I'm so glad! It'll be lovely having you here!' She leaned forward and gave him an enthusiastic hug.

He grinned as her arms went around him. 'If you're that happy to have me around, maybe we should get married again.' He wiggled his eyebrows at her cheekily when she drew back.

That made her laugh. She cupped his cheek and said with a smile, 'I love you with all my heart, Bhima, but I'm not marrying you ever again. You'll have to find someone else.'

He clutched his chest and let out a tragic sigh that was better suited to a stage. 'Very well.' In the next instant, he was smiling again.

Just then, Narad Muni's voice called out, and they were inundated with lunch orders by dozens of workers from a nearby factory who had been told by Karan's contacts that the food at the orphanage was tastier and better value for money than the lunch cart down the road. And that they served meat, which the food-cart vendor hadn't done in years.

Both Bhima and Draupadi rushed into preparing plates, working side by side with silent efficiency, while Narad Muni shouted orders in a harassed voice. Every now and again, he would screech, 'Why is everyone asking for change? There is only mutton and rice. *No change!*'

Draupadi stuck her head out of the window. 'Change is leftover money, old man! If they give you a high-value note, subtract the lunch price and give them the rest.'

Narad Muni scowled at her. 'Do I look like a mathematician to you, woman?

'No, you look like a man in need of a job!' thundered Bhima from somewhere inside the common room.

Narad Muni was significantly more subdued after that.

19

Scooping spoonful after spoonful of rice and ladling curry over them was just the kind of easy, repetitive job that Draupadi needed to get her mind off her situation. For some strange reason, however, it wasn't working.

She had come to the orphanage to take some pictures for publicity, but it looked like they were doing just fine on their own. Bhima had dropped a bombshell in typical Bhima style, announcing that he was staying on earth without any kind of discussion, angst or theatrics.

Why couldn't the rest of her ex-husbands be equally uncomplicated and straightforward?

And by 'the rest of her ex-husbands' she meant Arjuna.

He had dropped a bombshell or two himself the other night. Even considered the possibility of not going back to heaven for a brief moment before she'd yelled at him that it was the worst idea he'd ever had.

Draupadi sighed softly. She *would* be happier if he went back. Her life would certainly be less complicated, and she wouldn't spend all of her bloody time thinking about every half-coherent thing that came out of his mouth.

Ugh. She just realized she'd been spending all her time thinking about him. Thousands of years of constantly seeing Arjuna, talking to him occasionally, living just a short walk away from him in heaven, and she hadn't felt a damned thing. A few days of watching him prance around in jeans on earth and boom, she'd been reduced to an adolescent. It was pathetic.

She sighed again. This time, it was too loud to be missed.

'Something troubling you?' asked Bhima as he filled plates with food and handed them over to Narad Muni.

Draupadi dumped a large spoon of rice on a plate with a little too much force. The banana-leaf plate wobbled over her fingers.

'Yes. But I can't tell you about it.'

'Why not?'

'It's about your brother.'

Bhima shrugged. 'Which one?'

She huffed. 'Which one do you think?'

He frowned in thought and then asked, 'Arjuna?'

'Yes.'

'What's he done now?'

'I can't tell you.'

'Yes, you can.'

She turned to him. 'I can't talk to you about other men, Bhima. We used to be married.'

'We're not married anymore. Maybe we could be friends.' Bhima looked up briefly from plating the food and smiled at her. 'Trust me.'

She finished pouring curry on a plate and handed it outside the window.

'Ever since all of you came down, I've been having confusing thoughts about Arjuna.'

Bhima hummed as he worked. 'And him?'

'I think he's having them too.'

'Has he told you so?'

'We kissed.'

Bhima froze, and Draupadi immediately regretted her words. For all his talk about being friends, Bhima wasn't ready to hear about her kissing other men. She had never crossed that line in her last life, treating each of her husbands as if they were the only one during her allotted year with them. It was a delicately balanced, carefully choreographed charade that all six of them had faithfully kept up until the day they died.

'I'm sorry.' She cleared her throat. 'Forget I said anything.'

'No.' Bhima put the plate down, flattened his palms on the table and hung his head as if he were unwell, giving off a low growl in the process. 'Just give me a minute.'

'Seven more plates!' came Narad Muni's voice from outside.

'In a minute!' Bhima roared at the window.

Draupadi launched back into serving up the plates and handing them outside. Bhima's temper was quick and often destructive, although he had never been violent towards anyone he didn't consider an equal adversary. However, there was no guaranteeing that the mutton curry wouldn't end up on the floor.

By the time she completed the order, Bhima's breathing had steadied, and he turned around to face Draupadi, clearing his throat loudly.

'As much as the thought of you kissing a man makes me want to tear his throat out, it's something we *should* talk about. We're not married, we're friends. It's an easy thing to say, but more difficult to put into practice. I'll need time to get used to the idea. So, talk.' He took a deep breath. 'You kissed Arjuna.'

'Yes.'

'And?'

'And then he asked what if he didn't go back to heaven.'

'What did you say?' Bhima frowned at her.

'I told him he was crazy, but ...' She shook her head.

'But what?'

Draupadi fisted her hands and groaned. '*I don't know!* One minute, I want him to go, so my life can get back to normal. But then the next minute, I want him to stay so we can have another chance. And even as I'm saying this out loud, I know how stupid and unrealistic it is to hope that we could *ever* be together without any kind of baggage from the past. I mean, yes, we're ridiculously attracted to each other, but we can barely be in the same room without bickering like cats. And then there's Subhadra, who's sitting in heaven and whom he's always loved more than me, as much as he might deny it. Does he only want me now because *she* doesn't want him anymore? Or is their time truly past? If he stays down here, he'll never know! Neither of us will. And, as for me—I don't *need* a man, I really don't, but now that I'm not trying to manage all five of you at the same time, I feel like I might *want* one. Is that so wrong? To want someone to share my life with, to be in a loving, monogamous relationship? Other people do it. Everyone, except *me*! Don't *I* deserve to have a chance at true love, just like everyone else? Or will I forever be written off as the woman who was so scarred by her marriage to five men that she was unable to have a one-on-one relationship?'

Bhima put his hands up, his expression horrified. 'Whoa! This is too complicated for me.'

'You *said* I could talk to you!'

'I changed my mind.'

Now Draupadi felt like throwing the mutton curry on the floor.

Eyeing her as if she were a skittish mare, Bhima said placatingly, 'Look, maybe you can talk to Mother about the details, but from my side, I want you to know,' he held her eyes and continued in a gruff voice, 'if you want to be with Arjuna, you have my support.'

They stared at each other for a long moment without saying anything.

'Two more plates! And there's someone who wants to speak to you!'

Bhima stepped to the window, looked out and grunted softly before saying in a measured tone, 'Amit Sharma. Nice to see you again.'

An annoyed-looking Amit Sharma stood outside with two other men, glancing at the small crowd of people gathered around, eating their lunch hungrily.

He greeted Bhima with an air of injury and said, 'I've been informed that you're operating a food establishment without a licence, my friend. Some of the people in the neighbourhood have objected and threatened to call the police, but since you're Guruji's brother and Kuntiben's son, we thought we would come over and speak to you instead.'

Frowning at the smaller man, Bhima asked, 'Who has objected?'

'The food cart vendor down the road.'

Bhima scratched his chin. 'Why did he call you instead of the police? Aren't you operating a youth centre?'

That made Amit smile and bob his chin in a patronizing manner. 'We at the BYBM Centre feel responsible for maintaining community standards. The locals understand this. Now, I'm very sorry, but you'll have to shut down since you don't have a food establishment licence.'

Draupadi stepped forward and stuck her head out of the window. She gave Amit a mildly scornful glance and said, 'Mr Sharma, I'm Draupadi Kuru, and I work for NPTV, the news channel. My friends here are simply cooking and serving a few lunches within the confines of the orphanage, which is a residence, not public or commercial property. The food cart vendor is just upset because he's losing customers.'

Bhima gave her a grateful look, and she squeezed his hand under the window sill.

Amit Sharma transferred his patronizing smile to Draupadi. 'I'm sure you're a very important person, Miss Kuru, but all food establishments need a licence to operate, even if they are on private property. That's the law.'

Draupadi tilted her head. 'And I'm sure you're aware that small-scale home vendors only need to register with the licensing authority in order to operate. As per the law. I'm sure the police will agree with me.'

'Have you registered?'

'Yes.'

The look on Amit's face turned unpleasant. His friends shifted uncomfortably on their feet.

Draupadi smiled at them. 'Perhaps you'd like to have lunch now that you're here?'

One of the men asked, 'What are you serving?'

'Mutton curry and rice.'

Amit's eyebrows flew towards his hairline. 'You're serving meat? Here?'

'Yes. Is there a law against serving meat?'

This time, the look on Amit's face turned positively sinister. 'No, no law at all against serving meat, Miss Kuru. Even though most of the respectable residents of this community are vegetarians, *you* are free to eat what you please. Tell me, what kind of meat is this?' He pointed to a plate of food.

Draupadi resisted the temptation to roll her eyes. 'I just mentioned it was mutton.'

'From a goat,' added Bhima, whose temper had been kept in check so far by Draupadi surreptitiously squeezing his hand every time she felt him about to lose it.

Amit raised his brow again. 'How can we be sure it isn't beef?'

This time, Bhima couldn't be quietened. 'Because it's not! It's mutton, from a goat. Look at the bones.'

A look of distaste crossed Amit's face. 'How dare you ask me to look at bones? I'm a Brahmin!'

Bhima shrugged. 'I'm not asking you to eat it. I couldn't find a single butcher who even sold beef, by the way; so I don't know what you're getting so worked up about. If you can't buy it, you can't cook it.'

'Why are you looking to buy beef? Do you intend to serve it?'

Draupadi didn't wait for Bhima to answer that. Instead, she yelled 'Kunti!' towards the common room door and turned back to Amit. 'We have no intention of buying or selling beef, Mr Sharma.'

Kunti came rushing into the common room. Seeing Draupadi's troubled face, her smile fell and she asked, 'Is everything all right?'

'Kuntiben, I'm glad you're here,' said Amit, folding his hands in Kunti's direction from outside the window.

Kunti walked up to the window and folded her hands in return, saying in a strained voice, 'Amitji, thank you for visiting. Please let us serve you some lunch.'

'No, no,' replied Amit with a pained look. 'I'm a pure vegetarian, Kuntiben, and your son is serving meat. I'm sure you know that the BYBM Centre promotes wholesome, *Hindu* values in the community. This,' he pointed at the plates of food with a wince, 'is not the purpose for which we donated money to the orphanage.'

Kunti began to look worried. 'Of course, Amitji. We would never use your kind donation for anything except the basic welfare of the children. The money for this small lunch service has been given to us by my daughter, Draupadi. As you know, donations to charitable organizations like ours come and go. We have started this as an extra source of income, to help support us during times when funds are low. I hope you understand.'

Amit shook his head with an affronted air. 'If you had just come to me, Kuntiben, I could have helped pave the way for this lunch service. But to go behind my back, and then have the effrontery to serve this questionable animal flesh—'

'It's *mutton*, you fool!' Bhima shouted, finally giving rein to his temper. 'Who the hell do you think you are? You think just because you opened a two-bit centre and donated some money that you own the bloody neighbourhood?'

Moving faster than anyone would expect given his bulky frame, Bhima strode out of the common room and exited the building.

Marching up to Amit and his friends, Bhima loomed over them threateningly. The three men stepped back, fear written all over their faces. Bhima leaned towards Amit, who was less than half his size.

'I'm finished trying to be polite to you, so consider this a warning, Amit Sharma. The next time you come here, it better be to either eat the food or to pay your respects to my mother. Because if you want trouble, I will give you trouble.' He put his finger on Amit's shoulder and gave a gentle, but deliberate, shove. 'Am I making myself clear?'

Amit, clearly flustered and frightened, stammered out, 'How d-dare you threaten me? I'll call the police!'

'You threatened me first. I'm just protecting what's mine.'

Kunti hurried out of the building and stepped between Bhima and Amit. Given that the top of her head barely reached Bhima's chest, it was a rather futile attempt to block the two men from each other. Still, she put a hand on Bhima's torso and pushed until he stepped back willingly. Then, she tried to mollify Amit.

'My son can be hot-headed. Please forgive him, Amitji. We will stay out of everyone's way and quietly conduct our business. We're not trying to create trouble in the neighbourhood.'

From behind the window, Draupadi added, 'We're also not doing anything illegal.'

But Amit wasn't listening. Secure in the knowledge that Bhima wouldn't hurt him in front of Kunti, he pointed a finger at him with an almost-snarl, 'You will regret your actions today. Just wait and watch.'

He swivelled around and tramped away with the two men trailing behind him.

For a moment, no one said anything. Then, Bhima turned to Kunti. 'Why are you kowtowing to him? He's nothing but a bully!'

Narad Muni muttered from his seat behind the table, '… pot calling the kettle …'

Kunti shook her head, in obvious distress. 'You don't understand, son. It's not just a centre. Karan told me the other night that they have links to the ruling political party. They've started policing the neighbourhood, and apparently one shopkeeper paid for a gang from the centre to vandalize another shop down the road. The boy behind the counter was beaten with rods within an inch of his life. We can't afford to upset Amit or we'll have his mobs on our heads. And he will have the police and politicians on his side. I have to think about the children and their safety. Our best hope is to stay under the radar and keep him happy.' She took a deep breath, tears pricking her eyes. 'I'll go to the centre and apologize to him tomorrow, once he's cooled down.'

'Mother.' Bhima put his hand on her shoulder. 'We have faced mobs before. Forget mobs, we've faced burning houses, demons and armies! Armies that have wanted us to submit to their rule, silence our voices and forfeit what is ours. We have faced insurmountable odds, and have come out on the other side. Because we've never lacked for courage. You taught us to be brave, Mother, to fight for what is right. Remember?'

Now the tears were flowing freely from Kunti's eyes. 'I remember, my son. But the world is different now and we are alone. Against an army on the other side. And I have all these orphaned children to think about. What will happen to them without me?'

'We're not alone. We have each other. And I don't need an army when I have my mother's blessing,' said Bhima with forceful conviction.

Draupadi cleared her throat, having also exited the building, and stepped forward. 'As heroic as that sounded, Bhima, things are done a little differently these days. You can't just kill people willy-nilly anymore. However, you're not alone, Kunti. You have something as powerful as an army in a fight against Amit.'

Kunti wiped her face. 'What's that?'

She grinned. 'A media person in the family.'

20

He ran his hands down to her backside and lifted, wrapping her legs around his waist and pressing her up against the mirror in the fitting room, so he didn't have to bend down to kiss her properly. Angela was a pocket-sized tempest whose body fit his perfectly in this position, as he'd discovered the night of the music festival, when they had snuck into one of the green rooms backstage and made love.

Made love?

Nakula chuckled and drew back, gazing at her sleepy eyes and swollen lips. 'You've turned me into a romantic.'

Angela smiled back lazily as she ran her fingers through his hair. 'Good. One of us should be.'

A frantic tapping of fingernails on the door interrupted them. GT's high-pitched voice sang plaintively from the other side, 'We all know what you're doing in there, Angela darling. And we're jealous as hell. Come out so we can also drool over your gorgeous piece of man-meat.'

Shaking his head with a bemused look, Nakula asked, 'Does he have to talk like that?'

Angela laughed. 'I'm so used to it that when I hear GT speak in his normal voice, I get freaked out. He's got a bit of a chip on his shoulder about the gay thing, so he postures to be provocative. Attack is the best defence, right? Don't mind him. He's a really good person. Once you crack his walls, he'll be your friend for life.'

'It doesn't sound like he only wants to be friends with me.'

Nakula didn't really know how to deal with Gautam Thakur. In his day, if a man preferred other men, he did whatever he did without talking about it. Everyone else pretended they didn't notice. Life was neatly divided into roles, and men were expected to take a wife and bear children, irrespective of their personal inclinations. Now, with everything out in the open, and GT constantly directing sexual innuendos towards him, Nakula couldn't help but feel uncomfortable.

Angela shook her head. 'Don't worry about that. He knows you're straight; he's just doing it to fluster you. Next time, just say the words "hashtag me too" and he'll shut up immediately.'

'What's 'hashtag me too?'

Rolling her eyes, Angela replied, 'You ashram people! It's like you're time travellers from another century!'

More like another millennium, but he wasn't going to tell her that. Instead he ground himself against her one last time, reaffirming to both of them where his sexual preferences lay, before putting her down. He held up a brightly pattered, glittery garment and made a face. 'Do I really have to wear this?'

She sighed. 'I'm afraid so. It's an editorial fashion photo shoot, so the clothes are going to be really bizarre and unwearable, and they'll slap a ton of make-up on you, but in the end, the photos will look great. So will you. This is actually a really big deal—most models don't get to be in a magazine, wearing an A-list designer, until they're well into their careers.'

As he put on the garment, Nakula digested the fact that this was actually a lucrative career choice. He knew he was a handsome man, with an attractive face and physique, but he had never appreciated his appearance for anything more than the advantage it gave him when seducing women. He'd never thought of it as a professional instrument before now.

Imagine, he could teach an unbroken horse to respond to the lightest tug of a rein, steer a chariot smoothly through the thickest of battles, and wield a sword with consummate skill and precision, but in this day and age, it was his pretty face that had the most value.

'Okay,' said Angela as she finished buttoning him into a long jacket of sorts, with slashes, asymmetrical lines and glittery spikes. 'Now we go out and let them take your measurements, so they can alter the clothes to fit your body for the photo shoot. Remember, they'll be touching you and the clothes. It doesn't mean anything—that's just them doing their job. So, simply stand still, relax and follow their instructions.' She put a hand on the fitting room door. 'Ready?' She smiled, her eyes twinkling.

She looked so pretty when she smiled that way. Like they were about to embark on an adventure together. He couldn't wait to get her alone again. 'Ready.'

They exited the fitting room to the waiting group of people outside, including GT, his assistants, his tailors and Sahadeva.

Nakula met Sahadeva's eye, hoping to share a brief moment of humour at the utter ridiculousness of his clothing with his twin. Instead, he got a disapproving stare.

He didn't know why Sahadeva was behaving with such uncharacteristic petulance, intent on sucking all the joy out of their adventure. What he did know was that he was done feeling guilty.

'Very nice, but a thousand things we need to change, people,' said GT in a deeper, more natural voice that sounded positively business-like as he stared at Nakula with an expert eye. He stepped up and started pulling and pinching the outfit with practiced ease, rattling off a stream of instructions to his team about cuts, fits and alterations. It was as if he didn't see Nakula anymore, just an incomplete work of art in progress. His assistants ran around doing his bidding, the tailors measured and took notes, and Angela stood back and watched the scene with a keen eye. It was the first time Nakula had seen GT in his professional element, and he liked him the better for it.

He looked over at Angela and caught her beaming at him. Nakula smiled back, even as he felt a twinge of melancholy. Sahadeva would go back to his beloved wife and idyllic life in heaven when they returned in a few days, but Nakula would go back to a bevy of nymphs, none of whom would ever match up to Angela. In a few, short days, she had come to mean more to him than he had ever anticipated. Tireless and up for absolutely anything, she pushed him when he needed pushing and called him out when he got too full of himself. As a lover, she was as generous as she was exacting, without the slightest hint of artifice or the coquettish fawning he'd come to associate with nymphs. He liked her intelligence and vivacity, her strength and wisdom, and the fact that he could lean on her when he needed to. In every way that mattered, she was his equal, something no other woman had ever been before.

How could he go back to eternity after this? Knowing that the perfect woman for him was out there, but he couldn't be with her.

'Well, Nakula, I have to say, you've really elevated this look. It's the perfect combination of upper-crust and home-grown that we're looking for.' GT rubbed his hands together as he looked between Angela and Nakula. 'I was planning to do around four or five looks for the photo shoot. Each one will require detailed preparation, so we're looking at two days.'

He turned to Nakula. 'I know you're a "special friend" of my BFF here, but we still do need to sign a contract, darling. Just for the shoot days. After all, if we're going to fit the clothes for you, then we need to be sure you're available. Can we sign today? I know you're not represented by an agency yet, but Angela can take a look at it for you. You know, make sure I'm not cheating you or anything. What say?'

Nakula looked at Angela.

She nodded and turned to GT. 'Show me the contract.'

He gestured to one of his assistants, who pulled out a small stack of papers from a folder she was holding. Angela leafed through it carefully.

'Seems in order. Except, I don't think Nakula has a bank account. Draupadi didn't, when she came to Delhi. It'll have to be cash, GT.'

'No problem,' said GT. 'You'll get 50 per cent of the payment today. I can have one of my people run to the ATM to get it. So, can we sign?' He raised his impeccably shaped eyebrows at Nakula.

Two days of this 'photo shooting' was more than Nakula had accounted for. Today was supposed to be about trying something new and spending time with Angela. However, signing a contract meant money exchanging hands, a commitment.

'Nakula.' Sahadeva's voice came from the corner.

He didn't have to turn towards his twin to know what that meant.

'Give me some time to discuss this with my brother,' he told Angela and GT.

He walked over to the corner and sat down next to Sahadeva. The outfit ballooned awkwardly around him as he sat, bringing an inadvertent smile to both their faces. It really was a ludicrous garment.

Sahadeva cleared his throat, looked conflicted for a moment and then asked in a gentle tone, 'Are you coming back to heaven, Brother?'

Surprised, Nakula blinked. 'What do you mean?'

'I mean, I see the way you look at her.' Sahadeva nodded towards Angela.

Nakula chuckled. 'Is it that obvious?'

'It's not obvious to others, perhaps. But I'm your twin. I know better. You've never looked at a woman like this before.'

'I've never felt like this about a woman before either.'

Sahadeva nodded. 'So, what does that mean for you? For your future?'

'I don't know.' Nakula really didn't.

A pained look crossed Sahadeva's face. 'If you stay here, we'll never see each other again, Brother.'

'I know. I don't want that.'

'Then don't consider staying. Please, Nakula. You're not only my brother, you're my other half. I've never asked you for anything—'

'No, Brother. Don't do that,' Nakula interrupted. 'Neither of us gains anything by holding the other hostage to our relationship. This has to be my decision. Just like going back to Vijaya is yours.'

'How can you compare? Has she become that important to you?'

Nakula shook his head. 'No. It's not only Angela. I wasn't truly happy in heaven, Brother. Not for a long time.' He sighed down at the floor. 'Look, I'm going to sign this contract and ask them to do the photo shoot next week. It's only two days. I can decide about the rest later, once things become clearer.'

Shaking his head, Sahadeva looked close to tears. 'Things are becoming clear already. Everything is changing. I'm losing you, my brother.'

Every part of Nakula wanted to comfort Sahadeva and tell him that they would never be apart, that they would spend the rest of eternity together as planned. But he knew he wouldn't mean it. He'd been on a different path from his twin ever since they had begun their afterlife. Going back to heaven wouldn't change that. He put his hand on Sahadeva's shoulder and squeezed.

'Whatever happens in the future doesn't diminish the past we've shared. We will always be a part of each other. Forever.'

A tear welled up in the corner or Sahadeva's eye. 'Why does this feel like a goodbye?'

'Nakula?' Angela's voice broke into their little bubble from the other end of the room.

Nakula nodded at her, turned to his twin and murmured, 'I can't do this right now.'

His brother nodded wearily, the fight leaving him. 'Go and sign your contract, Nakula. We'll talk later.'

Every step Nakula had ever taken in the past had been in the name of duty, for the greater good. For Sahadeva, for his family. All his life, he had done what was expected of him, irrespective of what he wanted personally. As he turned away from his brother and started walking towards Angela and GT, for the first time in his life, Nakula felt what it was like to be in charge of one's own destiny.

It felt good.

21

If he wasn't his older brother, he would have his hide.

Arjuna fumed as he strode through the streets near the orphanage, on his way to the BYBM Centre, where Yudhishtra had apparently taken up residence.

It had taken them all by surprise. This morning, when Arjuna had returned to Draupadi's apartment after his usual run and cricket game with the neighbourhood youths in the park, he had been confronted with the aftermath of Yudhishtra's utterly uncalled for conduct. Draupadi sat on a sofa in angry tears, while Nakula paced the living room looking harassed, and Sahadeva awkwardly tried to console Draupadi.

Apparently, Yudhishtra had woken up this morning and announced that he was moving to the BYBM Centre because of Draupadi, Arjuna and Bhima's insubordination. He told Draupadi he was extremely disappointed in her and the woman she had become, and that she was leading his brothers astray. Draupadi had retaliated, saying that she had nothing to do with Bhima's decision to move to the orphanage and that Arjuna had merely tried to protect her at the music festival, but Yudhishtra was beyond reason. The argument had deteriorated, with Yudhishtra accusing Draupadi of trying to break up his family and Draupadi calling Yudhishtra a stubborn, self-important coward who refused to face reality. She had also, in a fit of temper, screamed that she'd hated being married to him. Upon which, according to Nakula, Yudhishtra had thrown a glass at the wall, called her a whore and stalked out of the apartment.

Arjuna couldn't believe that word had actually come out of Yudhishtra's mouth. What had happened to his brother? He'd handled a lifetime's worth of upheaval with wisdom, dignity and stoical confidence. Surely he could handle a few more days' worth of disruption without completely losing it or lashing out at the people who had been nothing but supportive of him as long as he had lived. This was the height of ungrateful behaviour.

By the time Arjuna reached the BYBM Centre, he was seething.

He walked through the main door into a hallway, ignoring the curious stares he got from the young men who were sitting around. There were quite a few of them, and many had their noses buried in their phones. He tapped a passing man on the shoulder and asked, 'Do you know where Yudhishtra Kuru is?'

The man frowned at him. 'Don't call him by his name. It's disrespectful. He is Guruji.'

Now it was Arjuna's turn to frown. Guruji? 'Do you know where he is?'

The man nodded. 'He is taking darshan in the MPH. But only for special donors. Public darshan will be later in the afternoon.'

This was getting alarming. 'What is an MPH and where is it?'

'Multi-purpose hall. Go straight to the end and turn right.' The man gestured to the left as he spoke.

Confused, Arjuna asked, 'Turn right or turn left?'

The man impatiently pointed left again. 'Turn right.' Then he walked off.

This place is crazy, thought Arjuna. No wonder Yudhishtra was acting strange. He walked to the end of the hall, paused for a moment and decided to turn left. He was rewarded a few steps later by a sign outside a door, which said 'Multi-purpose Hall', and underneath it, another sign on paper, which read 'Private Meeting in Progress. DO NOT DISTURB'.

Ignoring the sign, Arjuna opened the door and entered, only to come face-to-face with a sight so extraordinary, it stopped him dead in his tracks.

Yudhishtra was dressed in what looked like a billowy stage costume, while he brandished a toy spear in one hand and sat on a throne that could only be called an abomination. His hair, perfectly black this morning when Arjuna had left for his run, was now streaked with grey. To top it off, he looked like he had Bhima's moustache stuck on his upper lip.

Confounded, Arjuna started walking up to his brother when a hand shot out from the side and stopped him.

'This darshan is private,' said a young man who stood a head shorter than Arjuna, looking up at him with righteous indignation.

'That's my brother,' replied Arjuna, as he gestured towards Yudhishtra.

'Guruji is occupied,' said a voice. Amit Sharma stepped towards Arjuna and put a hand on his arm. Arjuna stiffened.

He also noted, with increasing frustration, how each devotee walked over to Amit Sharma after speaking with Yudhishtra. Inevitably, they handed him either a roll of cash or a rectangular slip of paper, which Arjuna assumed was in lieu of cash. Amit then handed the proceeds over to another man, who stashed it away in a shoulder bag and scribbled something in a notebook. Like a well-oiled machine.

After all the devotees had spoken to Yudhishtra, the elderly woman behind him offered him a drink of water and a plate of snacks, which he refused. She touched his feet, and went and stood behind the throne again, ready to offer sustenance at a moment's notice.

Then Amit went to the front, bowed low in front of Yudhishtra and said to the devotees, 'Thank you for attending this darshan. Guruji will now finish with a few words.'

Obviously, Yudhishtra wasn't expecting to make a finishing speech, because he raised his eyebrows in surprise. To Arjuna's horror, Amit eyed Yudhishtra pointedly, silently instructing him to say something, whether he liked it or not.

Arjuna groaned inwardly. Yudhishtra, who now stood up to say a few words in that ridiculous inflated dhoti, was clearly being taken advantage of by Amit Sharma. He needed to do something.

Finally, after Yudhishtra was done talking, the devotees were herded out by Amit and his underlings. Arjuna strode up to Yudhishtra, resisted commenting on his get-up and asked his brother, 'Can we go somewhere and talk privately?'

Before Yudhishtra could reply, Amit walked up to them and told Arjuna in an authoritative voice, 'Guruji needs to rest. He has another darshan later today.'

Oblivious, Amit continued in a voice that was anything but friendly. 'He's meeting with his devotees.'

'I don't care.' Arjuna shrugged Amit's hand off his arm and walked on, saying, 'Brother,' in a loud voice. For the first time he noticed that Yudhishtra was surrounded by a group of about twenty men and women, all of whom were sitting on cushion on the floor. An elderly woman stood behind him, holding plate with food on it, waiting patiently for Yudhishtra to sto talking to a middle-aged man who was kneeling at his feet.

Now, Arjuna had seen his older brother in court, dress in full regalia and being declared an emperor, so he was stranger to Yudhishtra being revered by people. But t particular scene looked so contrived and ridiculous, it uncomfortable to watch. And, given the look on Yudhisht face just before he turned his head, Arjuna wasn't the only feeling discomfited by the whole spectacle.

For a brief moment, when the two brothers' eyes across the room, Yudhishtra's looked happy and relie Then, he obviously remembered the events of the past days, and a hard, stubborn wall arose around him. Gestu towards the audience of devotees, Yudhishtra said in a voice, 'Come, Arjuna. Be seated. I will be with you sho

Arjuna watched as each of the devotees went Yudhishtra, crouching low with their hands folded, kissi fingers and asking him questions as if he was a fortune One woman even asked him if her daughter-in-law ever get pregnant because they needed someone to tak the family business. He couldn't hear Yudhishtra's muttered as it was in an irritated undertone, but he d the word 'destiny' a few times.

That annoyed Yudhishtra, who looked down at Amit and frowned. 'This is my brother.'

'Yes, we've met.' Amit gave Arjuna a look of dislike.

It was ironic. Yudhishtra might have actually chosen not to talk to Arjuna before Amit's interruption. After all, things were still contentious between them. But Amit acting as if he had some authority over whom Yudhishtra could and could not speak to acted like a catalyst, spurring Yudhishtra to assert himself. 'I will talk to my brother in my room, Amitji. Please excuse us.'

For a brief moment, the brothers were in accord as they strode out of the room together. However, the moment they entered what Arjuna supposed was Yudhishtra's bedroom in the guest-wing of the building, that united front tumbled down.

'Why are you here?' were the first words out of Yudhishtra's mouth, uttered immediately after he shut the door and flung his toy spear on to a table with unnecessary force.

Arjuna wanted to rail at him, ask him what on earth had happened to him, and why he was behaving against all logic and decency. Unfortunately, the look on Yudhishtra's face told him that his older brother would respond to his anger with anger of his own.

So he took a deep, calming breath and said, 'I've come to apologize.'

That took Yudhishtra by surprise. He had clearly been expecting an argument. 'Continue,' he said with a small, wary nod.

'I'm sorry for not regarding your feelings ever since we descended.'

'Is that all you're apologizing for? What about for raising your hand against me, your eldest brother?'

'I didn't raise my hand against you, Brother. I would never do that. I was merely protecting Draupadi.'

Yudhishtra winced. 'You think I would ever hurt her?'

Arjuna threw up his hands. 'You tell me! The Yudhishtra I know would never harm a woman. But you have been behaving so strange lately, I don't know what to expect. I mean, look at you.' He pointed at the dhoti and fake moustache. 'My eldest brother would never reduce himself to wearing a childish costume for money.'

'It's not for money! I'm talking to people; giving them guidance. Helping them cope with the Kalyug. Trying to utilize my time here on earth for a higher purpose.'

'Well, that's not what those leeches around you are doing,' Arjuna replied in anger as he waved at the door. 'They've been taking money from the people who come to meet you. I saw them hand over cash to Amit Sharma with my own eyes. And then I saw Amit Sharma do something that no mortal has ever dared to do since we won the Great War. Order you around like an underling!'

'He did not do that!'

'You and I both know he's telling you what to do, what to wear, how to ...' Arjuna's eyes squinted as he focused on Yudhishtra. 'Are you wearing *face-paint*?'

Yudhishtra glared back, looking embarrassed. 'It's only because I look too young. Besides, the clothes and make-up are to reinforce the message. That's how mortals do things these days.'

'That's just what they're telling you—'

'It doesn't matter,' Yudhishtra interrupted in a firm voice, turning away. 'There is one thing that has always been more important to me than life itself, and that is respect. Ever since we descended from heaven, Arjuna, I have gotten scarcely any of it from my own family. Instead, I find myself being respected and valued by strangers. I'm simply going where I'm wanted.'

'We do respect you!'

Yudhishtra swivelled around, his face a furious mask. 'How? By disobeying me at every turn? By refusing to listen to my opinion? By raising a hand to me? This morning, my own wife said she hated being married to me!'

Arjuna felt the reins on his own temper give way. 'You called your wife a whore!'

'She called me a coward!' Yudhishtra roared at him.

'Well, you behaved like one!' Arjuna roared back.

The two men launched themselves at each other, grabbing the other's arms and locking heads. Pushing at each other and grappling for control, they moved around the small room, knocking into the furniture. A ceramic lamp crashed to the floor, sending shards flying everywhere as Arjuna pinned Yudhishtra to the sideboard it sat upon. A chair went flying after receiving a wild hit from Arjuna's foot, after Yudhishtra kicked his knee in an attempt to make him fall. Fists flew in between twisting and turning, each trying to get the upper hand.

'I'll show you who's a coward,' Yudhishtra wrung out from clenched teeth, raising a knee in a bruising blow to Arjuna's chest.

Grimacing in pain, Arjuna wound Yudhishtra into a stranglehold with a snarl, only to have him curl out of it. 'Says the man with a toy for a weapon.'

Now it was Yudhishtra's turn to snarl. 'The only weapon I need against you, little brother, are these arms.'

Arjuna twisted Yudhishtra's arms and locked them behind him. 'This arm? Or this arm? You forget, big brother, I'm not a puny Kaurava!'

And on they went, in a tireless struggle until the other ceded and admitted he was wrong. Still, even as they burned with fury, neither tried to injure the other severely. There were no punches to the face, no pulling of hair or strikes at the groin. Arjuna, the larger and stronger of the two, instinctively held back a little so his brother was not at an unfair disadvantage. Bhima would have done the same for him. At the end of the day, their sense of fair play and their bond of brotherhood were too deeply ingrained for even the fieriest of arguments.

Finally, after a large table laden with papers, snacks and a jug of water toppled over with a resounding crash, the door to the room flew open.

'Stop! *Stop!*'

Arjuna could hear Amit Sharma's voice shrieking next to his ear as he felt a multitude of hands pulling him away from his brother. Breathing heavily and reeling with pain, he looked at Yudhishtra, who was also being held back by a group of men.

'You attacked our Guruji, you bastard! We'll teach you a lesson,' screamed Amit.

Suddenly, Arjuna felt a blow to his cheek. One of the men restraining him had thrown a punch. He began to struggle, but there were too many of them and they were holding him down. Expletive-accompanied blows began to rain on his body, pushing him towards the ground.

In the background, he heard Amit Sharma shout, 'Get the lathis!'

22

Yudhishtra looked on in horror as Amit and his men began beating his brother mercilessly, an entire crowd converging upon him with the bloodlust of lions who smelled fresh prey.

'No!' he yelled as he pulled away from the loosened grips of the men who were restraining him and flew at the group of attackers, who were trying to kick Arjuna to the floor.

Punching his way through the circle, Yudhishtra grabbed each man and flung him back forcefully.

'Get away from my brother!'

He caught one of the men who was kicking Arjuna and punched him in the face. Another man who was striking at Arjuna's head was wrenched back and Yudhishtra's knee battered his nose, breaking it instantly.

'Stand back!' It was the bellow of a man who had commanded armies.

Everyone in the room froze.

Yudhishtra pushed the remaining men off Arjuna and shielded his brother who, remarkably, was still standing after that vicious, one-sided assault. Glaring at them, Yudhishtra bared his teeth and growled, 'The next man who touches him will die.'

The men, slowly coming down from their frenzy, blinked at Yudhishtra with stunned confusion. Then, they looked at Amit, who stood back and scowled.

'But, Guruji,' he said plaintively, 'we were only trying to protect you.'

'I don't need your protection,' snapped Yudhishtra. 'I'm perfectly capable of fighting for myself. As for you all.' He looked around, 'You think you serve your guru by attacking a man ten-to-one? That was the most dishonourable assault I have ever seen. You should be ashamed of yourselves!'

Yudhishtra turned to Amit. 'Send your men out, immediately!'

Amit looked like he wanted to argue, but he nodded at the others. Slowly and reluctantly, they filed out, still looking bewildered. Filled with righteous indignation on behalf of their guru, they had obviously been looking forward to a lynching. This was a bit of an anti-climax. Some of them clutched bleeding lips and one had a broken nose. None of them had thought Yudhishtra was capable of such strength or violence. They cast him nervous glances as they left the room. Only Amit stayed behind.

Shutting the door with a slam, Yudhishtra turned to a badly bruised Arjuna, who swayed on his feet a little. He knew better than to offer his brother a supporting hand. Instead, he said, 'Brother, sit on the bed please.'

It was a testament to how much pain Arjuna must have been in that he quietly walked over to the bed and sat down, favouring his right leg slightly as he did so. Yudhishtra felt a blast of shame and sorrow. What was he doing? He needed to fix this. Now.

Turning to Amit, he spoke in a livid undertone, 'What your men did was inexcusable.'

'But—'

'You will apologize to my brother.'

Amit started to object, but his shrewd eyes caught the fury in Yudhishtra's and he capitulated, saying to Arjuna in a sullen voice, 'I'm sorry. It was a misunderstanding.'

Arjuna laughed without humour. 'You're not sorry, Amit Sharma. We both know what kind of racket you're running here. Unfortunately, my brother seems well and properly caught in your web.' He looked at Yudhishtra with a bitter expression. 'It seems I'm fighting a losing battle.'

Yudhishtra huffed. 'Brother ...'

'No,' said Arjuna in a firm voice as he rose to his feet unsteadily. 'I think we've said enough, and I refuse to stay here a minute longer. If you need to speak with me, I'll be at the orphanage for the rest of the day. Draupadi will be there too.' He stared at Yudhishtra with hard eyes. 'She was so upset that she couldn't go to work today.'

It was pointless arguing right now. Yudhishtra nodded. 'I'll come to the orphanage later. We'll speak then. Do you need assistance getting back?'

'I think the beating was enough for now.' Arjuna walked out without turning back.

The two men in the room waited until Arjuna's departure before looking at each other. Yudhishtra knew there was no point in shouting at Amit anymore than there was in trying to convince Arjuna that this was all a big misunderstanding. Modern mortals were horribly misled creatures, but that was to be expected. This was the Kalyug, after all. Chaos, spiritual and moral decay, abandonment of the dharmic way of life were the very underpinnings of this age.

It was that very reason why mortals needed Yudhishtra's guidance even more. Even if he did need to wear a stupid costume to get his message across.

He sighed. 'Amitji, we will talk about the principles and rules of combat during this afternoon's discourse. About honourable ways to fight and to resolve conflict. Please ask all the young men in the centre to attend.'

He felt a tickling on his lip and realized that he was still wearing the fake moustache. The one that Amit had insisted he wear, along with grey streaks in his hair, because otherwise he looked too young and devotees associated wisdom with advanced age.

Pulling off the offensive tuft of hair, he added, 'And I will not be wearing any make-up or costume. Please provide me with a plain length of cloth, any colour will do, and I will drape my own dhoti.'

Amit's eyes hooded for a moment, but he soon realized that any argument was futile. He folded his hands. 'Very well, Guruji.'

Yudhishtra nodded and turned away. 'You may go.'

'Er, Guruji.'

'Yes?'

'Are you going to the orphanage later today?'

Nodding, Yudhishtra said, 'Yes, I will go after the discourse.'

Amit frowned and cleared his throat, as if he were getting ready to be the bearer of bad news. 'I'm extremely sorry to criticize your family members, Guruji, but I think you deserve to know about the unsavoury activities going on there.'

That was news to him. He knew Bhima was helping Mother with the orphanage and that Narad Muni was the temporary caretaker, but nothing more. Truth be told, he was still upset with his mother and had barely spoken to her since the day he had stormed out of the common room and gotten into Amit's car. As guilty as he felt about his intractability the past few days, he didn't think their rift was his fault. If she was intent on breaking time-honoured ties for the sake of temporary gratification, then he had little to say to her.

'What unsavoury activities?' he asked Amit.

Amit took a deep, dramatic breath. 'Your brother, the large one, is operating an illegal food business. The neighbourhood people have threatened to call the police. In fact, the only reason they haven't already is because he is related to you. Also,' he shook his head with a disparaging expression and said in a scandalized murmur, 'they're serving forbidden meat.' He said no more, as if discussing it was as forbidden as the meat itself.

Yudhishtra pursed his lips in disapproval. Bhima was serving human flesh? Surely not. His brother was hot-tempered and unpredictable, but certainly not cannibalistic. However, he did enjoy his food, and was currently residing with mortals in the midst of a Kalyug. Who knew what deviances were considered acceptable these days.

'You're sure?' he asked Amit.

'Of course,' replied Amit. 'I went down there myself, but your brother threatened me and my friends and forced us to leave.'

That he could believe. Bhima was well-known for picking fights with people. Sighing, he nodded. 'I'll go there later and sort this out.'

Amit smiled. 'Thank you, Guruji. We must all do what we can to protect our Hindu values.'

Yudhishtra had no idea what the word 'Hindu' meant, but didn't feel like asking. He gestured for Amit to leave.

A few hours later, once he had given a gathering of men and women a rather forceful talk on how to resolve conflict without being adharmic, he made his way to the orphanage. He was a bit apprehensive about facing them all, given his altercations with Draupadi and Arjuna, but it was time they finally sat down together and discussed things calmly and rationally, no matter how unpleasant. And it was up to him, the eldest, to take the lead.

He found them all in the common room. Kunti and Draupadi sat with Arjuna at the dining table, while Bhima stood next to a large, simmering pot on one end of the room, which had been converted into a makeshift kitchen. Nakula and Sahadeva stood around rather aimlessly near Bhima, at hand to help.

Yudhishtra's entrance was greeted by a tense silence. Bhima glared at him while the others looked away. He gulped involuntarily. This was going to be more difficult than he had imagined.

'I think it's time we talk,' he announced, as he looked around the room.

For a moment, it looked like everyone was going to continue ignoring him, but then Kunti nodded.

'Yes,' she said, gesturing for Yudhishtra to sit at the dining table. 'I agree.'

She waited for him to be seated before she continued, 'I was shocked and saddened to hear that you and Arjuna came to blows today. And by the unpleasantness that occurred in Draupadi's home this morning.'

Yudhishtra nodded. 'I am saddened by it too. The last thing I wanted was for us brothers to separate or fight with each other. Or for there to be any discord between Draupadi and myself.'

At the mention of her name from his lips, Draupadi looked up at him with a face streaked with tears. This surprised him, given that she wasn't a woman who cried a lot.

'You called me a whore today, Yudhishtra,' she said softly, prompting everyone else in the room to grimace.

She took a shuddering breath. 'All through my previous life and even afterlife, I was made aware, in ways big and small, by everyone we ever met, that I was an aberration. One woman married to five men at the same time. People called me a whore habitually, not only behind my back, but in full view of my husbands and my elders. I was used to it, to the anger that it provoked inside me. I even expected it to a certain extent. After all, none of those people knew how I came to be married to the Pandavas. How it was never my choice, or how much we all struggled with it. None of those people knew the details, and so their judgement, their contempt, held no weight in my mind. I have been called a whore millions of times, Yudhishtra, and have not shed a single tear over it. Until today.' She swallowed unsteadily. 'Today, a man whom I once called my husband, the very man responsible for me being the shared wife of five men in the first place, the one who claimed my virginity on our wedding night and crowned me his empress—called me a whore.' Fresh tears began to flow from her eyes. 'I gave up *everything* for you. My freedom, my dignity, my life, my legacy. And now, finally, I know what you really think of me.'

Draupadi laughed bitterly. 'If I am a whore, Yudhishtra, it is only because you made me one.'

Yudhishtra looked down at the floor, his eyes skimming over Draupadi's feet, encased in floral slippers. She had always had such pretty feet. The first time he saw her, properly, was when the six of them were walking back to their Brahman's hut, immediately after Arjuna had won her hand in her swayamwara. He had felt desire, immediately followed by guilt for coveting his brother's bride. As they walked, his guilt had slowly fostered resentment. After all, he was the eldest. His marriage should have come first, before Arjuna's. Unfortunately, nothing in his life until then had happened as it should. Instead of sitting on the throne of Hastinapur as its king, he had become a prince in hiding, without prospects and constantly being outshone by his younger brothers. So, when his mother had unwittingly presented the opportunity for him to claim Draupadi, he'd taken it.

Knowing it was the wrong thing to do. But doing it anyway.

'I'm sorry, Draupadi. I never intended to make you suffer during our life together,' he said softly, looking up at her tear-stained face. 'Perhaps I was wrong to claim you as my bride, but I have always cherished you. Despite my demands.' He looked between her and Arjuna, and sighed. 'I knew you preferred Arjuna, and it made me angry. God knows I've tried to fight it, tried to extend myself beyond base desires and petty jealousies, and cultivate an unpolluted mind, but I'm just a man, Draupadi.'

He shook his head. 'I have always tried my best.'

That made Draupadi chuckle. 'That you have, except you keep getting in your own way.'

Her words were not what he wanted to hear, but he had to accept that they were at least partly true. He had many regrets, many things he wished he'd done differently. Of course, he would never admit that to anyone but himself.

'Forgive me for calling you a ... you know. It was said in anger. Perhaps, even though Mother made us, I hadn't quite let you go yet. I don't understand your life right now, Draupadi, and I may not entirely approve of it, but I must accept that I'm not a part of it anymore.' Yudhishtra attempted a small smile. 'I will work towards that. And wish you the best.'

Draupadi nodded, not quite smiling back but not scowling either. 'And I'm sorry for calling you a coward. You're not. You're delusional, stubborn and self-important,' now she smiled a little, 'but not a coward.'

He chuckled ruefully. Trust Draupadi to turn an apology into an insult.

'There are still a few things to discuss, Brother.' Arjuna's annoyed voice came from the other side of the table. His lip was cut, his cheek swollen and he was hunching slightly. Not to mention that he was glowering at Yudhishtra.

'I'm very sorry for what happened to you today, Arjuna.' He spoke with sincere contrition.

Arjuna shook his head. 'That's not what I'm talking about. It wasn't your fault they attacked me. However, I just don't understand what you're doing over there. Those people are clearly taking advantage of you, charging people money to meet you, telling you how to dress, when to speak. It isn't right.'

Yudhishtra ignored Arjuna's words, stood up and began pacing the room. Slowly, he looked each brother in the eye. 'What happened to us?'

He got no answer, so he went on, 'We were an unbreakable force, all our lives. Right up until the moment we left heaven for this little sojourn, nothing and no one could have come between us. However, from the moment we landed, it's as if I don't know any of you anymore. Why? How?'

None of his brothers said anything in response, even though both Bhima and Arjuna looked like they wanted to say something.

Finally, Kunti broke the silence. Looking around, she said, 'It's a credit to all of you that you are here, talking to each other, after everything that's happened.' She gazed at Yudhishtra with a fond look. 'My son. Come, sit with me.'

Yudhishtra walked to Kunti and sat on the floor next to her feet. She shook her head and guided him to a chair at her side. Stroking his cheek, she said, 'There is much I did wrong in my previous life, Yudhishtra. Not only did I abandon Karna as a baby, but I didn't tell you he was your brother until after his death in the Great War. Had I done so, you would have stopped the war instantly and handed over your kingship to him. You would have obeyed him and fought for him, and treated him with the same loyalty and respect that your younger brothers show you, despite him having taken your position. That is the kind of person you are, and I am so proud of you for your principles.'

Shaking her head sadly, she continued, 'However, you always expected your brothers and wives to be exactly like you. They tried, they really did, at great cost to themselves. But, at the end of the day, it has left them feeling unfulfilled. Well, all except the baby of the family.' She glanced at Sahadeva, who smiled at the old nickname.

Kunti turned back to Yudhishtra. 'The reason they have gone their own ways now is because, in this short window of time, they are trying to find some personal fulfilment. Surely, my son, you can't begrudge them that.'

Before Yudhishtra could say anything, Sahadeva spoke up. 'What if this short window of time isn't enough?' He looked at Draupadi and Kunti. 'It wasn't enough for both of you.'

Kunti sighed. 'That's true. There was still much to do when it was time to leave, so I decided to stay. Knowing that my decision would hurt you all. But I realized that each of us has to face our own destiny. That is how birth and rebirth work—we live as a family, but we pay for our karma individually, and our soul's journey is undertaken alone. For thousands of years in heaven, my earthly failures haunted me day and night. I was unfulfilled. I stayed here not only for Karan, but also for myself, to mend my karma and finally have peace of mind.'

Sahadeva frowned. 'Are you saying you would support any of us who wanted to stay back?'

Kunti shook her head. 'I would have no part in it, son. Each of you must decide for yourselves.'

Yudhishtra huffed. 'Mother, I have made no secret of the fact that we came down here to try and persuade you to come back. The decision to stay together or not should be a family one. Draupadi no longer wants us, but you are still our mother. All our problems can be easily resolved if you come back to heaven with us now.'

Kunti shook her head firmly. 'I'm sorry. I can't do that.'

'She's not the only one who's staying.'

23

'When you say "family decision", what you actually mean is *your* decision.' Bhima turned around from his cooking and faced Yudhishtra. 'I'm sorry, Brother, but you are not going to decide my fate either. I've made the decision for myself.'

Yudhishtra's eyes widened. 'Bhima, no.'

Crossing his wide, muscular arms across his chest, Bhima levelled his eyes with his elder brother. 'I am staying here, with Mother and Draupadi.'

He watched as Yudhishtra spun around to Kunti and cried out, 'See? This is the problem! This is why you should never have come down here, Mother. Why you need to come back up now. Or Bhima will sacrifice his own future for you!'

Kunti quickly looked at Bhima and held her hand up for him to be silent, knowing that Yudhishtra's words would make him angry. 'Your brother is right, Bhima. You shouldn't stay because of me.'

Bhima was indeed angry, but not with her. He glared at Yudhishtra and said, 'I'm not sacrificing anything. I want to stay.' He waved a hand upwards briefly and continued, 'I was wasted up there. Here, I'm useful, my hands and mind are busy, and I get to do what I love. It's an easy decision. One I won't reconsider.'

'What about the upcoming war with the demon world?'

Bhima shrugged. 'Demons aren't half bad when you get to know them.' After all, he'd married one in his previous life. He'd also had a half-demon son who fought by his side in the Great War.

Yudhishtra gave Draupadi a plaintive look. 'Draupadi, talk some sense into him. He listens to you.'

Draupadi shook her head. 'I've spoken to him already. It is his choice, and I won't interfere.'

Yudhishtra threw his hands up. 'This is madness!' Looking around at Arjuna, Nakula and Sahadeva, he asked, 'Are any of you also planning to stay?'

Sahadeva gave Nakula a look before saying, 'No.'

'Thank god.' Yudhishtra nodded. He thought Sahadeva had spoken for all three of them, but Bhima noticed that neither Arjuna nor Nakula had replied. In fact, they both stared ahead with inscrutable expressions when the question was asked. Were they thinking about staying? He needed to speak to them.

Taking a deep breath, Bhima tried to make his tone a respectful one. 'Brother, let's talk about you. Arjuna came back from your centre this morning having been beaten up by the very men you are now living with. I should tell you, that Amit Sharma also came to the orphanage the other day, while we were serving lunch, and threatened us. What on earth are you doing allying with these people?'

With a huff, Yudhishtra replied, 'You start an illegal business, serve human flesh and you expect mortals to not have a problem with it?'

'*Human* flesh?'

Yudhishtra frowned. 'Amit said you were serving forbidden meat.'

That made Bhima laugh. 'Since when is mutton a forbidden meat?'

'Mutton, as in a goat?'

'Yes!'

Draupadi added, 'The lunch service is perfectly legal, Yudhishtra. We've already registered with the authorities. Amit Sharma is just trying to create trouble.'

Confused, Yudhishtra asked, 'Why?'

It was Kunti who answered. 'He's running the BYBM Centre like a gang and is intimidating the neighbourhood, Yudhishtra. He is the one involved in illegal activities, not us.'

This obviously troubled Yudhishtra greatly, from the look on his face. He sat down and hung his head in contemplation.

Kunti pressed on. 'Come and stay here at the orphanage, son. We can spend a little time together, before you leave.'

She said it kindly, but there was a pinch of hurt in her tone. Yudhishtra had been avoiding all of them lately.

If he noticed his mother's tone, Yudhishtra didn't acknowledge it. Instead, he slowly shook his head. 'I have given my word, Mother. Since both you and Draupadi are staying back, I have nothing left to do here. My brothers have each found an alternative mission, one that fulfils them personally. I accept that. I will then pursue my own path. It won't give me any personal fulfilment, but I will do it for the greater good. I'll continue to speak at the BYBM Centre, and will try and counsel Amit Sharma and his men out of their unprincipled behaviour. That will be my purpose until I leave.'

He stood up and looked around at the stunned expressions of his family, a resigned but resolute look on his face. 'Needless to say, I am disappointed at the outcome of this meeting. But perhaps this too is destined.' With that, he walked out without looking back.

Arjuna shook his head, grimacing at the movement. 'He's still upset.'

Turning back to stir his pot and check the progress of the curry in it, Bhima replied, 'We tried. Nothing's left to say.'

Nakula then spoke for the first time, only to say quickly, 'All right, if we're finished here, I have an appointment, so I'm heading off.'

Draupadi looked up at that. 'What's happening between you and Angela?'

'Nothing, if I'm late for our appointment.' Nakula grinned.

Sighing, Draupadi said in a weary voice, 'I've had a difficult day, so please tell me you're not going to break my dear friend's heart when you leave.'

Nakula's face grew serious. 'Actually, it might not be just your friend's heart in question. Anyway, I have to run, and I won't be back tonight. But I'm starting a photo shoot for GT tomorrow, so drop in if you want to chat.' With a quick look at Sahadeva's now-sullen face, he hurried out.

After the door had closed behind him, Sahadeva ran a hand through his hair and said softly, 'Well, if I'm not needed here, I'll get moving too.'

Kunti asked, 'Where will you go?'

He sighed. 'I'm not sure. I need time to think.'

'About what, my son?'

Sahadeva smiled at Kunti with affection. 'A lot is about to change, Mother. I need to prepare myself.' And with that cryptic statement, he left.

'I should be going too,' said Draupadi. She turned to Arjuna. 'Come, let me take you home to rest.'

'Actually,' said Bhima without turning around, 'I wanted to talk to Arjuna, so you carry on without him. He'll make his own way home.'

Draupadi huffed. 'He's injured, Bhima. Surely you can talk tomorrow.'

That made Bhima laugh. 'This is nothing. He's endured much worse and he's been fine. Don't coddle him.'

Both Draupadi and Kunti left fairly quickly after that. Bhima carried on cooking for a while in silence, trying to figure out exactly what he wanted to say to Arjuna. Draupadi's admission that they kissed had shaken him. He'd automatically assumed that just as the Pandavas had shared her equally as a wife, they would relinquish her equally too. Obviously, Arjuna had made no such assumptions.

A little miffed, he turned the cooker off and covered the pot. 'This is ready. Let's go for a drink. I need to get out of here for a while.'

They found an establishment that served alcohol within a short walk from the orphanage. It was almost empty, given that there was still some daylight outside. Sitting in a darkened booth, the two brothers sipped a frothy beer each and sighed with pleasure.

'God, I've missed alcohol.' Bhima took a hearty sip that emptied his glass. He signalled for another.

Chuckling, Arjuna said, 'Me too. I can't stand amrith.'

'Hah! A child's drink.'

They drank in silence for a while, listening indifferently to the music that was playing in the background.

Finally, Arjuna asked, 'What is it, Brother?'

Straight to the point. Bhima smiled. That was what he liked about his younger brother. Arjuna had quietly accepted Bhima's decision and wasn't going to try and talk him out of it, or harp on about immortality or the cycle of rebirth. However, he still had to answer to Bhima for his actions.

'You kissed Draupadi.'

Arjuna stiffened. He obviously hadn't expected Draupadi to tell Bhima. Slowly, he looked up and met his brother's eyes.

'I did.'

There was no trace of remorse in his eyes.

'What are your intentions with her?'

With an irritated look, Arjuna retorted, 'What are *your* intentions with her?'

Bhima was confused. 'My intentions?'

'Well, you've decided to stay back on earth. What does that mean for you and Draupadi?'

Arjuna's eyes glittered with what Bhima recognized as jealousy.

He shook his head and said in a firm voice, 'It means that we will continue to be family, in whatever capacity she wishes.'

Anger arose in Arjuna's eyes. 'So, if she decides she wants you after we leave, you'll have her?'

Despite the fact that his younger brother was obviously itching for a fight today, Bhima saw no reason to lie.

'Let me be clear about one thing. I'll have Draupadi any way she'll take me. However, it's not me she's kissing, is it? Despite her love for me and mine for her, it has never been me she wanted to kiss. So, you can put your hackles away and tell me what's going on with you two.'

He leaned back and drained his glass, signalling for another. Draupadi wanted him as a friend. And, as her friend, he would need to look out for her in her relationships. With other men. He took a deep breath, willing himself to be calm.

Now Arjuna drained his beer glass. 'I don't know.'

'That's not a good enough answer. Did you kiss her first or did she kiss you?'

'She did.'

Calm, stay calm. Don't crush the glass. Bhima took another breath and cleared his throat. 'I noticed you didn't answer Yudhishtra's question, about whether you're staying here or going back to heaven.'

'No, I didn't.'

'Well?'

The server put two fresh beers in front of them, and Arjuna picked his up to drink immediately, obviously buying time.

'I don't know what I'm going to do.'

Bhima grunted in frustration. 'Stop saying you don't know!'

He got a glare from Arjuna in return. 'If I knew, I would tell you, Brother.'

They were quiet for a while. Finally, Bhima put his glass down with a thump and said, 'Fine. You still have some time to decide. But I warn you, don't play with Draupadi. If you decide to stay, and both of you want to be together, you'll have my support. But, if you hurt her, you'll find out what a real beating feels like.'

Arjuna frowned at him. 'You'll actually support Draupadi and me becoming a couple? What about your relationship with her?'

Bhima shrugged. 'I'm not blind, Brother. It was always you she wanted.'

'But what will you do?'

He shrugged again. 'I'll live.'

The ire in Arjuna's eyes immediately dissipated, only to be replaced by its close cousin, anguish. He hung his head and exhaled in an unsteady breath. 'I'm so confused. I feel like—'

'Oh no you don't,' Bhima interrupted. 'Don't start rambling adolescent drivel at me. I already got enough of that from Draupadi. All you need to know is this—were you happy in heaven?'

Arjuna's eyes hardened. 'No.'

'Can you be happier down here?' asked Bhima.

'Maybe. Or maybe I could try to change things in heaven. Make them better, keep my promises.'

'Is it Subhadra?'

Arjuna nodded. 'She expects me to return, and I promised Krishna I would take care of her. I love her, but things haven't been the same between us in a very long time. And Draupadi ...' He smiled. 'Draupadi's different now. I think it's because she's happier and doing what she loves. But there's no guarantee we would be a couple if I stayed.'

Bhima shook his head. 'She's not the most predictable of women. But she did kiss you. And you won't have to share her this time.'

His brother didn't say anything, but Bhima knew by the look on his face that it was something he wanted. He took a large gulp of his beer, set his glass down firmly and looked Arjuna in the eye.

'As mother said, we are each responsible for our own destiny. Don't base your decisions on what other people want or feel. Do what will fulfil your own soul. Guilt-free.'

Chuckling, Arjuna murmured, 'Guilt and I are good friends so it may take a while. But you're right. I need to do this for myself.' He smiled at Bhima. 'Thank you, Brother. For the advice and ... everything else.'

Bhima grunted. 'Don't thank me yet. The second you leave, I'm going after Draupadi.'

24

The sun was setting rapidly, only a few dregs of orange left on the horizon. He really should be getting home, thought Sahadeva. The slum near the orphanage wasn't exactly the best place to be roaming around after dark. It was daunting to navigate during the day, but it became positively dangerous at night.

Sahadeva looked around at the crowded, ramshackle structures, with their dirty curtains and putrid gutters. It pained him to see people, especially young children, living in conditions like this. So much had gone wrong in the mortal world. He sighed.

'Why so sad, Philosophy? Come, I'll make you happy.'

The voice was a loud one, husky with a nasal inflection. It had come from a plump woman of indeterminate age, who was sitting on the stoop of a dilapidated hut. She wore a low-cut, faded sari blouse that was too loose for her, giving the impression that her large breasts would fall out at any moment, and an equally faded skirt that reached her calves. She chewed something habitually and adjusted her hair as she regarded him with an amused expression.

'You're so cute; I'll give you a discount.' She winked.

Sahadeva smiled politely and shook his head.

'Come on! I'll let you do whatever you want. At a very reasonable price.'

Sahadeva chuckled ruefully. 'That's not what I need right now.' He turned to go.

'No, it looks like you need someone to talk to. I can do that too, you know,' she said.

That stopped him in his tracks. He did need someone to talk to. He had walked aimlessly for over an hour, trying to figure out what to do, what to say to Nakula that would convince him to return to heaven. Normally, it was his wife, Vijaya, who advised him on how to deal with his brothers. After all, the older Pandavas weren't easy people to get along with. Each one had a strong personality that tended to overshadow his own. Even Nakula, who knew him better than anyone, and whom he loved better than anyone, wasn't always easy to get along with.

God, he missed Vijaya. She'd have known what to do. How to deal with Nakula's fickleness.

'Tell you what,' the prostitute on the stoop said, scratching her chin and then spitting out whatever was in her mouth. 'I'll give you half-rate for only talking.' She patted the space on the stoop opposite her. 'Come and tell Vijaya your problems.'

Sahadeva started. 'Your name's Vijaya?'

She smiled suggestively. 'My name can be whatever you want it to be.'

He chuckled. Providence certainly worked in interesting ways. 'Vijaya is fine. Better than fine.' Approaching the stoop and sitting atop it gingerly, he handed over the small amount of money in his pocket. 'This is all I have.'

Vijaya took the money from him and looked it over. 'It's barely enough for a chat, Philosophy, but I like you, so I'll accept.' She looked up at him. 'What's bothering you?'

'My brother.'

She laughed and shook her head. 'Usually, it's about a woman. Go on.'

Sahadeva sighed again. 'He's my twin. We're here on holiday and are supposed to be going home at the end of the month. But I'm pretty sure he wants to stay here.'

'So? What's wrong with that?'

'Nothing, except that we won't be together.' Sahadeva wrung his hands, his voice pained, 'We lost our parents when we were infants. We've only ever had each other. I don't want to lose him.' He looked up at Vijaya. 'I want him to come home with me, where he belongs.'

'What does your brother want?' she asked.

'He hasn't told me yet.' Sahadeva clenched his jaw. 'He's met a woman.'

'Aha! See, I told you,' snorted Vijaya. 'It's always about a woman.'

Sahadeva was beginning to regret his impulsive decision to take advice from a complete stranger just because she had the same name as his wife.

'Never mind,' he said, shaking his head and getting up to depart.

'Sit,' ordered Vijaya, looking at him intently. 'Let me tell you a story, Philosophy.' She looked around to make sure no one was listening. 'I gave birth to a baby two years ago,' she said. A small smile stretched her lips. 'A girl. She was beautiful. Too beautiful. This place would have ruined her.'

She stared at Sahadeva with hard eyes. 'Do you know what life is like for girls born in this part of the slum?'

'No.' But he could imagine.

'The pimps make them take customers, sometimes even before they learn how to speak. They give them drugs, starve them. The unlucky ones are maimed and sent out to beg. It's a fate worse than death.' She shook her head. 'Even so, many of the prostitutes here choose to have daughters anyway. They take care of you later on, when customers don't want you anymore. Some, the more compassionate ones, abort the pregnancy. I couldn't afford to abort her, and when I saw her face, I was glad I didn't. But I couldn't bear the thought of her suffering the same fate as me. So I gave her up.'

She nodded in the direction from which Sahadeva had been walking. 'There's an orphanage down the road, with a kind warden. I left my daughter on the doorstep early one morning and walked away. I haven't seen her for two years, Philosophy. She's my blood, the only thing I love in this world, and I don't even know what she looks like.'

Sahadeva struggled to swallow the lump in his throat. He stared at the ground, his vision blurring. 'How can you bear it?' he whispered.

Vijaya sniffed lightly, her eyes as dry as they had been at the beginning of the conversation. 'I bear it because I know she's better off now. Because this way, at least she has a chance. It's the only thing I can give her.'

'What about you?'

Vijaya smiled. 'I go to sleep every night with the knowledge that there is a part of me out there that hasn't been tainted by this life. It keeps me going.'

Sahadeva stayed quiet, watching her fingers absently play with the folds of her skirt.

'Here, take this.'

He looked up to find her holding out the money he had given her earlier. He reached out and pushed her hand back.

Vijaya shook her head, looking slightly annoyed. 'Keep it,' she said firmly. 'I know it's strange to hear this from a prostitute, Philosophy, but here's some advice, no strings attached. Do the right thing. Even if it hurts.'

Sahadeva nodded. 'Thank you, Vijaya.' He got up and walked away.

25

The next few days passed without any further confrontations or baring of hearts. Nakula completed a successful, and surprisingly enjoyable, photo shoot for Gautam Thakur in a forest a few hours' drive from Delhi. Even though he'd had to wear an absurd assortment of clothes, he had also posed with a beautifully carved golden sword and had a chance to show Angela some of his sword-fighting moves. Moves that had paid off generously when they got back to their hotel room at night. Not to mention the significant amount of money he had been given at the end of it, which he'd given to Kunti for the orphanage.

Sahadeva, on the other hand, seemed to be in a meditative mood. He stayed in Delhi on the days of Nakula's photo shoot, quietly helping Kunti with her children. He said little during this time, except the one night he went drinking with Bhima. Intoxicated and barely coherent, he had shed a tear and admitted to Bhima that he was sad but refused to say why.

Bhima didn't push him. The twins had their own dynamic, and he thought it was best to stay out of it.

The lunch service at the orphanage did well, to no one's surprise. Bhima was a talented cook, and in a community that had few options for culinary variation, his reasonably priced curries and roasted meats became the talk of the town. Everyone from local workers to college students and their professors, and even housewives, started filing in at lunchtime, and the food often sold out within the hour. Latecomers cursed the closed window, and even wrote reviews requesting that Bhima expand his business and cook on a larger scale. Men from the BYBM Centre walked in one day with a police constable, questioning the origin of the meat being sold and trying to convince Bhima to either shut down his service or serve vegetarian food, but Kunti told them to call Draupadi at NPTV and they left soon afterwards.

This did nothing to help Yudhishtra's case at the centre. Amit Sharma was indeed a scoundrel, as his family had warned him, and was almost impossible for Yudhishtra to manage. He tried turning down donations, but then discovered that Amit had been taking them in secret. He then tried to ensure that donations were actually sent to charities, but there was no way to ascertain which charities were genuine. Meanwhile, Yudhishtra met people every day who were suffering and full of questions. He tried to counsel them, but most just wanted quick fixes. They wanted a guru to tell them that their luck would change after a particular date, or if they undertook a pilgrimage or fast. Most of them weren't willing to learn, take responsibility or change their behaviour. Yudhishtra went to bed every night completely drained and despondent. This Kalyug really was appalling.

Meanwhile, Arjuna accompanied Draupadi to and from work every day, playing bodyguard. Each was so muddled in their own mind that neither tried telling the other what to do, which made for a pleasant change. It was an enjoyable, albeit temporary, truce. They watched TV at home, went out to try new foods, and Arjuna accompanied Draupadi to a party at a hotel, where the rooms were bedecked in gold. In fact, the party and venue were so over-the-top, Arjuna joked that it was more luxurious than heaven itself. Draupadi had laughed, agreeing that while heaven might have immortality, this party had alcohol and biryani. Dressed in a long, flowing ruby dress with sparkling jewellery and glistening red lips, Arjuna thought she looked good enough to eat. Given the way she got all flustered after eyeing him in his new navy suit, her thoughts probably weren't too different either. But he kept his thoughts to himself. Their new harmony was delicate, sitting on a ticking time bomb. Each held their heart close, afraid of what would happen when the clock stopped.

Arjuna still didn't know what he wanted to do. Bhima had no one to go back to heaven for, so staying on earth was an easier decision for him. Arjuna had commitments in heaven, making his decision more complicated. Then again, was Subhadra really waiting for him? Between her various quests to become a Vidyadhari or be reborn as a gypsy, did she really care about his future and what he wanted? Did he care more about their marriage than she did? Arjuna wasn't the type of man who gave up easily, but was it time to give up on Subhadra? Had their relationship run its course?

These were the questions that tormented him during the taxi ride all the way from the NPTV office to the cricket stadium, where he was due to meet Rohit Jadeja and the Indian cricket team.

A young woman in uniform met him at the entrance, hung a 'Visitor' card around his neck and led him to the field, where the team was practicing. The stadium itself was the biggest arena he had ever seen. The field was massive, but the stands were awe-inspiring, probably accommodating tens of thousands of people. Nothing like it had existed in his own time.

People, mostly men, crowded around a large group who were doing warm-up exercises. Everyone wore the same uniform with a few slight variations, so Arjuna was unsure how many of them were players. During fight training sessions in his own time, there were typically elderly commanders and field hands present, along with the warriors, either to train them or to facilitate the process of training. Generals and senior officers often stood on the sidelines, watching and assessing the individual capabilities of fighters. He imagined this wouldn't be too different.

He was led to a group sitting under a blue tent. Five men sat on chairs and laughed at something one of them had said.

'Sir,' said the woman to one of the men, a portly man in his fifties. 'This is Arjuna Kuru.'

The man smiled and stood up, walking up to Arjuna and thumping him soundly on his back. 'Arjuna! Pleasure to meet you. I'm Sunil, the bowling coach today. Rohit has told me all about you. I'm looking forward to seeing you play.'

'Thank you,' replied Arjuna. He couldn't imagine how this man bowled well enough to coach the Indian team with such a large, protruding stomach, but he supposed appearances could be deceptive. The Indian cricket team was one of the best in the world right now, so Sunil was obviously good at his job. 'Where is Rohit?'

Sunil shook his head. 'He'll meet you later with the rest of the team. The practice session is in progress. I'll be assessing you first with my assistant, Mansi.' He pointed to the woman who had escorted Arjuna on to the field. She smiled and gave him a friendly wave.

He followed Sunil and Mansi to some flimsy-looking nets set up in one corner of the field. The wooden stumps here were attached to a base instead of dug into the ground. Absently, Arjuna wondered if he could make the entire base fly off the ground.

Mansi handed him a cricket ball, just as Sunil said, 'Okay, Arjuna. Show us what you can do.'

There was a hint of condescension in the man's tone. As if he were humouring Arjuna because Rohit Jadeja, one of the team's best batsmen, had personally recommended him, and so it was difficult to refuse. Arjuna knew that it took years for most cricket players in the country to rise through the ranks of the circuit, slogging it out at every level from the time they were old enough to hold a bat. For Arjuna to simply walk in here and take what other players had worked an entire lifetime towards, he would need to dazzle Sunil, the bowling coach.

Really dazzle him.

So he took a little time to warm up with a few exercises. Then, he examined the ball, the undulation of the ground and the stumps closely, and planned his delivery. Gripping the ball, the way Rizwan the scout had shown him, he trained his vision on the exact spot where he wanted the ball to bounce and replayed its trajectory in his mind. Then, taking a run up, he whipped the ball through the air with all the strength and accuracy his body could summon.

The ball careened through the air, bounced just about where the batsman's feet would stand and collided into the stumps, knocking the base down and breaking the middle stump in half.

Arjuna supressed a smile at the sight of the broken stump lying on the ground, and turned to Sunil and Mansi. By the looks of their hanging jaws, he assumed he'd gotten their attention.

'Mansi,' said Sunil softly, without looking at her. 'Get another set of stumps and a speed gun.'

Mansi turned and began running towards the stands. Meanwhile, Sunil walked up to Arjuna, congratulating him on an excellent delivery. 'You've never had any formal training, have you?' he asked.

Arjuna shook his head. 'No. How do you know?'

Sunil smiled. 'Your body isn't conditioned to your action. Which is full of flaws, by the way. They're not affecting your speed, but are unacceptable in international cricket. Don't worry though, they won't be difficult to correct because your muscles haven't gotten habituated yet. Also, while it's amazing that you're able to instinctively gauge the wicket and your delivery, if you thought more about the smaller details—pitch, angle, grip, swing, seam, line, wind, humidity, ground density and a hundred other things—you could do even better.'

Tilting his head to one side, Arjuna thought about what Sunil had said before replying, 'You're right that I'm not used to throwing the ball like this; however, don't you think that overthinking the details actually interferes with instinct? What if I already feel all those things without actually knowing what they are? After all, sporting games are similar to battle—you can't fight without instinct.'

Sunil grinned at that. 'Yes, instinct does matter a lot, but so does strategy, temperament and consistency. Now, I'm going to show you a different way to grip the ball and also alter your action a little. Then let's see how you do.'

As Mansi came running with the equipment, Sunil positioned Arjuna's body and made adjustments, talking constantly while he moved limbs around. 'Relax this muscle ... relax more. Lean into it. You see this in your wrist? It twists a little before it flicks. That's taking units off your speed. So is that little hop mid-stride in your run-up to the crease. Try it without. The aim is economy. You already have precision, but your action could be streamlined. Like this.' He moved Arjuna's arm back and forth, again and again. 'See how that feels different to what you were doing? Now, practice like this a few times and see if it makes a difference.'

Arjuna nodded, his respect for the bowling coach soaring with all this new information. The coach may not be able to throw the ball himself, but he knew what he was talking about. He practiced throwing the ball gently, trying to incorporate Sunil's suggestions. All the while, the bowling coach kept talking him through it in an undertone.

It took Arjuna some time to amend his delivery style and then more practice to relax into it. Finally, after a few rounds that satisfied them both, Sunil suggested Arjuna try with the stumps.

After Mansi positioned a speed gun on its stand, Arjuna started bowling at the stumps. At first, because the new action felt less natural, his deliveries were slower and less accurate than before. He looked at Sunil, who nodded patiently and suggested he keep trying.

Arjuna shook his head and focused his mind. The trick was to combine his natural instinct with the new techniques that Sunil had taught him. He'd begun concentrating too much on the technicalities and less on how he felt. That was the problem. Stroking the ball absently, he channelled his energy into it, becoming one with it. He scanned the wicket again, tuning out the world, seeing it first with his own eye and then adding Sunil's factors into his vision. When he did his run-up and moved, it was with the intense single-mindedness of a tiger charging towards a deer in the forest.

With a swing of his arms and a flick of his wrist, Arjuna sent the ball flying through the air. When it collided with the stumps and flung the base off the ground, it was with such finesse that all three of them jumped up in the air and exclaimed.

Sunil strode over and thumped Arjuna's back again. 'Well done, my boy!'

'C-Coach.' Mansi's unsteady voice came from a few paces away.

Sunil ignored her. He said to Arjuna, 'That was almost perfect. Still a lot to learn, though, but you have excellent potential.'

'Coach.'

He carried on talking. 'Of course, I'm unsure how this works, since you're technically a beginner and an amateur.'

'Coach.'

'You know, there is a usual base of clubs and tournaments that we select players from, which you've never played in, so it might be difficult with the Cricket Board.'

'Coach!'

Sunil swivelled around, glaring at Mansi. '*What?* Can't you see I'm talking?'

She stuck her head out from behind the speed gun, an apologetic look on her face. 'He just broke the world record.'

Sunil looked stunned. 'What?'

She gestured to the stumps and spoke slowly, 'Um ... he broke the world record. For the fastest ball ever bowled,' she added. Just in case there was any doubt which world record she was talking about.

Scowling, Sunil looked back at her. 'That can't be. Are you sure?'

'It's what the speed gun says.'

Arjuna smiled, pleasantly surprised that modern mortals had a way of measuring how fast a ball flew through the air. He wondered if one could use a speed gun with arrows. He would love to know how fast he could shoot them.

There was no time to ask though, because Sunil shook his head and said, 'Can't be. Let's try measuring again. Arjuna, throw a few more please.'

Arjuna proceeded to bowl the ball repeatedly, while Mansi measured the speed of each delivery and shouted it out after it hit the stump. Not every ball was as fast as the first one, but a couple of them were.

'Mansi!' Sunil finally barked with what looked like the beginnings of mild hysteria. 'Get another speed gun!'

Mansi went sprinting full pelt towards the stands, her excitement palpable. When she came back with a bigger gun that featured a screen and separate stand with wires, Sunil and Arjuna waited patiently as she set it up, doing stretching exercises to keep Arjuna's body warm.

When it was set up and Arjuna started bowling again, the new speed gun produced the same results as the old. Sunil slumped until he was sitting on the ground. Looking up at Arjuna's tall, strapping form, he whispered, 'I've never seen anything like it.'

Arjuna couldn't help a rush of pleasure at those words.

Sunil gave an unsteady laugh as he stood up. 'We have to sign you up, my boy.'

The pleasure dissipated. 'I don't know about that.'

Eyes widening, Sunil said, 'No, you don't understand. You're a match winner, Arjuna. With the right training, you can play international cricket in a matter of months perhaps. This is a phenomenal opportunity for you!'

Arjuna shook his head. Playing for fun and a little glory was one thing. Signing a contract and making commitments was another. 'I don't know where I'm going to be in the next few months, Coach. I might be out of ... the country.'

'Then stay in the country!' Sunil's tone was exasperated. 'There are hundreds of millions of Indian men who would sell their souls to be in your shoes right now. To play cricket for India is to be like a king in this country. No man in his right mind would refuse.'

'I'll have to think about it.' Along with everything else.

Sunil looked at him as if he was insane. Then he turned to Mansi. 'Go get Rohit Jadeja. Quick!'

In a few minutes, a sweaty and tired Rohit Jadeja came running up to them and was told about Arjuna having broken the world record. After that, it was three against one, all of them trying to break down Arjuna's defences.

'It's a great life, bro. The money is good, and you'll get to travel the world,' said Rohit. He cast a quick, slightly apologetic glance at Mansi before adding, 'And women love cricket players.'

Mansi rolled her eyes and beamed at Arjuna. 'With your looks, you'll probably make a fortune in endorsements too.'

Sunil waved his hand at the other two. 'Forget all that. You're a born sportsman, Arjuna. Whatever else you do in life will never make you happy. I know people like you. You need to move, be outside, push your body and your mind. You know that rush you get every time you bowl a great ball, every time you make the stumps fly? That's adrenaline, my boy. For a sportsman, adrenaline is like water and air; you need it to stay alive. To feed your soul. Now, imagine a life where you could have that regularly, doing what makes you happy, what you excel at it. What could possibly be better?'

Nothing. It was exactly the kind of life that Arjuna wanted. A life that gave him a mountain to conquer, and nourished his mind, body, heart and soul. A life of purpose.

At the cost of immortality. Of eternal youth and freedom from the cycle of rebirth and karma. Of his promise to Krishna.

'I'll have to think about it,' Arjuna repeated. He wasn't ready to decide yet.

The others finally realized that he wasn't going to give an answer today, so Sunil did the next best thing. He gave Arjuna a tour of the stadium, complete with a sack full of free merchandise, and introduced him to all the players. He even told them that Arjuna had broken the world record, a fact that led to much revelry. Players congratulated him and said they couldn't wait to unleash him upon their international rivals. Coaches were eager to work with him. He hadn't had a similar moment of glory since the last time he'd been alive.

And may never have one again.

26

It had been a good day, all things considered.

Draupadi smiled as she parked her car in the parking lot of her apartment building. It had been pretty intense at work, but everything was lined up for the shooting of next week's episode. Draupadi would be interviewing a group of feisty college girls who were developing new technologies to deal with climate change. Apparently, the earth was getting hotter by the second, a fact attested to by the sweltering heat that hit her when she stepped out of her air-conditioned car.

In her last life, the air around them had been light and clear, the sky blue, and rivers and forests lush and teeming with life. Not to mention it had been much cooler, even in the hottest summer months. The winters, on the other hand, were milder than the biting cold of just a few months ago. This last January, she'd needed to wear five layers of clothing for a week. It had been unprecedentedly frigid and windy.

Which was one of the reasons they were doing episodes on climate change.

She gave a quick greeting to the guards and made her way to the lift lobby with a spring in her step. Arjuna had gone to meet the Indian cricket team today, and while she wasn't exactly thrilled about that, things had been so much better for them lately. He was charming and friendly and energizing, not to mention ridiculously attractive. There was none of the old baggage that had plagued them in their previous life. A part of Draupadi wished he did stay, even as she knew that was highly unlikely. Arjuna was a man of his word, and if he had told Subhadra he would return, then he probably would. Despite everything.

Still, she wasn't going to let that weigh her down right now. She would live in the moment, enjoy this time with him. And when he left, she would shed her tears and let Angela fix her up with a nice man. The funny thing was, until her five ex-husbands had landed up in her living room, she hadn't even considered entering into a relationship. At the back of her mind, she'd still felt like a married woman. No man she had met this last year managed to change that feeling, despite the concerted efforts of many. Until now.

It was ironic that the man who finally made her feel ready for a relationship was one of her ex-husbands.

Even more ironic was the fact that said ex-husband was also the prime candidate for said relationship.

Draupadi chuckled ruefully as she unlocked her front door. Stepping inside, she heard footsteps running down the stairs near the lift. Instinctively, she pushed her front door shut when something on the other side shoved it open again. Without warning, the man who had been stalking her for the last few months entered her apartment and shut the door behind him.

Cold fear washed over Draupadi. She backed away slowly, as if he were a wild animal. The man had a plain, boxy face and was about the same height as her, but his body was barrel-shaped and would definitely be strong enough to overpower her. The scariest thing, however, was the look in his eyes.

They looked hungry and angry at the same time.

'Nakula! Sahadeva!' she shouted towards the hallway. No one replied.

Taking a deep breath, she tried to stay calm. If she made a dash towards one of the bedrooms to lock herself in, chances were that he would give chase and catch her before she reached. No, if he intended to rape her then running or struggling would only arouse him into expediting his attack. The only option was to try and gradually talk him down. She had to brazen it out.

'Welcome,' she said with a tight smile. 'Come, sit please. Tea?'

The man looked confused. He had probably expected a cowering, begging and possibly even hysterical woman. He certainly hadn't expected to be invited in for tea. So he just stood there and stared at her, unsure.

'Not tea? Juice then? Come, sit please. What's your name?' She tried another smile.

But the man didn't respond, except to keep standing and staring at her.

Draupadi didn't know what to do. She took a step backwards and he followed, a glint of excitement in his expression. It was then that she knew he was going to attack, and no amount of talking would make a difference. This wasn't a man set on revenge or driven by extreme lust. This man was unstable.

She grabbed the closest thing she could use as a weapon, a lamp from a side table. It had a long, thin brass body with a wide, circular base. She yanked it out of the socket just as the man reached her and swung it with as much force as she could at his head.

The man ducked before the lamp could hit him and grabbed its body. Draupadi held on with both hands, trying to get it out of his grip and take another swing. But he was even stronger than she had anticipated. He wrenched it out of her hands and threw it on the floor, advancing towards her.

'Look,' said Draupadi, as she walked backwards, one hand in front of her. 'You really don't want to do this. You'll go to jail, be hanged! It's not worth it. Do you want to ruin your whole life?'

The man just kept walking towards her, clearly enjoying the fear written all over her face.

She edged her way around a large sofa, trying to find something else to hit him with in her peripheral vision. She'd been attacked by men in the past, but she had never actually feared for her life before now. To have it end just when things were looking up for the first time in thousands of years. Surely, the gods wouldn't be so cruel.

Well, if it was her time to die, then she would go down fighting.

Snatching a large silver bowl off the table, she hurled it at the man's head. He deflected it with his arm, but not before grimacing with pain as the bowl struck his wrist. Then, he charged at her.

Draupadi turned to run, but the man came up behind her and locked his arms around her torso. She pushed and struggled, striking at his face and kicking at his legs with everything she had. He grunted in pain and locked her arms behind her, pushing her to the ground with the weight of his body.

'No! Help! Somebody help!' Draupadi screamed at the top of her voice as she felt her face crash into the carpet. The man's weight on her back pressed her down, and she felt a hand pull at the hem of her dress, yanking it upwards. She turned her face to the side and screamed again.

Suddenly, the weight left her back, her arms were freed and she heard a yelp of pain. Turning around, she saw that Arjuna had pulled the man off her and was now punching him senseless. She sagged on to the carpet, her body shaking in relief.

Arjuna rammed a fist into the man's nose and broke it with a loud crunching sound. As much satisfaction as the sight of the man's blood flowing down his face gave her, Draupadi knew Arjuna would probably kill him if she let it go on. Whereas that would have been perfectly acceptable in the past, these days, it was more complicated. If you wanted to kill someone without consequences, you either needed a lot of money or be a policeman.

'Stop, Arjuna!' she shouted from the floor, her shaky legs unable to support her just yet. 'You can't kill him!'

Arjuna stopped and held the man hanging lifelessly in the air, his eyes burning with fury. 'Give me one good reason.'

'We'll go to jail. Just restrain him while I call the police.' She kept her voice calm and rose up, letting Arjuna see that she wasn't hurt.

With a snarl of aggravation, he shook the man violently and threw him on the floor, where he lay limp. At this point, it was difficult for her to tell if the man was still conscious or just pretending to be unconscious. He hadn't put up a fight with Arjuna at all. Like most rapists, he probably saved all his aggression for women.

She quickly fished her phone out of her bag and called the police. When they heard who she was, they showed up within twenty minutes, arrested the man, filed a report, and took the guards and building personnel to the police station for questioning. They assured her that everything would be taken care of and the man would stay behind bars while the case was undertaken in court. Before leaving, the inspector in charge also genially mentioned that he was a big fan of Draupadi. He didn't watch her show, but he followed her page on social media, the one run by NPTV's public relations department. Maybe, he suggested, she could give their police station a shout out in her future posts. Seeing as they had been so professional in handling her case.

Draupadi was too weary and shaken to tell the inspector that the last time she'd gone to a police station, before becoming a celebrity, the policeman on duty hadn't even bothered to listen to her, let alone file a report.

By the time the police left, and both Draupadi and Arjuna had showered the stench of the ordeal off themselves, night had fallen. They sat in silence at the dining table, and ate their dinner without tasting it.

Rinsing and leaving their dishes in the kitchen sink for her cleaning lady to wash in the morning, Draupadi sighed and turned to Arjuna. 'Wine?'

He nodded. They returned to the living room, where Draupadi discovered that the lamp she had tried to use against her attacker still worked. Bathed in its warm light, the living room looked soothing and inviting, a sharp contrast to the events that had occurred in it earlier.

Arjuna eyed the carpet where he'd seen the man holding Draupadi down. 'Are you sure you want to sit here?' he asked, pointing to the carpet.

Draupadi nodded shakily. 'It's my home. I'll be damned if I let him spoil it for me.'

She wouldn't let him win. She poured the wine into glasses and handed Arjuna one.

His jaw clenched after he took a small sip. 'I'm sorry,' he said.

'For what?'

'I should have been with you. I'm supposed to be your bodyguard.'

She shook her head. 'Don't. I know you feel guilty, but there is no way you can be with me around the clock, Arjuna. Besides, you came home before he could hurt me.'

She put a hand on his cheek. 'Don't torture yourself over it, please. I'm fine.'

He nodded, but she could see he was fuming as he glared at the carpet. She bit her lip and said, 'Actually, I don't want to sit here, and it's hot on the balcony. Let's go to my room.'

Given that she hadn't invited any of them into her room until now, Arjuna looked at her with wide eyes. 'Are you sure?'

Draupadi smiled determinedly. 'Yes. We'll stretch out, and drink wine and celebrate.'

'Celebrate what?'

'That my stalker is in jail, of course.'

Some of the tension left Arjuna's shoulders with those words. He followed her into her room, closing the door behind him, slipping off his shoes and sitting back against the headboard. Instead of joining him, Draupadi stood and eyed the bed, which now looked a lot smaller with him on it. Since there were no chairs in her room, she would have to sit next to him on the now-small bed. What had she been thinking, inviting him in here?

As if he sensed her discomfort, Arjuna frowned. 'Do you want me to leave?' There was a hint of tension in his tone.

It provoked her own ire. Which was a shame because they hadn't fought lately, and it felt so good.

'No. Stay right there,' she snapped.

Striding over to the other side of the bed, she plonked down on it and drank a big gulp of wine from her glass.

He looked at her and shook his head in amusement. 'What?'

She huffed. 'Nothing.'

'You're angry with me again. Why?'

Draupadi didn't know what to say. She wasn't angry with Arjuna, she was angry with herself. She glanced at him. He looked so at home on her bed, so desirable in a T-shirt that stretched across his chest and arms, his legs tightly encased in a pair of those bloody tight jeans. She knew that he found modern clothing restrictive, that he would strip when he went to sleep in the study, and suddenly, she began to picture him. The study in the background fell away and became the forest, and his lithe, strong, naked body looked so at home as it lounged on a bed of soft grass. She sighed. They had made love so many times on the forest floor that she could still remember the fresh smell of the grass, the slight sting of pebbles against her back and the rich blue of the sky behind Arjuna as he moved over her. Inside her.

That was it. She was done fighting.

27

When Draupadi turned to him, Arjuna was expecting a tirade, filled with fury that would match his own. He should have been there with her when she returned from her workplace. Every other day, he'd made it a point to accompany her to and from work. But today, because of his cricket appointment, he had been preoccupied.

And that snake had seized the opportunity.

The sight of him atop Draupadi had made Arjuna's blood boil to the point of madness. Brought back images he had firmly locked away in the recesses of his mind. When he'd struck the man, he saw the faces of all the men who had touched her in the past. He would have killed him within moments of Draupadi stopping him. He still might, if the police didn't deliver justice.

However, Draupadi didn't rail against him. Didn't shout or deliver a sarcastic rejoinder in a voice as sharp as a demon's tooth.

Instead, she kissed him. Again.

Instinct and relief took over. The taste of her, the smell of her, so familiar and yet forgone for so long, cast all thought from his body. He wanted to fill her, inundate her senses with him, so that nothing remained but this and them. So that the memory of every other man was wiped from her mind and body. Only him. Only ever him.

Their hands moved fast and furiously, reacquainting themselves with the bends and dips of each other's bodies, young and firm like they had been in the beginning, in the years after Draupadi's swayamwara. Arjuna had been with an uncountable number of nymphs in heaven and still hadn't come close to feeling the hot blaze of lust that shot through him every time she let out a gasp or moan. His movements became rougher, more demanding. Next time he would be gentle, he promised himself, worship every part of her body like the goddess that she was. But right now, he could barely control himself as he tore off her clothes and leaned back to look at her.

Hair that waved and licked around her glossy shoulders like an inverted bonfire, bewitching eyes that had inspired the greatest poets in the world, smiling lips swollen from his nips and kisses. Skin like silk and breasts that would spill over even in his hands. A tapered waist that had kindled almost as much poetry as her eyes, and serpentine hips that told a man he didn't need to hold back. She was breathtaking.

He reached for her as if his life depended on it, pushing her back on the bed. She threw her head back on to a pillow and moaned as he bent over her in an urgent exploration. Soon though, he moved back to her face and they met in a deep kiss as he parted her legs with his own. It had been too long, and he couldn't wait anymore. He moved to join them when she gasped and put a hand on his chest.

'Wait!'

He groaned and held himself taut, suspended over her like a bowstring a second before it snapped. 'Are you trying to kill me, woman?'

She was breathing as heavily as him, but there was a glint in her eyes. 'I could get pregnant!'

The words barely penetrated the haze of lust that enveloped him. 'I'll pull out.'

She shook her head, her face flinching with the same exasperation he was feeling. 'That doesn't always work, and I can't get pregnant right now, Arjuna.' Then, her eyes lit up. 'Wait, I have a condom!'

He frowned as he leaned back, still braced over her. 'What's that?'

She pushed at his chest. 'I'll show you. Get off me.'

She *was* trying to kill him. He closed his eyes and commanded the throbbing, feverish rod between his legs to subside for long enough that he could summon the strength to stand. It didn't work. Groaning, he rolled to one side and covered his eyes with one hand. 'This is it. Going back to heaven now.'

He didn't have to look at Draupadi to know she was rolling her eyes.

'Always so bloody dramatic,' she murmured as she scurried to her cupboard and began to rummage through her things.

He half-opened one eye, gazed at her perfectly rounded bottom and smiled, feeling something undefinable tug at his heart even as he felt ready to burst in other areas.

She returned to the bed with a small, square packet in her hand, holding it up like a trophy. Grinning, she said, 'Angela gave it to me last year. She said every woman needs to have at least one, just in case. I forgot I had it!'

He couldn't help grinning back, even though he had no idea what she was talking about. 'What is it?'

She sat down, ran her eyes over his naked body and kissed him briefly, pulling back before he could deepen it. 'It's a condom. We have to roll it on your ... member.'

He frowned. Sitting up, he took the square packet from her and examined it. 'How?'

She grabbed it and opened the packet. Inside was a yellowish, extremely thin circle made from a material he couldn't identify. She held it up, looked at it carefully and cleared her throat. 'We start from the top and then roll it down apparently. At least that's what Angela said. I haven't actually done it before.'

They both looked down at his member, still eager for the proceedings to continue. The poor bastard.

He sighed. 'All right,' he said, as he took the condom from her. 'Let's try.'

Slowly and gingerly, he rolled the thing over himself and then eyed the disturbing picture it presented. 'Is there supposed to be that extra material at the top or have I done it wrong?'

She shook her head. 'I have no idea.'

He looked down again. Not only did it look bizarre, it felt strange too. And not in a good way. 'So, mortals can fly hundreds of people halfway to heaven in enormous tubes, but *this* is how they prevent pregnancy?'

Rolling her eyes again, Draupadi said, 'It'll catch your seed. It also protects people from disease.'

That, he could appreciate. In his time, prostitutes had been notorious for carrying diseases that could be transmitted to their patrons. He'd known men who had not only lost their own lives to such diseases, but had also unwittingly been responsible for the deaths of their wives. However, since neither he nor Draupadi had taken a lover since their time in heaven, disease prevention didn't really apply to them. Also, he wasn't going to tell her, but the condom felt a bit noose-like. And, although they had yet to put it to the test, he was pretty sure it would mean less pleasure for both of them. Which was a shame, given how much he was looking forward to being with her again.

Still, it was a lot better than not being with her again.

'I guess we're good to go then,' he said, as he grabbed her waist and lifted, moving her to the centre of the bed and laying her down, his eyes gleaming playfully. 'Now, where were we?'

She grinned and opened her legs, locking them around his waist. 'Right here.'

He was right. It didn't feel exactly the same, but he couldn't have given a damn. Nothing had ever felt as good, as right, as being with Draupadi. As he watched her gasp and keen in pleasure, felt her body writhing under his, and her soft, sweat-slicked skin shiver under his hands and mouth, as she clenched around him in release and called out his name, he knew nothing would feel as good, as right, ever again.

They were made to fit each other perfectly.

Later, as they lay in bed, their limbs entwined and sleep closing in quickly, he breathed in the scent of her hair and asked in a murmur, 'Aren't there other ways to not have a baby?'

She hummed sleepily. 'There are, but they take weeks to work.'

He kissed her forehead lightly. 'Let's get those then.'

She yawned and cuddled closer. 'But you're leaving soon.'

After a moment of silence, he said, 'Let's get them anyway.'

28

'Sir, I'm a poor man. If I give free coriander and chillies to every customer, then I still have to pay for it, no? They'll pay hundreds to eat a burger or see a movie in a mall; yet they grudge me my small margin. But, for you and the orphaned children, I'm happy to give extra!'

Bhima nodded absently as they loaded the vegetables he had bought into the back of an autorickshaw. This vegetable seller talked a lot, but he had the best prices in the market. When you bought food for as many mouths as Bhima did, the cost determined everything.

Although, their budgets had eased a bit lately, because of the lunch service. They'd achieved modest returns since opening, which enabled Bhima to buy better quality ingredients for the children's meals. No more potato and dal broth over rice. They now ate carrots and beans, cabbage and gourds. The other day, he had added dried fenugreek leaves to the kids' curry, giving it an entirely new dimension in taste. Still, there was so much he could do with more money. Green, leafy vegetables and fruit were still a pipe dream. So was paneer, which the children regarded with almost as much awe as the chicken, mutton and fish they saw him cooking for the lunch service. Karan had suggested increasing the price per plate to increase profits, but Bhima knew that the majority of his customers were either students without jobs or workers who earned little. Good food at cheap prices was his biggest advantage over the competition.

He also refused to spend more money to expand the business for the moment. At some point, he would love to open an eatery of his own. But his mother needed him right now, while she struggled to make ends meet. Draupadi didn't make enough to support the orphanage, even though she did help with some of the costs. And Kunti was extremely reluctant to take more money than necessary from her former daughter-in-law. Just the other day, Bhima had suggested asking Draupadi to buy the orphanage a vehicle, but Kunti refused. 'Draupadi already does enough,' she had said firmly. 'The girl deserves to enjoy the life she's sacrificed so much for.'

Bhima lifted a sack of onions and balanced it on top of a few other sacks, while the vegetable seller bound them all tightly together with a rope. Bhima would then hold the entire bundle precariously while the autorickshaw drove to the orphanage, praying that nothing fell out to be run over by other vehicles. It was incredibly inefficient, which was one of the reasons he had suggested buying a vehicle in the first place.

He shook his head before something occurred to him. From the looks of it, Nakula was probably going to stay on earth too. If he did well for himself with this modelling thing, then he could help with money too. That woman he was with,

Angela, sounded like she could be just the kind of stabilizing influence Nakula needed. Bhima had a good feeling about her. Given the open-mouthed adoration with which his baby brother talked about her, he obviously did too.

It made Bhima smile. Little Nakula was in love.

As for the woman Bhima loved, it had been pretty clear from his talk with Arjuna where things were headed with him and Draupadi. While he was not exactly thrilled about it, he wasn't going to waste time feeling sorry for himself either. Mortal life was short and he had enough to do already.

He sat in the autorickshaw, making conversation with the driver and occasionally chastising him for making sharp turns, which made the sacks he was clutching tilt to the side. When they reached the orphanage, Bhima was surprised to find a large crowd outside.

He frowned in confusion. The lunch service didn't start for hours. Who were all these people?

Narad Muni came running towards him, panic written all over his face. 'They're breaking the windows and the furniture!'

'*What?*'

Narad Muni cried, 'Masked men! They came in after you left and forced their way inside. They've got lathis!'

Bhima felt a white-hot blaze of fury burn through him. 'Mother?'

'She's locked up in one of the dormitories with the children.'

Pushing Narad Muni aside, Bhima mumbled, 'Stay here,' and began to run. He barrelled through the onlookers, threw open the doors and began to comb the rooms.

Everywhere he looked, there lay pieces of broken wood, smashed lights and fans that had been pounded out of their sockets with lathis. Offensive slurs marked the previously whitewashed walls. The common room was the worst hit of all. The furniture had been destroyed and pieces of his cooking equipment lay strewn all over the floor. The lunch service window was broken and shards of glass were everywhere. It was a wreck of a room.

Bhima roared into the hallway, 'Where are you, you cowards? I'm going to tear you apart!'

He heard men's voices and dashed towards them. Turning into one of the dormitories, he found six masked men breaking the children's beds and windows. He charged into the man closest to him, grabbing him by the neck and slamming his face into a wall. A satisfying crunch filled the room, coupled with a screech of pain from the man, before Bhima elbowed the back of his neck, making him lose consciousness. He fell limply to the floor.

The other five men turned and saw Bhima. Their faces were hidden by some kind of face glove that covered their entire heads, leaving only their eyes visible. They held sturdy lathis in their hands. Together, they attacked Bhima.

Growling with rage, Bhima met them in the middle of the room. As the man closest to him swung his lathi, Bhima caught it before it could make impact, yanked it out of the man's hands and used it to block the other four lathis that were about to strike him. Before the first man even registered what was happening, Bhima had grabbed his head by his hair and used him as a human shield. One of the attackers' lathis hit the man in the face and blood spurted out of him.

The other men stopped, seeing that they had just assaulted their own by mistake. Bhima threw the bleeding man down on the floor and faced the others.

'Two down, four to go,' he growled at them, his teeth bared and lathi positioned in the air. He beckoned them with his fingers. 'Come on. Are you scared? You should be. I'm about to do to you what you've done to my rooms.'

The men cast nervous glances at him and then at each other. One of them shouted in a muffled voice, 'Close the lunch business and we'll leave you alone!'

Bhima curled his lip menacingly. 'The lunch business will carry on. In fact, now I think I'll probably expand it. After I send you lot back to the BYBM Centre in white shrouds.'

That made three of the men look at the one who had spoken with panic in their eyes. One of them whimpered a soft, 'Dada …'

Their leader glared at Bhima, but obviously thought the better of attacking him. He squinted and snarled, 'We'll be back. With a mob next time. Let's see who puts who in a white shroud then!' He turned to his men, 'Go!'

The men sprinted out of the room, not stopping to attend to their two unconscious comrades on the floor. Bhima gave chase until the front door, where he barked, 'Cowards!' at their retreating backs before holding his lathi up and glaring at the crowd that had gathered to watch the men vandalize the orphanage.

Bhima spat in disgust at the ground near his feet and shouted, 'A crowd full of able-bodied men just stood here while a group of scoundrels attacked a building full of defenceless children. You outnumbered them, could have taken them down within seconds had you tried; yet, you chose to watch instead? You're nothing but impotent cowards, just like those masked losers, who were too afraid to show their faces.' He glared at the embarrassed faces of the men in the crowd, his face full of wrath.

A voice shouted back at him from the gathering, 'They'll come after us if we interfere. Our homes and families.'

Bhima shook his head. This neighbourhood was obviously living in fear of Amit Sharma. And, as he well knew from his previous life, despots used fear to terrorize innocents and create anarchy. It was time to step up and rally these people. Bhima wouldn't let those BYBM goons win.

He spoke in a booming voice, 'They'll come after no one if we stand up and fight back together! We outnumber them a hundredfold. Today, you let them dictate where and how you can conduct your work, tomorrow they will decide your entire life. My name is Bhima, and I am named after the Pandava Bhima, who stood up for the downtrodden, who fought against the forces of evil. I will protect and fight for any person here who fights with me!' He held up his lathi in the air and waved it over his head.

Cheers rang out from the crowd, many of the men who had stood back and done nothing when the vandals started their destruction now waved their fists in the air. Bhima knew their zeal would be temporary, triggered by his words, and forgotten when they returned to their homes. There was a reason generals gave impassioned speeches immediately before a battle began. Bloodlust in a soldier was a useful addition to his training, but it was unreliable and easily spooked by the sight of a sizeable enemy army.

Still, it looked like Bhima now had a battle on his hands. And he would need as many fighters as he could muster.

'Friends,' he said in a thunderous voice to the men who had cheered. 'Those men vandalized a home for orphans. Only the most evil forces in the world attack children. Two of those villains now lie senseless inside, and the rest have fled in fear for their lives!'

Murmurs filled the crowd, which began to look at Bhima with new eyes. Earlier, he had been a man with big words, but now they saw he had strength to match.

'But they will be back, and there will be more of them! We need to organize, arm ourselves, create a chain of communication and command. I will be holding a meeting in an hour, in our common room, after we have had a chance to clean up the damage and ensure the children are safe. I hope many of you will join me for this meeting, with your weapons.'

He bared his teeth and pointed his lathi in the direction of the BYBM Centre. 'Together, we will give a befitting reply to their next attack. Go, tell your families that you have decided to take back control of your livelihoods. Tell them we won't let them trespass upon our lives, instruct us on what to eat, how to dress and who to believe in. Tell them you are ready to fight for your self-respect, for your children, for your community. Tell them not to be afraid, for you fight with Bhima!' he roared.

The crowd roared in response. Bhima pointed outwards. 'Go!'

The moment people started dispersing, Bhima turned around and went looking for Kunti. He found her in the furthest dormitory from the front, huddled with a large group of young children. They looked terrified.

'Where are the others?' he asked Kunti, pointing at the children.

Kunti replied in a shaky voice, 'I sent the older ones away. They climbed out of the windows at the back. I was worried they would be beaten.'

Bhima nodded. 'Did they know where to go?'

'Yes. We have friends in the slum who will hide them temporarily.'

'Good.' Bhima walked up to his mother, sat her down on a small stool and kneeled next to her. 'Mother, they've broken most of the furniture and fittings. And windows.'

She let out a soft sob of despair and let the tears flow. Money was so tight to begin with, and they would need a lot to repair the damage. But, first things first.

'Mother, there will be time later to cry. Right now, I need you to listen to me. There were six of them. Four have escaped, and they have promised to bring back more to take revenge.'

Kunti's watery eyes widened. 'Bhima! You haven't killed two men, have you?'

He shook his head. 'They are merely senseless. I need you to take the children somewhere safe for a few days. We have a fight on our hands, and I can't let you be caught in the middle.'

'No, Bhima!' said Kunti in a pleading, frantic voice. 'We will report them to the police. Times have changed. You cannot fight them by yourself!'

'They are in cahoots with the police, Mother. I must.'

'Then we'll call Draupadi!'

Bhima shook his head. 'We called her last time, but it didn't scare them away, did it? They'll keep coming back, Mother. Until we respond in kind.'

She began to argue, but Bhima shook his head again, saying, 'Don't try and change my mind. I know you're scared for the children. Here is what I need you to do. Call the police and hand in the two men we have. Make a complaint if you have to, or call Draupadi to highlight our situation in her workplace. Either way, I need you to leave the orphanage with the children for the next few days. Narad Muni and I will take care of the mess.'

Perhaps she saw that there was no talking Bhima out of it, or maybe she accepted that things had come to a head and he was right. Either way, Kunti kept her thoughts to herself as she nodded in resignation.

'I'll get started.' She got up from the stool she was crouching on, leaning down and cupping his cheeks. 'These children aren't the only ones I'm worried about. You're my child too. Take care of yourself, my son.'

Bhima smiled at her and put his hands over her own. 'I will. Don't worry, Mother. The world may change, but right and wrong, good and evil, always stay the same. We've done this before, and it wasn't easy back then either. But we won in the end. Remember?'

She nodded. 'I do.' Then, with a determined look on her face, she wiped her tears, fished her phone out of her pocket and began to press buttons on it. 'I'll call the police and also arrange for a bus to take the children to Draupadi's house. We can camp there for a few days.'

Smiling, Bhima got up. 'Good,' he said. Then he stalked out. Where was Narad Muni?

He found him outside, hiding at the back of the building in a drain ditch. Bhima swore in exasperation as he pulled him out, none too gently.

'Listen, old man, I have a job for you.'

'I won't fight! I'm a Brahman!'

'Nobody is asking you to fight. I need you to find my younger brothers. Arjuna, Nakula and Sahadeva. Tell them I need them. Immediately.'

'And if they ask why?'

A glint shone in Bhima's eyes. 'Tell them we have another battle on our hands.'

29

'I thought I told you that all donations have to go through me!' Yudhishtra snapped at the man sitting behind the table as he held up the wads of cash he'd found in the man's shoulder bag.

He had good reason to be angry. Yudhishtra had held a meeting with all the BYBM Centre 'associates' as they were called, including Amit Sharma, when he'd returned from his last visit to the orphanage. He had specifically told them that all donations going forward were to be handed directly to him by the donors. He had laid out a structure for how the money was to be accounted for, processed, and, most importantly, how it was to be utilized. Yudhishtra had also drawn a line in the sand about the way he would conduct himself in the future. No costumes, no thrones and no telling of the future!

Amit Sharma was visibly unhappy that Yudhishtra had taken charge of his own activities. His response had been seething silence during the meeting. There was, however, not much he could say because Yudhishtra's following had grown exponentially since the day they had launched their public relations campaign. Not only did far more people watch and follow Yudhishtra on social media now, they also flocked in huge crowds to hear him speak. Private darshans had to be held in the large hall, and the local media were beginning to knock on their doors. All of this, Amit tried to explain to Yudhishtra, cost money to keep going, keep growing. A fact Yudhishtra refused to accept.

'It doesn't need to grow, Amitji,' he had replied in an authoritative voice. 'It just needs to be useful. That's where the charities come into the picture. Use the money for the purpose it was donated.'

His firmness had not been appreciated. And today, when he had caught the man with the shoulder bag slinking away again after a private darshan, he stopped him and checked its contents. It was, as suspected, full of money, and Yudhishtra had lost his temper.

Shoulder-bag man folded his hands and said in a plaintive voice, 'But, Guruji, I was going to give you the money after I counted it!'

Clearly, a lie. Yudhishtra had no idea what Amit and his men were doing with the money, but it stopped now. 'Then count it in front of me.'

The man looked at Amit Sharma, who was standing next to Yudhishtra with a scowl on his face, for instructions. Amit stayed quiet so he reluctantly sat back down on the table. Taking the wads of cash and opening his notebook, he began to count them.

Yudhishtra turned to Amit, whose scowl quickly turned into a wary expression. 'I know you aren't happy with my approach, Amitji. But the Kalyug has swayed your better judgement. It's not your fault, but you must allow someone with a superior moral code to supervise you. In time, you will relearn your lost dharmic values.'

Amit looked like he had just swallowed a lemon. He mumbled, 'Yes, Guruji,' with about as much enthusiasm as a cat getting an enema.

'Oh, and one more thing,' said Yudhishtra. 'I will not be going on that tour thing you were talking about. I'll be returning to heaven in a few days, so I cannot travel.'

Amit's eyes narrowed as he asked, 'Heaven?'

'Yes, heaven. You remember I told you we came down to visit earth for a month.'

Normally Amit agreed, readily or reluctantly, to whatever Yudhishtra said. Now, a mocking look crept over his face and drawled, 'Ah, yes. Well, Guruji, you'll just have to delay your return to *heaven* because you signed a contract with us.'

Yudhishtra frowned. 'I have signed no such thing, Amitji. I made a commitment to you for the course of my visit, and I have kept my word.'

'But, we've invested a lot of money in you!'

'Money I told you to give to charity, remember?'

Amit's face screwed up in a grimace, as if he were dealing with a petulant child. 'And, when will you return from ...' he rolled his eyes, '... heaven?'

Yudhishtra always told the truth. Always, irrespective of the consequences. So, it was without hesitation that he replied, 'I will not be returning.'

There was silence for a few moments. Even the man who was counting the money stopped what he was doing and looked up at Amit with fearful eyes. The rest of the men in the room exchanged nervous glances. While Amit looked like he was about to explode, Yudhishtra was unperturbed by the potential effects of his declaration on the men in the room.

To everyone's surprise, Amit took a long, deep breath. He bared his teeth at Yudhishtra in a sinister grin and said, 'You tell me on the day you plan to leave, Guruji. I wouldn't want to miss saying goodbye.'

'Of course! I would never be so impolite.'

The grin stayed in place as Amit added, 'Good. In fact, I can even organize your transport arrangements to go to heaven, Guruji.'

A snicker sounded from somewhere in the room, followed by a cough. Most of the men stared at their feet, a couple of them with shaking shoulders. Amit seemed to be perfectly fine with Yudhishtra's departure, a fact that made Yudhishtra decidedly suspicious as he declined Amit's offer of transportation. However, before he could pinpoint exactly what he found disconcerting about Amit's reaction, another associate entered the room and addressed him.

'The hall is full, Guruji. We have started the devotional songs, so you can come any time to begin the talk.'

Yudhishtra glanced at the man who was supposed to be counting the money. The one who had stopped counting for some reason. 'Have you finished?'

The man shook his head. 'Not yet, Guruji.'

Amit stepped forward and put a light hand on Yudhishtra's back, trying to herd him towards the door. 'Don't worry, Guruji. We will keep it here until the end of the talk, after which you can watch him count it again. You have my word.'

There were men whose word you could trust and there were men whose word you couldn't. Yudhishtra knew Amit fell in the second category, but he had a large crowd of people waiting to hear him speak, and he was looking forward to it. After all, that was the primary purpose of his mission, to spread the word of dharma. So Yudhishtra nodded at Amit.

'Very well. There are nineteen clipped wads of money now, and there should be the same number when I return,' he instructed shoulder-bag man before turning and walking out the door.

In the hall, he waved to the audience, which had started applauding the moment he entered. Loud, wailing songs played in the background, while hundreds of people, some standing in the back and others crowding into aisles because there wasn't enough seating, all beamed up at him. Men, women and children, young and old, rich and poor. Yudhishtra smiled. Every time he gave one of his talks, he felt a little bit like a king again.

He stepped up to the microphone, a contraption he had become quite attached to in the last few weeks, and tapped it to check if it was working. A piercing squeal reverberated off the walls, which, when combined with the applause and the devotional music, created a cacophony of sound that hurt the ears. Irritated, he signalled for the music to be turned off and for the audience to sit down.

It took a while, but eventually everyone was seated and rapt with attention. Yudhishtra began to speak.

'We are all products of the time during which we have been raised. When Krishna, an avatar of Vishnu, left earth for his heavenly abode, mortals were plunged into the Kalyug. It has been thousands of years now and many of you have no idea what is right or wrong anymore. It's not your fault—you have been beaten down by circumstance, blinded by the greed and systemic corruption you witness all around. Friends and family who are immoral and adharmic get ahead, while honest men and women are left behind. You begin to measure your success and happiness in material wealth rather than spiritual wealth. You become accustomed to chaos. These are the hallmarks of the Kalyug, my friends.'

The crowd was silent, some of them nodding and some of them staring at Yudhishtra in scepticism.

He continued, 'Today, I'm going to talk about the difference between accumulating material wealth versus spiritual wealth. I have lived both as a beggar and as an emperor, so I hope you will appreciate that I know what I'm talking about.'

'Tell us about the war at Kurukshetra!' someone shouted from the crowd.

Yudhishtra fisted one hand and prayed for patience. These mortals were really getting on his nerves today. 'I will tell you about the war after the discourse.'

'The discourse is boring!' It was a boy, whose head was covered in a hood attached to his T-shirt. Yudhishtra saw a lady sitting next to the child cuff him on the back of his head.

He sighed. 'You see what your mother just did, boy? By slapping you, she taught you about karma. Your words were rude and brought forth punishment. That is how the universe works.'

For the next hour, he spoke non-stop about his favourite themes, not allowing anyone else to interrupt him. The associates and Amit stood on the sidelines patiently, but the audience began to fidget by the end of it. Perhaps it had something to do with the fact that today's talk was about how they were all delusional and materialistic, weak and immoral, seemingly incapable of redemption. It was a bitter pill to swallow for even the most devoted of them. Not to mention the fact that Yudhishtra no longer looked like a Pandava. Gone was the dramatic saffron-coloured dhoti and the gilded throne, gone too was the aristocratic moustache and princely spear. In their place stood a plain man wearing a plain piece of cloth, just like the rest of them. He didn't look special.

Which was probably why, at the end, when Yudhishtra was riding high on a wave of post-talk elation, many of the audience members called out, requesting he do a question and answer session. He smiled and agreed, much against the vigorous head-shaking of Amit and the other associates. He had never done this sort of session with such a large gathering before. It was something reserved exclusively for private donors. Surely, thought Yudhishtra, the common man deserved answers to his spiritual questions too. Even if he couldn't afford to pay for them.

'Raise your hands to ask a question,' stated Yudhishtra magnanimously.

Dozens of hands went up in the air, much to his delight. He pointed to a middle-aged woman in a sari, who was seated at the back. 'You may ask your question.'

The lady stood up and folded her hands, bowing. She asked in a loud voice, 'Guruji, many other gurus can perform magic and miracles. They can walk through fire, hover above the ground and create jewellery from thin air. They can do impossible yoga positions. Some of them can even cure illnesses with a single touch. Can *you* do something miraculous?'

And, just like that, Yudhishtra's irritation with the mortal world returned with a vengeance.

'Yes,' he said with uncharacteristic sarcasm. 'I can teach you how you can ascend to heaven after your death. In your case, that will be a miracle indeed. Sit down, dear lady. Next question!'

He pointed to a large man sitting in the front. The man stood up and cleared his throat. 'I'm sorry to bother you Guruji, but I have lost so much sleep these last few years. My brother works on our family farm in our village, and for the last two years, the monsoon has been very late. Our crops have suffered and our family has barely made ends meet. We need the rains badly this year, Guruji, or we will have to sell the land. Please, tell me what to do.'

Yudhishtra thought about that. 'Have you approached the authorities to help with grants and subsidies until your land is profitable?'

The man huffed bitterly. 'The government doesn't care about poor farmers like us, Guruji.'

'In that case,' said Yudhishtra with a sad smile, 'You must deal with what is to come. When my brothers and I were faced with the corrupt administration of Uncle Dhritarashtra, and the house we were given was burned down by my cousin Duryodhana, we disguised ourselves as Brahmans and lived off alms until we got back on our feet again. There is no point railing against things you can't control, like the monsoon. Sell your land if the rains don't come, and keep trying to forge your destiny. Setbacks are disheartening, but they teach us valuable lessons, and the person who perseveres despite failure is usually successful in the end.'

The man didn't look happy with that answer at all. Yudhishtra had essentially told him to become a beggar if the rains didn't come on time this year. 'Don't you have a prayer we can do, a mantra we can chant, or a ritual that will ensure the rains come on time?'

Yudhishtra smiled. 'My good man, in my lifetime I did a lot of that. I even conducted the great Rajasuya sacrifice, which not only hurled the entire Aryavarta into war, but also lost me my kingdom, and sent my brothers and wife into exile. So you may recite whichever prayers you want, but you will walk the path the gods have set for you.'

The crowd began to fidget. Yudhishtra wasn't playing ball, and they didn't know how to react. Yudhishtra knew he wasn't giving them the answers they wanted, but they needed to understand that it wasn't the job of a guru to provide quick fixes. No, a guru's job was to educate, advise and comfort. He pointed to a small man in a faded kurta. 'Your question?'

The man stood up and Yudhishtra could see tears flowing down his cheeks. He folded his hands. 'Guruji, I am in a terrible predicament.'

'What is it?'

The man looked around in apprehension before he spoke again. 'I'm a poor man, Guruji. I hope you can understand.'

'I understand. Ask your question, without fear.'

The man wiped a tear from his face. 'Guruji, I'm a milkman. I have four cows, and I love and worship them like my mother. But I also have children and elderly parents who live with me. There are a lot of mouths to feed, Guruji.' He paused for a moment and then continued, 'Two of the cows are old and have stopped giving milk. I've tried to keep them, but I just can't afford it anymore. My children are going hungry because I have to buy fodder for the cows. Other milkmen just set their cows free to scavenge, but I don't want to abandon mine. All the cow shelters I spoke to are full, and the cows there don't look any better fed than the cows on the street. What can I do?'

Yudhishtra frowned. 'Are you a Brahman or a priest of some sort?'

'No.'

'Were the cows given to you as a tribute by a pupil of yours?'

'No, Guruji. I bought them both.'

He nodded. 'In that case, it is more straightforward. I can see you love these two aged cows dearly. Indeed, it is part of our culture to revere the cow like a mother, for she nourishes us with milk, just like our mothers do. I'm happy to see that you have such respect for the animals you keep. However, animals are not humans. You are a family man, and therefore, your greater duty is to your family. You must make difficult choices in this case.'

He smiled at the man, hoping it would ease the pain of his words. 'A milch cow can live for twenty years after its teats have dried up. Once the milk has gone, it has already served its life's larger purpose. The scriptures tell us that the best way for an animal to be consecrated, to be rewarded for a life well-lived by the gods, is by giving it a new life. Through sacrifice. Therefore, I suggest you gift the cows to an experienced priest, who will sacrifice them during a yagna, performing all the necessary rites in accordance with Vedic scriptures. Agni, the god of fire, particularly enjoys eating the flesh of barren cows. By offering your cattle to him, you may even elevate them to rebirth as humans in their next life. And Agni will confer his blessings upon your family as well. It is beneficial to all.'

The man gawked at him, and the rest of the audience froze in shocked silence. Something dropped to the floor with a loud clang, but nobody moved.

Yudhishtra eyed the gathering with some confusion. Had he said something wrong? Did they not know how to perform a yagna these days? Surely they hadn't completely abandoned the scriptures? He asked the milkman, 'Does this solve your problem, my good man?'

The man looked around like a scared rabbit. 'Y-Y-You want them to be *killed*?'

'No,' replied Yudhishtra in a steady voice. 'I suggested they be sacrificed, not killed.'

The man shook his head frantically. Without a word, he pushed his way out of the audience and ran out of the hall as if demons were after him.

Now Yudhishtra began to get worried. He turned to Amit, who was also staring at him in shock. 'What's the problem?'

'*Anti-national!*'

It was the man whose nose he had broken the other day during the scuffle with Arjuna. He was a junior associate who had kept his distance from Yudhishtra since the fight. Now, he was staring at him with unreserved hatred as he shouted, 'Cow is our divine mother! You're nothing but a fake guru! A jihadi!'

The audience began to murmur amongst themselves. Then, another associate who had been beaten during the fight jumped up from his seat. 'You want us to eat beef! You're anti-Hindu!'

The rest of the associates and audience began to get riled up. Shouts echoed from all around.

'He's posing as a guru to fool us!'

'Infiltrator! Undercover terrorist!'
'Go back to your own country!'
'Defiling our Hindu culture!'
'Pretending to be a Pandava!'
'Beef eater!'
'Feminist!'
'You're the same as your brother. We'll teach you both a lesson!'

That last one had come, to Yudhishtra's utter surprise, from Amit Sharma, who was now glaring at him with the same venom as the rest of his men. He pointed at Yudhishtra with an accusatory finger. 'We trusted you, took you from nothing and made you what you are. But you turned out to be a snake, like your brother who serves beef to innocent children in the orphanage!'

The audience gasped in a loud, scandalized rumble. It was blasphemous to suggest sacrificing an old cow, but it was completely heinous to be poisoning the minds and bodies of destitute, defenceless children. Suddenly, these orphans, whom nobody in the hall had given a damn about just a few seconds earlier, became victims of monstrous tyranny in their minds. Helpless, persecuted *Hindu* children who needed to be rescued from beef-eating fiends immediately.

'We must save the children!'
'Kill the jihadis!'

'Now look here,' said Yudhishtra sternly, 'my brother Bhima is serving mutton, not beef. The orphaned children are well cared for, and at no point did I suggest eating the milkman's cows. This is just a misunderstanding.'

But the audience was past listening to reason. Bloodlust had started boiling in their veins, and they began to advance on Yudhishtra. Amit whispered something to one of his men and joined the crowd, a nasty look on his face.

Yudhishtra quickly realized that the situation was beyond redemption. He already knew that Amit was trying to cheat him out of donation money, so he wasn't surprised that he had turned on Yudhishtra. The absence of loyalty, integrity or respect was another attribute of the Kalyug.

So was violence, which would ensue fairly quickly unless he got out of there. There were too many people for him to take on by himself, and he was sure that after the crowd was done with him, they would head to the orphanage and attack Bhima. And possibly his mother.

It was at this point, faced with disappointment in the mortals who had turned on him, and apprehension that his own family may be in danger, that something changed within Yudhishtra. He finally realized that he'd been wrong.

He couldn't rescue these people from the Kalyug. Because this was the Kalyug! It was exactly how it was meant to be. Everyone's collective destiny.

Yudhishtra recognized, with not a small amount of shame, that despite preaching non-stop about shouldering one's inevitable fate, he hadn't been practicing it himself. Change was essential, the very bedrock of destiny. His brothers had easily accepted that the mortal world had changed from their time. That Draupadi and their mother had changed. In the past few weeks, his brothers had changed as well, their individual desires and dynamic as a group shifting as a result. Only Yudhishtra had been trying to hang on to the past. And hold everyone else back too. Refusing to see what was right in front of his eyes.

Draupadi was right. He had been acting like a coward.

He chuckled to himself ruefully, keeping a close eye on the people who were approaching him while screaming things that he had by now tuned out.

Yudhishtra grabbed the mic one last time. It was the only thing he would miss in this godforsaken world after he left.

'Friends,' he said cheerfully to the audience. 'My time is over. Today, I am no more a guru or a king than you.'

Dropping the mic, he picked up its stand. He had to get to the orphanage, quickly. Waving the base of the stand threateningly at the people in front of him, Yudhishtra gave Amit a sardonic look.

'You want to go first?' he taunted.

Fear shone in Amit's eyes for a split second before he realized that he was in the majority, hundreds to one.

'Get him!' he screamed to the crowd.

A few men in the front attacked Yudhishtra, who swung the stand, hitting them in the face. The crowd hesitated briefly. Swinging it rapidly in front of him so the spindly, weak stand looked like a deadly weapon, Yudhishtra calculated the distance to the chairs in the front row. There was no time to lose. He struck the man directly in front of him with the stand and waited for the moment when everyone looked at the injured man to sprint to the nearest chair. He leaped on to it and used the momentum from its backrest to push himself over the heads of the crowd. Unwitting members of the audience who had stood back now felt the blow of Yudhishtra's nimble feet or the mic stand on their heads and shoulders. He bounced off them so fast that no one had time to react, let alone catch him.

Finally, he vaulted off the people at the back and sprinted out the door. Given that the most aggressive members of the crowd had been in the front, it took some time before they gave chase. Yudhishtra had time to run out of the complex and down the street before they followed him.

'O Krishna,' Yudhishtra laughed up at the sky as excitement streamed through his blood, waking up the warrior in him who had led armies into battle. 'When I get back up there, I will drive your chariot against the demon army myself!'

30

'No, don't throw the shards of glass away,' Arjuna told a man with a bucketful of broken glass from the orphanage windows. 'Put them on the roof.'

The man, one of the neighbourhood residents, looked thoroughly confused. 'The roof?'

Arjuna nodded. 'They can be thrown along with the stones and bricks. Won't do much damage, but they'll help scare away the nervous ones.'

Bhima stopped tying his kitchen knives to the ends of sticks and rods, and eyed the glass. 'Remember, no killing. Mother made me promise.'

Waving the man with the bucket away, Arjuna grinned at Bhima. 'Relax, Brother. We'll just rough them up a little. Enough to give them a good scare.'

Bhima grinned back, 'Hah! They won't know what hit them.' The two brothers shared a look of comradery.

Narad Muni shook his head as he sat curled up in one corner. He had done what Bhima asked of him and summoned the younger Pandavas after the attack on the orphanage. Since they'd arrived and held a meeting with a group of about two dozen neighbourhood men who had volunteered to resist the goons of the BYBM Centre alongside them, Narad Muni had done little other than fret.

Now, he asked in an unsteady voice, 'Why can't I go to Draupadi's house to help Kunti with the children?'

'Because I'd rather have you skulk in the shadows here than over there. Mother has enough to deal with already,' replied Bhima as he ran a finger over a blade to test its sharpness.

That made Arjuna frown just before he kicked the leg of a tall chair in to break it. His mother was trying to manage over a hundred children in that small apartment. The police had filed a report, but had yet to actually do anything, and Bhima was fairly certain that the vandals would be returning to seek revenge soon. Probably under the cover of night. Which meant that all fighting men had to camp here for the next few days, ready to go at a moment's notice.

Hopefully, once they understood that the Pandava brothers were a force to be reckoned with, they would crawl back to their little centre and stay there. After all, the Pandavas had fought armies that far outnumbered them, demons who were bigger and stronger, and even, occasionally, gods. A puny bunch of hooligans certainly didn't scare them.

He added the broken chair leg to a pile of wooden pieces that could be fashioned into weapons. Apart from the lathis the neighbourhood men had brought, they had slats from beds, legs from tables and chairs, and blades from ceiling fans. Chair seats and mattresses were made into shields, bricks from a nearby construction site had been moved to the roof along with stones collected from around the neighbourhood. Bhima was making spears with his kitchen knives and had fashioned a mace using one of the heavier cooking pots.

Nakula and Sahadeva strode into the room. Sahadeva quietly gathered the wooden weapons and left the room, but Nakula stayed back, fidgeting on his feet.

'What is it?' asked Arjuna.

Nakula took a deep breath. 'Don't tell Sahadeva, although I think he probably knows, but I'm not going back to heaven.'

Both Bhima and Arjuna stopped what they were doing. Narad Muni stared at Nakula as if he'd gone mad. 'You've gone mad,' he said.

Nakula shook his head. 'I'm actually thinking more clearly than I have in a long time. Angela ... I think I can make this work.'

That made Narad Muni raise an eyebrow. 'You're going to give up immortality for a *woman*?'

Quelling the old man's remonstration with a hard glare, Nakula looked at his older brothers. 'So, what do you think?'

'*Are* you giving up immortality for a woman?' asked Bhima.

'No,' Nakula returned his gaze steadily. 'I'm giving it up because I'd rather die trying to be happy than live forever with regret.'

Bhima nodded. 'That's good enough for me.' He got up and hugged Nakula, slapping him on the back. 'Don't spoil that pretty face of yours in the fighting. I need money to get this place repaired.'

Laughing, Nakula picked up a few of the homemade spears and shields. 'First things first. I need to give these mortals the fighting lessons we got when we were five.'

'Training going that badly?' asked Arjuna.

'They have the reflexes of a rhinoceros.' Nakula blew out a sharp breath and left the room.

The two remaining brothers locked eyes in unspoken understanding. The neighbourhood men had no fight training. The Pandavas would have to keep them on the sidelines as much as possible, so they didn't get seriously injured.

The room was silent for a while, except for the sounds of weapon-making. Then Bhima spoke, 'Somebody suggested that a few people should take videos with their phones. As evidence.'

Nodding, Arjuna turned to Narad Muni. 'Please go to the roof and find four or five of the older, weaker-looking men. They'll be in charge of recording everything for evidence.'

Narad Muni was still shaking his head over Nakula's declaration. It seemed to have distracted him from his fear. He barely acknowledged Arjuna's request as he left, mumbling, 'Heaven! Crazy people … why would anybody … should never have created women …,' to himself as he walked.

'Speaking of heaven, are you going back?' Bhima asked without looking up.

Arjuna was about to answer when there was a commotion at the front gate. Yudhishtra's voice could be heard shouting for everyone to either get inside and lock the front door, or leave the compound immediately. Bhima and Arjuna got up and ran to the hallway just as Yudhishtra burst in.

'Get in! Quickly!' he ordered as he shepherded the few men who had been outside through the front door. He pushed the last of them into the hallway and shut the doors, sliding the heavy bolt into place and locking it.

'What's going on?' asked Arjuna. Yudhishtra was dressed in just a dhoti and didn't have any shoes on.

'They're coming,' replied Yudhishtra in a steady voice.

'Who?'

'A mob. From the BYBM Centre. They will be here any second.' Yudhishtra stopped talking and looked around in shock. 'What happened?'

Bhima shrugged. 'Courtesy of the BYBM Centre.'

Yudhishtra clenched his jaw, his hands fisting at his side. 'Mother?'

'Safe. With the children at Draupadi's.'

He let out the breath he was holding. 'The mob. They're armed.'

'So are we,' said Bhima, holding up one of his spears. 'Projectiles are on the roof. And two dozen fighters.'

'Windows and back entrance?'

'Sealed.'

'Water and blankets for fires?'

'Ready.'

'Hot oil?'

Bhima shook his head. 'No killing. I gave Mother my word.'

Yudhishtra nodded. But, before he could say anything, Nakula and Sahadeva came running down the hallway, confusion written all over their faces.

'What's happened?' asked Nakula. 'The men are clucking like chickens on the roof.'

Sahadeva frowned at Yudhishtra and asked, 'Why are you barefoot, Brother?'

'It doesn't matter,' said Yudhishtra. 'There's a mob coming.'

Then, he took a deep breath and looked all four of his brothers in the eye. 'I have much to say to you, but we will talk later. Bhima, Arjuna, Nakula and Sahadeva, sons of Pandu and inheritors of Bharata's blood. Mighty warriors, bulls amongst men, my brothers. I have to ask you for something. Not as your king or even your elder, but as your equal. For now, and forever.'

Extending one hand out in front of him, he asked, 'Will you fight this battle by my side?' He looked at Bhima and swallowed. 'One last time.'

For a moment, time stood still. Then, Bhima covered Yudhishtra's hand with his own much-larger one. He grimaced with the effort to hold back his tears. 'It would be my honour, Brother.'

'Mine too,' whispered Arjuna, unable to summon his voice as he put his hand on theirs.

'Mine too,' said Nakula, clearing his throat and adding his hand.

'Mine too,' said Sahadeva, as he put his hand on the top and squeezed.

The five brothers grinned at each other and everything clicked perfectly into place. The world made sense again. The Pandavas were about to do what they did best. Fight a battle, together.

One last time.

31

The mob had obviously whittled down, thought Yudhishtra as he stood on the roof and watched it make its way down the street. There had been a diverse audience in the hall at the BYBM Centre—middle-aged men and women, some elderly people and a few children. The large group of almost a hundred approaching the orphanage, however, was made up almost entirely of young men. Many of whom Yudhishtra couldn't remember ever seeing at the centre or at his talks.

This wasn't a spontaneously assembled, revenge-seeking crowd of people. These young men weren't wronged believers, or 'ideological warriors' as Amit Sharma had called them.

No, this was a well-planned operation. These were trained fighters.

'It just got a lot more complicated,' murmured Yudhishtra softly to Arjuna, who was standing next to him. He didn't want any of the neighbourhood men to hear him or they might get alarmed and run away.

Arjuna nodded, not taking his eyes off the approaching horde. 'They'll aim to kill. Which means we not only have to be careful not to kill them, but protect our own from being killed too.'

'Precisely.'

'The twins?'

Yudhishtra nodded and Arjuna beckoned the twins over to whisper in their ears. Nakula and Sahadeva were both accomplished swordsmen, but they'd had little time to prepare the mortals under their tutelage. They would be tasked with the protection of their fighters, while Yudhishtra, Arjuna and Bhima took on the bulk of the fighting.

Turning, Yudhishtra assessed the roof full of men, most of whom were looking at the mob with unconcealed alarm. They had signed up to resist in a moment of fervour, but now reality was quickly sinking in. It wasn't any different to soldiers who faced an enemy army right before a battle.

Nothing gave a man more value for his life than the prospect of imminent death.

'My brothers,' he said in a loud, authoritative voice. 'I know you're looking down there and fear is taking hold of your mind. I want to tell you not to worry. You see, the only difference between you and those men is that right now you are scared instead of them. The second we turn that around, the second we make them realize that we are not afraid of them, they will surrender and run. Battles are never won because of bodily injuries. Battles are won when you injure the mind of your enemy.

'So, I want you to laugh and taunt them. Beat your chest and roar at them. Do not show fear! When they come at you, they will expect you to cower and beg, fall to the ground and be defeated. Do you know why? Because that's what has happened before. Every time they have executed an attack, they have met little resistance. If, however, you push back, they will be taken by surprise. Attack them with speed. When they strike you, strike back. If you fall, strike their legs. Your body will heal, but their minds will stay wounded.'

Yudhishtra smiled. 'Most importantly, do not worry. We are organized and prepared. My brothers and I have battled many, many times before. All you have to do is listen to our orders. With us by your side, you will prevail!'

The men looked less worried with those words. Yudhishtra would have liked more time to prepare them properly, stir up some passion within their chests, but the moment of reckoning had come.

The men at the front of the mob marched up to the gates of the orphanage and began to smash the fence with lathis. It seemed to be the weapon of choice these days. Some of them carried iron rods instead of wooden ones. Others carried stones.

Amit Sharma was with them too. Wearing a short wooden club strapped to his waist, he held a gun over his head and fired a shot into the sky.

'They have guns!' the men behind Yudhishtra exclaimed.

He heard Arjuna say to the men in an undertone. 'I'll take care of the guns, don't worry.'

Yudhishtra smiled and leaned over the roof's waist-high boundary wall. 'Amit Sharma!' he bellowed down to the street.

Amit and his men stopped what they were doing and looked up. Laughing, Amit shouted back, 'I'm here to send you to heaven, Guruji!'

The men behind him tittered.

Yudhishtra grinned, baring his teeth. 'How about I send you to hell first?'

'How are you going to do that if you hide behind closed doors, you jihadi? Come out here and fight!' Amit waved his gun in the air.

'Who will fight me, Amit? You?' Yudhishtra gave a mocking laugh. 'A weakling like you could hardly put a scratch on me.'

Amit snarled and pointed his gun up at Yudhishtra. 'I won't need to fight you if you're dead.'

But, before he could fire a shot, a stone struck his fingers with such intense force that it knocked the gun right out of his hands. He let out a loud 'Arrgh!' and clutched his fingers to his stomach, doubling in pain.

'See?' said Arjuna to their own fighters, who stood gaping behind him. 'I'll have you covered. Don't be afraid.'

Their faces changed, much to Yudhishtra's delight. What was a frightened, sceptical bunch just a few seconds ago had now turned into a fighting force who believed they could win. It was a welcome transformation.

'Amit Sharma,' he shouted again, with a contemptuous expression on his face. 'Stop bawling like a baby and heed my words. Since you have no regard for dharma, you probably won't concern yourself with the rules of engagement. However, I will give you one last chance to disengage. Leave now and do not return; otherwise my men and I will be forced to hurt you. Badly.'

Still bent over his hurt fingers, Amit screeched at his men, 'Get them! Attack! *Attack!*'

The mob surged forward, towards the front door. Yudhishtra waved an arm. 'Start throwing everything except the stones and bricks. Leave those for Arjuna.'

The men behind him rushed forward and began to pelt the attackers below with all the debris from the vandalized orphanage. Glass, pieces of broken furniture, parts of ceiling fans, cooking implements and utensils rained down on the mob. Many of the men who had reached the front door now stepped back, shielding their faces from the onslaught.

'Keep going!' said Yudhishtra, keeping his eyes on the scene below. He scanned the men at the back, realizing that one of them had drawn a gun. 'Arjuna, gun at the back!'

Arjuna threw the brick in his hand at the man, striking him hard in his face. He dropped the gun. One of his companions quickly stepped over and picked it up, only to have his face struck with a brick too.

Yudhishtra didn't stop to celebrate. 'Identify how many guns and keep disarming,' he said to Arjuna. 'I'll pick them up when I go down.'

'Don't shoot,' said Arjuna as he threw another stone at a man's hand with enough force to break a finger.

'I won't,' replied Yudhishtra. He looked down and saw that a few men were trying to break the front door down. Bhima was holding it shut, but it wouldn't last for long. They were running out of debris to throw anyway. Soon, the full force of the mob would descend upon the door. It was time to engage.

'Men!' he shouted. 'Pick up your weapons and follow me. We attack!'

The men ran to the back of the roof, and picked up their lathis, rods, clubs, shields and spears. Only Arjuna stayed in place, continuing to target the men below with a pile of stones and bricks behind him.

Yudhishtra and the fighters ran down the hallway, where they found Bhima with two other men, pushing at the door. It was seconds away from collapsing under the blows from the other side.

'Now!' he yelled at Bhima.

'Hah! Finally!' Bhima bared his teeth, grabbed his cooking-pot mace with one hand and a shield with the other, and took his weight off the door. Pulling the bolt free, he slammed the door open and let out an ear-splitting roar, startling the men outside into stopping their pounding for a second. Then, Bhima charged at them.

It was a sight he hadn't seen in so long that Yudhishtra had forgotten how spectacular it was. Bhima unleashed upon the enemy, his mace flying on all sides, making contact with men's faces. They went down like dominoes.

The neighbourhood fighters behind Yudhishtra cheered, now eager to join the carnage. Yudhishtra nodded to Nakula and Sahadeva, who nodded back. They would flank their twenty or so fighters and make sure no one was seriously wounded. The rest of the men, either elderly or weak, would take videos on their phones from above or run around picking up stones and bricks to return to Arjuna.

'*Charge!*' He ran out the door into the fighting.

Yudhishtra, lathi and chair-seat-shield in hand, began to strike down men from the mob. They came at him in groups, lathis held over their heads, ready to pound him into submission. However, he moved so fast that they felt his strike even before they were able to prepare their own. At all times, Yudhishtra kept a close eye on what was happening around him so that he could plan ahead.

It wasn't much of a contest, thought Yudhishtra as he saw Bhima ram his mace into men's faces and stop their attacks with his shield. After a while, mob members started running in the opposite direction when they saw Bhima approach. Nakula and Sahadeva bounded and vaulted about with the grace and precision of dancers, their lathis moving so fast they were a blur to the eye. Arjuna stood on the rooftop, his eye carefully calculating and anticipating the movements of the men below, and meticulously delivering knock after knock with his projectiles.

A surge of pride went through Yudhishtra. Thousands of years after they had left this world, and the Pandava brothers still had it.

He made his way quickly to a pistol he saw lying on the ground, next to an unconscious man who had been smacked in the face with a brick. A wooden club struck his back when he bent down to pick it up. Furious, he swivelled around and pointed the gun at the man who had hit him. The man's eyes almost popped out of their sockets and he ran away. Intrigued, Yudhishtra held the gun up over his head to make it clearly visible to everyone around him. They immediately scrambled.

Yudhishtra looked at the gun in his hand. Such a tiny thing that provoked such terror. He would have to study it a bit further before he went back, perhaps evaluate its usefulness against demon weapons. Right now, however, he had to find Amit Sharma.

He went searching amidst the melee, trying to identify Amit's face amongst throngs of men who all looked surprisingly like Amit. Average-looking, twenty-somethings in dusty T-shirts and jeans. A few weeks ago, when Yudhishtra first walked into the BYBM Centre, he had wondered why all these young men didn't have jobs. Now he understood.

This—roaming around in mobs, vandalizing buildings and intimidating ordinary people—was their job.

Apparently, in the Kalyug, criminals resided at lawful addresses and conducted their business openly while honest people were reduced to hiding.

He found Amit Sharma at the back of the crowd, flanked by his associates. Instead of fighting them away, Yudhishtra pointed a gun around and they scattered. Amit looked at him, horrified. He fished a smaller pistol out of his pocket and pointed it at Yudhishtra, his hand shaking in fright.

'Don't come any closer!' he shouted at Yudhishtra, his voice pitching high with panic. 'Get him!' he screeched, but nobody came near Yudhishtra. This gun was truly a remarkable weapon.

The two men stood at an impasse, each pointing a gun at the other.

'Coward,' Yudhishtra spoke evenly. 'How about we put down these toys and fight like real men?'

'Don't shoot! The police are coming. You'll be in jail for the rest of your life!' cried Amit. His lip trembled as he stared at Yudhishtra's gun.

The mob around them began to retreat, running away and disappearing into by-lanes and alleys. They had obviously realized this was a battle they couldn't win. Yudhishtra could hear Bhima calling out to those who ran from him, taunting and giving chase. His brother was never happier than when delivering a thrashing.

'Amit Sharma,' said Yudhishtra in a calm voice, despite the fact that he was fuming about his mother's orphanage being vandalized. 'I am no stranger to those who desire power and wealth at any cost, so I can fully understand why you terrorize your neighbours or why you steal money that isn't meant for you. But one thing I can't comprehend. What is wrong with opening a lunch business that serves mutton? Why all this fuss over meat?'

'Because it's wrong!' shouted Amit. 'It is not in our culture. Before this country was invaded by foreigners, our people were all Hindu vegetarians, pure in mind and body. Meat-eating is wrong. You are always harping on about dharma. Isn't the highest form of dharma non-violence towards other creatures?'

Laughing, Yudhishtra asked, 'So, you believe in non-violence?' He waved his hand at the riot around them.

'This is different!' shouted Amit. 'Ours is an ideological war! To bring back the native, natural and sacred ways of our people. To fight the invaders! If we don't, our way of life will die! Hindus will become extinct!'

Yudhishtra frowned. 'I've heard you say the word "Hindu" many times. What exactly does that mean?'

Amit's jaw dropped. 'You're joking, right?'

'Humour me. I've been in heaven for a long time.'

Shock turning into disgust, Amit snarled, 'Hindus are the native people of the land we call Bharat and the religion they follow!'

'The whole of Bharat?'

'Of course!'

Amazed, Yudhishtra shook his head. 'You are mistaken. Bharat is not a uniform place. Within it lie many different religions and cultures. They all interpret the scriptures differently. Some eat meat, others don't. You can't cover them all with the same ideological blanket.'

'Yes, we can!'

'No, you can't. Because, at the time the scriptures were written, Bharat was a pluralistic place. The scriptures, at least the ones that have not been altered over the ages, were chronicled in a non-prescriptive manner so that they could be interpreted by a diverse following. Unfortunately, that has backfired many times, with people in power interpreting them to their own advantage. During moments like that, usually an avatar would be born, but they changed the formula.' Yudhishtra shrugged and then gave the man standing opposite him a mocking look. 'You should know, you are not a protector of native ideology, Amit Sharma. You're exactly what you are fighting against. An invader.'

Amit's face went from anger to shock and then to unmitigated rage. 'You bastard, I'll kill you!' he screamed, right before the gun in his hand was knocked away by a brick. For the second time that day, Amit squealed in pain and clutched his fingers.

Yudhishtra laughed and picked up Amit's gun, turning to see Arjuna standing at a distance. 'Perfect timing, as always. Your skill is still as remarkable as ever, my brother!'

Arjuna grinned and replied, 'I've been practicing,' before charging at two men with a lathi. Both quickly turned and ran away, leaving Arjuna to grumble in disgust, 'I've missed all the action. Should have come down sooner.'

He'd indeed missed most of the action. The mob had more or less dispersed. Only those lying on the ground, injured or unconscious, remained.

Yudhishtra looked at Amit, showed him both guns and then threw them in Arjuna's direction. He caught them easily.

Yudhishtra turned back to Amit. 'I've fought many invaders, Amit Sharma. Killed them too.'

Amit shook with fear. 'The police are coming! You'll go to jail!'

'Let them come. It won't change anything.' He began to advance on Amit.

'Please,' Amit whimpered. 'Please don't hurt me.' He looked around frantically. 'Help! Help!'

'None of your associates can come to help you now. You will have to defend yourself today.'

Amit cowered, as Yudhishtra had expected him to. Men like him only puffed out their chests and strutted around in groups. Their bravado fled the moment they were alone.

'Guruji,' begged Amit as he folded his hands. 'Forgive me. I will stop doing this work, I promise. Give me one more chance. Please!'

'Make up your mind. Am I a guru or a bastard? Or both? Most gurus in my day were, indeed, born illegitimately.'

Yudhishtra got within arm's length of Amit and struck him square in the face. His lip split and blood spurted out. Yudhishtra felt an uncharacteristic surge of satisfaction. If anyone deserved a thrashing, it was this snake.

Now Amit was crying. He fell to his knees and clasped his hands together. 'Please, Guruji. I'm *sorry!*' he sobbed.

Yudhishtra grabbed him by the hair and pulled him to his feet.

'Stop begging. Fight back, damn you!'

'No!' Amit shook his head as he dropped back on his knees. 'You can't hit a man asking for mercy, Guruji. It's against your principles!'

He was right. Yudhishtra didn't have it in him. But that didn't mean his brothers couldn't deliver this man's reckoning.

'Bhima!'

'No! No, no, no, *no*!' Amit cried hysterically.

Bhima came over, and with one look at Yudhishtra, understood exactly what he needed to do. He picked up a panic-stricken Amit by the neck and proceeded to hold him high in the air, choking him. Then, when Amit's eyes looked like they would pop out, he let him fall to the ground. Yanking him up by his shirt, Bhima delivered a blow to Amit's stomach.

'This is for destroying my cooking equipment,' he growled.

He held Amit's face up and broke his jaw with his fist.

'And that was for wrecking the orphanage.'

He threw him on the ground.

'Enough,' said Yudhishtra softly.

Bhima scowled. 'It's not enough!'

'No, but look at him.' Yudhishtra pointed at a petrified, wailing Amit, trying to crawl away from them. Which was pathetic but also ridiculous really, given that his legs were fine.

Suddenly, the sound of a siren filled the air. Uniformed policemen surrounded them, pointing guns in their direction. One of them yelled, 'Hands up in the air! Everyone!'

Yudhishtra looked around. The scene looked disastrous, with dust, debris and blood everywhere. Most of the men who could run had run away, including their own fighters. Only the injured mob members on the ground and the Pandavas remained.

'Stand down,' he called out to his brothers.

Amit screamed, 'Terrorists! They attacked us!' before howling with pain and clutching his broken jaw.

Looking down at him writhing on the floor, Yudhishtra shook his head and said to Bhima, 'Maybe I shouldn't have stopped you. He is a worthy opponent after all. A regular Shakuni in the making.'

32

It was a large room, separated from the rest of the police station by thick bars of metal that ran from ceiling to floor. Those were encased in a net of metal wiring, so that people on either side could see each other clearly, but only touch with their fingers and nothing more. On their side of the metal barrier was nothing but stone benches protruding from the walls and a few other men lounging on them. On the other side was a bustling office full of policemen and other people.

So, this was what 'going to jail' meant, thought Arjuna, as he paced up and down the prison cell like a caged animal.

His brothers sat on one of the stone benches that had been cleared out for them. The other inmates had taken one look at the imposing, blood-spattered bunch and immediately moved over to the other side of the cell. After that, it had been hours and hours of waiting, followed by one policeman coming over to say that a police report had been filed against them by Amit Sharma. For assault, attempted murder, inciting violence and rioting, vandalism (of their own orphanage) and contributing to terrorist causes. Oh, and operating a food establishment without a licence. It would have been laughable had the policemen they'd encountered so far even bothered to ask them what happened. Instead, they had been cuffed and thrown in this cell, and ignored for the better part of the day, not allowed to make so much as a phone call.

They had become 'the accused'. Amit Sharma and his associates were now 'the victims'.

Arjuna chuckled. This was the last thing he'd expected to happen on this trip. So far, nothing had gone according to their original plan. Instead of convincing their mother and Draupadi to return to heaven, the Pandavas had ended up questioning their own futures.

He turned to his brothers. Nakula and Sahadeva talked quietly amongst themselves, while both Yudhishtra and Bhima seemed lost in thought. Arjuna went and sat next to them.

'Brother,' he said to Yudhishtra. 'What happened at the centre?'

Yudhishtra shook his head. 'I came to my senses, that's all.' He looked around. 'I owe all of you an apology. I suppose this is as good a time as any.'

Arjuna began to say something, but Yudhishtra put a gentle hand up to stop him. 'Yes, I do need to apologize. Hear me out. I have only recently appreciated, very belatedly, how much of your lives were inexorably altered by my decisions. I essentially chose your lives for you. At every turn, I made decisions without consulting you, decisions that were crucial to your futures. I forced you to live out a destiny that I thought was inevitable, and I never questioned it, never regretted it. I didn't think you did either, until we came down here.'

The Misters Kuru

He glanced down at the floor, took a deep breath and looked back up again. Deep sorrow resonated in his eyes.

'You have been unhappy, in your lives and afterlives. I take responsibility for that. You see, from the moment I was born, in the eyes of the entire world, I have been a number rather than a person. The first son. Dharma and duty were drilled into me from the beginning. I was taught that I knew what was best for everyone – not because of my intelligence or wisdom, but because of my position. I have believed this my entire life. In keeping us together, in deciding what we do, where we live, whom we marry and how we conduct our lives, I believed I was doing what was in everyone's collective interest. Thoughtlessly, I prevented any of you from carving out your own destinies.'

He chuckled without humour. 'Krishna went against the codes of dharma so many times during our mortal life. I should have learnt flexibility from him. Rules and duty are important, but so are discussion and collaboration, as are autonomy and independent thinking. I should have asked more and instructed less. Perhaps you all would have suffered less for it. Forgive me, my brothers.'

'There is nothing to forgive.' Arjuna put a firm hand on Yudhishtra's shoulder and squeezed. 'Just as you were taught to lead us, we were taught to follow and obey you. We all did our best, what we thought was right at the time. That is all anybody can do.' He looked around. 'I think I speak for all of us when we say we are sorry you felt isolated during this visit. However, just like a snake cannot shed its old skin without chafing against the earth, perhaps we needed a bit of friction before we could begin a new relationship.' He smiled.

'I thank you for your forgiveness,' responded Yudhishtra, smiling at his brothers. He let his gaze rest for a moment on each of their faces. 'I want you to know that I will support anything you choose going forward. Bhima,' he swallowed, 'I will miss you terribly. But I will not oppose your decision to remain here on earth with Mother.'

Bhima nodded. 'Thank you, Brother. I will miss you too. That is why I suggest we all stay back!'

That elicited a round of chuckles. The other inmates looked at them curiously, probably wondering what on earth this ragged-looking group had to laugh about.

Yudhishtra shook his head. 'I almost wish I could. There is so much to do here, and I have to admit, it felt good to be valued again, no matter how temporary or misguided. But I have committed to fighting in the heavenly army against the forces of Mara, and if I stay here, I probably won't make it back to heaven.' He looked at Arjuna, Nakula and Sahadeva. 'I hope I will get to fight with the rest of you, though. Not as your commander, but as a fellow soldier.'

Silence answered him. Yudhishtra's face fell in surprise and disappointment. He asked quietly, 'Bhima is not the only one staying, is he?'

Nakula took a deep breath. 'I'm staying too, Brother.'

Yudhishtra's eyes widened. 'Why?'

'I'm happier here.'

Yudhishtra looked at Sahadeva. 'You'll stay too, Sahadeva?'

Resignation and sorrow were written all over Sahadeva's face when he heard Nakula's quiet declaration. Not surprise, noted Arjuna. Sahadeva was by far the most intuitive of them all. He had probably seen it coming. Putting his hand on

Nakula's shoulder, Sahadeva shook it gently, compelling his twin to look up at him instead of staring at the floor.

'When did you decide?' he asked Nakula.

Not being able to meet his twin's eye, Nakula replied, 'A few days ago. I'm sorry.'

Sahadeva closed his eyes for a long moment. When he opened them, there was an ocean of pain inside. 'Look at me, Brother.'

Nakula looked up at Sahadeva, seeing his own pain reflected in his twin's face. 'Forgive me. I know this will hurt you. It will hurt me too, but I must find my own way, Brother. I hope you can understand.'

Sahadeva nodded. 'I do understand.' Then he chuckled humourlessly. 'I suppose now we will have to become two wholes instead of two halves.'

Nakula sighed. 'I suppose so.'

'So you'll return with me, Sahadeva?' asked Yudhishtra.

'Yes, I will,' replied Sahadeva. 'Vijaya and I are happy in heaven, and when the time comes, I shall fight in heaven's army with you.'

Yudhishtra exhaled, some relief evident in his expression. Then he turned to Nakula. 'I will miss you, Brother.'

Nakula extended his hand, which Yudhishtra grabbed and squeezed. 'As will I, my brother and king.'

'Just a brother. Always a brother. Irrespective of which worlds we inhabit.' Yudhishtra looked at both Bhima and Nakula with glistening eyes as he spoke.

Arjuna knew they would turn to him next. And he had no idea what he was going to say. Except, for reasons beyond his comprehension, he found his lips uttering the words, 'I've been sleeping in Draupadi's bed.'

From the way his brothers stared back at him, he almost wished he had stayed quiet. Almost. Taking a deep breath, he said, 'I know that's not something any of you want to hear, but I need you to hear it. Because I can't move forward otherwise. None of us have had any kind of marital relations with her since we ascended to heaven. I myself had no thought of rekindling our relationship until I came down here. I don't know what is happening between us now, or if she even wants a future with me, but whatever it is, it's happening.'

Yudhishtra looked very uncomfortable, but he asked quietly, 'Are you planning to stay here for Draupadi?'

'I haven't made a decision yet.'

'What about Subhadra?'

Yudhishtra's voice was light, but Arjuna felt the weight of his words on his shoulders. 'I haven't decided yet, Brother,' he said firmly. 'But, if I do decide to stay, do I have your blessing?'

'You've been sleeping with her and you still haven't decided?' asked Bhima angrily.

Looking his older brother squarely in the eye, Arjuna replied, 'I'm not taking advantage of her. I love her deeply. And,' he narrowed his eyes, 'you yourself said that I am the one she wants. Just the other day, when you gave me your blessing. Remember?'

Bhima grunted.

Yudhishtra frowned at Bhima. 'You knew about Arjuna and Draupadi?'

'I knew they kissed. I didn't know they had fallen into bed together.' Bhima looked away in disgust. 'Anyway, it doesn't change anything. You have my blessing. Provided you decide to stay. If you decide to go, however, I'm going to have to give you a thrashing like you've never had before.'

Ignoring Bhima's threat, Arjuna nodded. 'I would deserve it.' He turned to Nakula and Sahadeva. 'I'm assuming the two of you would have no objection?'

The twins shook their heads, neither of them looking particularly perturbed about the prospect of Arjuna and Draupadi becoming a couple.

Yudhishtra, on the other hand, would be a tougher nut to crack. It was one thing to sever your connection to your wife, but it was entirely different to be happy about her being with another man. Honestly, if it had been Bhima who had gotten together with Draupadi, Arjuna didn't think he would ever be able to accept it. Bhima was obviously the better man. He certainly didn't love her any less than Arjuna.

He turned to his eldest brother.

Yudhishtra had a harassed look on his face. With tight lips, he said, 'She belongs to herself now. So, I suppose she can choose anyone she wishes. Although, if I am being completely truthful, Arjuna, I wish it had been anyone but you.'

No one said anything for a few long moments, stunned as they were by his words.

His hands fisted in his lap, Yudhishtra whispered, 'I'm sorry I feel that way.'

Arjuna asked softly, 'Why?'

'Because I am the one who took her from you!' Yudhishtra's exclamation was made softly, but it was no less impactful. 'It was wrong, I know that now, but I won't apologize for it, Arjuna. Draupadi and I had a life together, she bore my children and ruled my realm beside me. I loved her. I still do. I *cannot* regret that.'

'I'm not asking you to regret it. The past will always be important, Brother. But I'm talking about the future.'

It was as if Yudhishtra didn't hear him as he continued speaking, this time in an angry voice, 'I knew she preferred you back then and I hated it. I cannot believe I still do!'

That made Bhima utter impatiently, 'So do I, Brother. But I'm not letting that stop me from doing the right thing.'

Yudhishtra gaped at Bhima, clearly stunned by that statement. Then, to everyone's surprise, he let out a wry chuckle. 'You are absolutely right. It doesn't matter how I feel, does it?'

Bhima shook his head. 'No. Just let them be happy. It's about time.'

Nodding, Yudhishtra repeated, 'It is about time,' before turning to Arjuna, taking a deep breath and saying, 'You and Draupadi have my blessing.'

33

It had been one hell of a day.

Draupadi had rushed home after a cryptic phone call from Kunti, only to find her apartment jam-packed with children. Jumping all over her light-coloured sofas, throwing her silk cushions at each other with food-stained hands, running wildly between the bedrooms, study and kitchen, and basically wrecking the apartment.

Now, Draupadi had birthed children of her own during her previous lifetime, but there had always been a gaggle of palace women around, ready to take them off her or Kunti's hands at a moment's notice. Now, as she beheld a harried Kunti trying to prepare a meal with whatever sparse provisions there were in the kitchen, while also trying to prevent the children from either killing themselves or each other, Draupadi would have given her right arm for a handmaiden.

'*Stop!*' she yelled at the top of her voice, startling all the children into pausing their rampage and peering up at her.

Draupadi quickly walked over to the TV and switched it on, scrolling to a channel that showed cartoons. 'Everyone sit down and watch!'

The orphanage didn't have a TV, so this was an unexpected treat. Over a hundred children crowded into her living room, spilling over the sofas and chairs, squeezing next to each other on the floor and standing with their backs pressed against the balcony door, all trying to get a good view of the cartoon in progress.

Thank god for television, thought Draupadi as she strode into the kitchen. Kunti was fumbling around with pots and pans. Chopped vegetables lay strewn all over the counter and there were a couple of eggs lying broken on the floor. Quiet sobs wracked Kunti's body.

'What happened?' Draupadi ignored the mess, walked over and put her arms around Kunti.

'The boys. The orphanage,' Kunti blubbered, before she began to weep violently. It was almost as if she'd been holding back, waiting for another adult to arrive before she could let go.

Draupadi hugged her tight, until Kunti rode out the worst of it. Then, she leaned back. 'You need to rest. The children are watching TV. Come to my room and we can talk.'

'No,' Kunti said, vigorously shaking her head. 'I have to make lunch. They'll be hungry soon.'

'Oh, for goodness, sake,' exclaimed Draupadi. Taking Kunti firmly by the shoulders, she scolded, 'Go to my room and lie down. I'll take care of lunch. No arguments. I'll be there in a few minutes.'

Kunti didn't argue and left the kitchen with stooped shoulders. Draupadi picked up her phone and dialled Angela.

'What's up, babe?' Angela's voice rang from the other end.

'If I told you I needed food for over a hundred children and I needed it in an hour, with plates and cutlery, do you have someone who could deliver it?'

'Er, that's somewhat difficult,' replied Angela. 'Are these your mother's orphanage children?'

'Yes, they're all at my place.'

'What? Why?'

Draupadi huffed. 'I don't know. I got a frantic call from her, and I got home to find her distraught. Help.'

'I'm on it,' said Angela. 'I'll come with the food. God knows you could probably use the help.'

A little tension left Draupadi's shoulders. 'You really are as your name says, an angel.'

'Now, now. Flattery will get you everywhere. Later, babe.' Angela hung up.

Draupadi took a bracing breath and walked to her bedroom. Kunti was pacing up and down, looking as upset as before. She grabbed Kunti and made her sit on the bed. Then, she sat beside her.

'Now, tell me what happened.'

'Masked men,' Kunti said in a trembling voice. 'They came this morning while Bhima had gone to the market. They completely destroyed the orphanage, Draupadi. Furniture, fittings, windows, all the new cooking equipment, everything. Bhima came back and fought them off, but they promised to return, with more men.'

'From the BYBM Centre?' Draupadi felt the hum of rage build inside her.

Kunti nodded. 'I think so. They've come a few times and threatened us, even brought along a policeman once. I knew they would return, but I never thought they would attack a building full of innocent children! And they call themselves a charity!'

'Did you call the police?'

'Yes,' replied Kunti. 'We also handed over two of the men to the police. Bhima gathered a group of neighbourhood them to camp out at the orphanage. He wants to fight them, Draupadi. I tried to stop him, but he wouldn't listen.' Tears began to flow out of her eyes again.

She needed to get over there, thought Draupadi. See what was going on and perhaps intervene. Force the police to do something. Maybe even call a camera crew to record the destruction so they could create public support, put some pressure on the BYBM Centre to back off before things got further out of hand. But Kunti wasn't going to be able to manage the children on her own, and Draupadi was loath to leave her in this state. Plus, there was the question of arranging a meal and bedding for tonight.

No, she would have to wait until nightfall. When all of them were asleep, she'd go down to the orphanage and assess the situation. Arjuna, Nakula and Sahadeva would probably go there too. If Bhima was preparing to fight, he would have called his brothers. Which meant they could all get into a serious amount of trouble, with both the centre goons as well as the police.

Draupadi had a bad feeling, a *really* bad feeling about it. It didn't go away when the food and Angela arrived, after all the children were fed, and they arranged bedding and the dinner meal to be delivered in the evening. Thankfully, she had enough money that she could afford to pay for all of it. At least temporarily. Angela had promised to advance a month's salary to her. She'd also promised to hold a donation drive at NPTV to repair the damage done to the orphanage. Overcome, Draupadi hugged her so tight, Angela had actually choked a little.

Hours later, just as she was thinking of leaving for the orphanage, someone began frantically banging on her front door. Draupadi's heart flew into her mouth. Something was terribly wrong. She ran to the door, only to find a shaking Narad Muni on the other side. He ran inside, saw the mass of children, and, for a brief moment, looked like he wanted to run back out. Then he shook his head. 'No, no. I must!'

He looked at Draupadi with panic-stricken eyes. 'A mob came, with weapons! There was a fight. Our side prevailed, of course, but the place is in a shambles. Wounded men everywhere. And the police has taken them away!'

A cold chill swept through her. 'The police has taken who away?'

'The Pandavas! All five of them! They clamped their hands in chains and drove away. That Amit Sharma was screaming that they were terrorists and blamed the whole thing on them. The police believed him!' He clutched his hanging forehead and moaned loudly, 'I *knew* this whole expedition would end in catastrophe. Time and time again I said, "Don't do this, don't go down there, the Kalyug will get you", but did anybody listen? No, of course not. Nobody *ever* listens to me ...'

Draupadi had certainly stopped listening after learning what happened. If the police had arrested all five of her former husbands and Amit Sharma had filed a report against them, it would take more than a media story and public support to set them free. Police reports, once written and filed, were extremely difficult to retract. Even if the others left for heaven soon, Bhima would still be stuck in jail. She couldn't let that happen. No, she needed to do something. Something that would not only get them out of jail, but get them all out of this impossible situation.

But what?

Her mind drew a blank.

'Come on, think!' she scolded herself under her breath.

'... after, all, who am I? Just someone who's been around for hundreds of thousands of years. Someone who's dealt with mortals, gods *and* demons. But no, why would my opinion matter? I can't break a man's nose or throw stupid balls at stupid sticks in the mud ...'

Throwing balls at sticks in the mud! That was it! Draupadi laughed out loud.

The sound of her laughter brought Narad Muni's diatribe to an abrupt end. He glared at her instead. 'Is this any time to titter, woman?'

'No,' replied Draupadi. 'It's time for action.' She turned to Narad Muni. 'Here's what's going to happen, old man. You're going to stay here with my mother and help her. I mean *actually* help. I have to go and get the Pandavas out of jail.'

Narad Muni gave her a dismayed look, but he nodded. Once.

'Oh, and don't tell her what happened. She'll worry unnecessarily.'

'You want me to *lie*?'

Draupadi exclaimed in frustration. 'No, just keep your mouth closed for once in your life!'

Then, she left.

Hours later, after night had fallen over the city and the bustle at the police station had dwindled to a light hum, Draupadi strode into the jailhouse with two men by her side. They walked up to a desk with a policeman on duty, and one of the men whipped out some papers from his briefcase. Upon taking a look at them, the policeman jumped up and ran further into the office. Soon, they were escorted into the private room of the inspector who was on duty at the time. He examined the papers carefully and asked the men some questions in a conciliatory tone. Finally, after about an hour of questioning, a few phone calls and far too much small talk for Draupadi's patience, she was led towards the cell where the Pandava brothers were being held.

She pushed down the anger she felt when she saw her former husbands sitting on stone benches in a cage. It was similar to what she'd felt when she had seen them shed their royal garments and wear the garb of forest dwellers just before they went into exile. They deserved better.

The policeman who walked ahead of them opened the heavily fortified door to the jail cell and called out, 'Yudhishtra Kuru, Bhima Kuru, Arjuna Kuru, Nakula Kuru and Sahadeva Kuru!'

The brothers looked up in surprise. They saw Draupadi standing behind the policeman. She quickly put a finger to her lips, and they each gave her an infinitesimal nod in return. Quietly, they stood up and followed her to a desk where their release papers were processed. They continued to stay quiet while Draupadi led them outside, profusely thanked the two men who had accompanied her and bundled them into her car.

Finally, when she began to drive the car, Bhima groaned from the front passenger seat. 'I need to eat.'

Draupadi nodded. Her relief at having them out of jail finally pushing her body into feeling the anxiety and exhaustion of the day. 'We'll eat something when we get to the orphanage. I can't take you to the apartment because there isn't an inch of space left.'

Yudhishtra said, 'That's all right. We should probably camp out there anyway, in case they come back.'

Draupadi shook her head. 'They won't come back.'

Arjuna asked, 'How did you get us out?'

Draupadi turned to smile at him briefly. Given that the car was still moving at the time, this caused every man inside to stiffen and hold on to their seats tightly until she looked back at the road again. 'It was because of you, Arjuna.'

'Me?'

She nodded. 'I called Rohit Jadeja. Oh, I forgot to tell you that he messaged me after we met at the cricket club. Asked me out for coffee.'

She knew Arjuna wouldn't like that, but the thought that he might be jealous gave her a small, inexplicable sense of satisfaction.

She continued before he could say anything, 'So, anyway, I knew the Indian cricket team was really keen to have you. When I told Rohit Jadeja that you were ready to sign with them if they could fix this, he called the head coach, who called the president of the Cricket Board. There are many industrialists who sponsor the team, including the richest man in the country, this billionaire who is apparently a *huge* cricket fan. And happens to be very close to the prime minister because he's a major donor to the election campaign. Anyway, the president of the Cricket Board called the billionaire and he called the prime minister's office. The PMO called the ruling party headquarters, who called the inspector general of police and dropped all charges against you. Turned out that the BYBM Centre is owned by cronies of the ruling party.'

She grinned. 'Also, given that there are viral videos all over the internet of the centre's men attacking a poor, defenceless orphanage, the party management recommended that, as of today, the BYBM Centre be immediately closed and repurposed. Your Amit Sharma will probably be sent to some party outpost to cool his heels until this dies down.'

The five men were stunned into silence. Then, after a few moments, Arjuna asked, 'All because of cricket?'

Chuckling, Draupadi replied, 'All because of cricket. It's the only thing that unites this country anymore.'

Arjuna shook his head in amazement. Then, something occurred to him. 'I suppose I have to sign with the team now?'

Draupadi stayed quiet for a minute before replying. She knew Arjuna had to go back to heaven. She had always known that. None of this changed anything. She replied in a slightly wobbly voice, 'For the moment, yes. When you leave, we can tell them you died. It would be the truth.'

Nakula grinned mischievously. 'It would. And then Rohit Jadeja could console Draupadi. Over coffee.'

There was a growl from the back seat that made Nakula laugh.

'Oh, and by the way,' she looked at Bhima, who glanced nervously at the road ahead. 'Angela started a crowd-funding page online for the repairs needed at the orphanage. After the videos of the mob attack went viral, the orphanage has raised a phenomenal amount of money.'

Bhima's eyes widened. 'How much?'

'Enough to repair and upgrade everything, *and* keep it going for at least a year.' She smiled. 'Also, enough to expand the lunch business.'

Bhima threw his head back and laughed. 'Does Mother know?'

'Angela called her while I was arranging your release. She's been a lifesaver today. I really hope you don't hurt her when you leave, Nakula.'

She heard the grin in Nakula's voice as he replied from the back seat. 'You don't have to worry about that. I'm not going anywhere.'

'Really?'

'Really.'

Well, that was just wonderful for Angela and Nakula, Draupadi thought with a smile. Then, her smile dropped. Arjuna hadn't said anything on the subject in the last few days, despite the fact that they had spent every night together. Would he consider staying, given that two of his brothers were giving it a shot?

She was too scared to ask.

She pulled up at an eatery near the orphanage where they quickly ate some food in wearied silence. Promising to return the next day to help get the place back in working order, she dropped them off and drove home. Tomorrow would be a busy day for all of them.

It would also be one of their last days together.

34

A large group of workers were clearing out just as Draupadi walked in through the front door of the orphanage. It had been four days since what they were now calling 'the little war'. They moved the children back yesterday, after a clean-up and partial restoration. More work would continue over the next few weeks, which would include fresh paint, new fittings and furniture, a brand-new kitchen, which could cater to both the orphanage and the lunch service, and, much to everyone's delight, a small van.

The best part was, not only was there plenty of money left over from their crowd-funding initiative but more was coming in every day! Not just money, but volunteers were showing up unannounced at their doorstep, ready to help with repairs or supplies. In fact, Bhima had announced just yesterday that if things continued this way, he might even look into starting a separate eatery in the neighbourhood, instead of operating his lunch service through the common room window.

Things were looking up around here, thought Draupadi. A part of her was thrilled. The rest of her felt like crawling back into bed and hiding from the world. She hadn't spoken to Arjuna alone since the morning of the little war. He was living at the orphanage with his brothers, working with them to repair and rebuild the place. Meanwhile, she'd been busy sorting out its finances with Angela. There had been no time to ask him what he was going to do.

It was probably too much to hope that he would give up eternity and Subhadra for her. Was it? Draupadi shook her head slightly as she walked down the hallway, determined not to drive herself crazy thinking about it. But it was hard not to. For a few short days, she'd known what it was like not to share, either her man or herself with anyone else. For a few short days, she'd felt happy in a way she never had before. Warm and sated. Wanted and cherished. Content. She shook her head again. Not thinking about it.

The common room was full of boxes, so she went to the kitchen. Since the children were back in residence, Bhima was busy preparing their evening meal, giving quiet instructions to Narad Muni, who was sitting nearby and chopping a big pile of greens. It was a relatively easy job, but Narad Muni managed to look and sound as if he were being tortured.

Draupadi shook her head. She definitely wouldn't miss him when he left.

'Ah, Draupadi,' said Yudhishtra from the other end of the kitchen. He stood over a half-assembled, flat-packed shelving cabinet looking utterly confused. 'The workers had to leave. Will you hold this for me while I attach the screws?'

'Of course,' she replied and walked over. Yudhishtra obviously hadn't followed the instructions properly because the legs of the cabinet were installed upside down. She stifled a giggle. If anyone *hated* being given direction by a woman, it was Yudhishtra. Bhima was just going to have to deal with a wobbly cabinet.

Holding the shelf while Yudhishtra inserted a screw into a hole with all the concentration and deliberation of a surgeon performing an operation, she asked, 'So, I still don't know how you ended up running to the orphanage from the centre before the little war? What happened there?'

Yudhishtra hadn't told any of them yet.

He smiled, but his lips were strained. 'You all were right about those men. I just couldn't see it until things came to a head.'

She waited for him to say more, but he stayed quiet. Obviously, whatever had happened, he wanted to keep it to himself. Fair enough.

'How do you feel about Bhima and Nakula staying back?'

He sighed. 'Sad, obviously. Remorseful, for the past and the last month. But also happy for them, I suppose. The time has come for the Pandavas to go their separate ways. I must accept that with as much composure as I can muster.'

Smiling, Draupadi put a hand on his arm. 'That's very gracious. I'm proud of how far you've come.'

Yudhishtra stopped what he was doing, stared at the floor and took a long breath. Then, he covered her hand with his own for a brief moment before he let it fall.

'I want you to know that I deeply regret every horrible thing I've said and done, or allowed to be done, to you. In the past and during this visit. The truth is, I am amazed at everything you have achieved in just one short year. And all on your own. It's a testament to what a remarkable woman you are, and I am very proud of you, Draupadi.'

Never in a million years had she thought she would hear those words coming out of Yudhishtra's mouth.

She cleared her throat. 'That means a lot to me.'

He looked up from the floor at her face, staring into her eyes, his own shining with regret. 'I know I'm not your husband anymore, and perhaps I have no right to talk about us, but I also want you to know that I have cherished our years together and always will. That will never change. Should you want to ... be with another man, whomsoever he may be, I wish you every happiness.'

Draupadi stiffened. Did he know about Arjuna? She studied his expression carefully but couldn't tell.

'I'll keep that in mind.'

'Draupadi.'

Thank god. She whirled around and faced Bhima. 'Yes?'

Bhima stirred his pot and waved her over. 'They told me I need a licence to drive the van. What is it with licences in this world?'

She laughed. 'Wait till you buy a house.'

That made Narad Muni mumble under his breath, '... giving up heaven to apply for mortgages. Crazy people ...'

Draupadi ignored him. She looked around. 'So, where are the others?'

Bhima and Yudhishtra exchanged a glance. Then Bhima answered, 'Nakula and Sahadeva are helping Mother in the dormitories.'

When he didn't volunteer anymore information, Draupadi asked, 'And Arjuna?'

'He's setting up Mother's new bed in her room.' Bhima waved at the cabinet Yudhishtra was assembling. 'It's another one of these furniture pieces that you have to pay for but build yourself.'

'Oh.' She shifted on her feet, undecided about what to do.

Bhima's lip twitched. 'You know, Arjuna must be getting hungry. He ate very little lunch.'

'… ate like a horse …'

Bhima glared at Narad Muni, who ignored him but stopped mumbling. Then Bhima ladled some curry into a bowl and held it out to Draupadi. 'Could you go give this to him?'

She glanced down at the half-cooked, rather meagre meal. 'Er … what about rice?'

'He's on a diet.'

Now it was Bhima's face she studied. It was perfectly bland as he held out the bowl. She looked at Yudhishtra again, who quickly turned around and started studiously inserting screws into holes, as if his life depended on it.

They knew!

She took an unsteady breath and looked at Bhima again, a questioning look on her face.

Bhima swallowed, exhaling slowly. Then, he smiled and nodded at the bowl. 'Take it to Arjuna, my love.'

Tears pooled in her eyes as she took the bowl from him. 'Thank you.'

He waved her away.

She looked at the hallway past the kitchen door. Time to go get her heart broken.

35

He was angry with a bed.

'What's up?' Draupadi asked as she walked into Kunti's small, unadorned bedroom. Everything here had been smashed to pieces, except for the small table with the statuette of Krishna on top of it. Apparently, the modern-day vandals thought it was acceptable to destroy everything in front of god, just not god himself.

Arjuna glanced up, seething. 'These instructions are wrong!'

She shook her head. 'No, they're not.'

'I've followed them to the letter! This is rubbish.' He rapped at a leaflet in his hand with frustrated fingers.

He had done everything perfectly, even though the instructions asked for the legs of the bed to be assembled first, when everyone knew you always started building a bed's base before its legs. It was simple common sense!

She took the instructions from him gently and put them on the table. Then she put the bowl in his hands. 'Bhima sent this.'

Arjuna stared at the bowl of curry in confusion. It wouldn't feed a cat. 'Are you sure this is for me?'

Nodding, Draupadi took a deep breath. 'Can we talk?'

He looked up, saw her expression, and his frustration with the bed dissipated. All the anguish that had preceded it, however, now returned in full force.

Draupadi didn't give him a chance to say anything. She quickly squared her shoulders and widened her stance, as if preparing for a fight. It would have been funny if he wasn't holding his breath.

'So, I'm just going to put my cards on the table,' she said.

Taking a deep, bracing breath, she announced, 'I'm in love with you.' Like an accusation. Almost as if she were angry.

Arjuna stared at her, blinking too fast. It was the first time she had ever said it. He knew she loved him, of course. But this was different. This was better.

'I'm in love with you too. You know that.' He'd certainly told her enough times.

Nodding, Draupadi continued, 'I want you to stay. I want us to be together. There, I've said it. Now it's your turn.' She crossed her arms, as if ready for the worst.

He took a step towards her, to envelop her in his arms when he realized he was still holding the bowl. Setting it down on one of the pieces of the bed, he turned to Draupadi and pulled her into a hug. Things had been so perfect since their first night together. Thousands of years of baggage had been shed in a handful of nights. They had talked, made love and realized how much the other had changed while they weren't looking. It felt so right, and the last thing he wanted was to give it up.

In fact, Draupadi wasn't the only thing that felt right. As agreed, he had signed a year-long contract with the Indian Cricket Board. They would pay him an enormous sum of money as a retainer, while training him to play international cricket. They would pay even more once he started playing for the team. Not to mention, he'd come to really enjoy the game. The thought of passing up such an incredible opportunity left a sour taste in his mouth.

He felt Draupadi's curves pressed against him and sighed. 'I don't want to go back.'

Draupadi leaned back and looked up at his face, her own lighting up in a dazzling smile that made the night sky look lacklustre. Then, she saw the torment in his eyes and her smile fell. He hadn't said he wasn't going back, only that he didn't want to.

There was a world of difference between the two.

Her anger, always quick to surface when he said something she didn't like, now sprung up. 'Just decide, Arjuna.' She tried to pull out of his arms, but he held her tightly, infuriating her even more. She struggled lightly against him before erupting. '*Why* does everything have to be so bloody complicated with you?'

She pushed against him, and this time he let her go. Draupadi turned away, fuming, but then swirled around. 'You know what, just leave! It's what you do best, isn't it?'

'That's not fair,' he whispered.

'Then what is it? You've already said you were unhappy in heaven. You're bored, not getting along with Subhadra and you don't think there's going to be a war of the worlds anytime soon. You've told me multiple times that you love me, that you enjoy playing cricket, that you've had more fun in the last month than you have had for thousands of years before that. So, what's stopping you? *What is it?*'

Arjuna's jaw clenched. 'When I abducted Subhadra and married her, it was against the wishes of her family. I even fought a battle against her brother, Balarama, to make her my wife. Things were never the same between them after that. At that time, I made a promise to Krishna that I would always take care of her; be with her forever. When she ascended to heaven, Krishna was already in his own realm, and I was all she had left. She's my responsibility.'

He locked eyes with Draupadi, silently pleading with her to understand. 'If I am anything, I'm a man of my word. How can I rescind for my own selfish reasons? What does that make me? Where does that leave her?'

Draupadi threw up her hands. 'Surely that promise doesn't hold true for every single one of your lifetimes, Arjuna? If you had chosen to be reborn, you wouldn't even know her anymore. You yourself told me she wanted to be reborn. She wanted to become a Vidyadhari, for god's sake! What does that tell you about her priorities?'

'You don't understand!' Arjuna exclaimed in frustration. 'It doesn't matter what *her* priorities are. This is about me, Draupadi. I need to do the right thing, even if it's not what I want. I can't live with myself otherwise.'

Draupadi stilled. She gazed up at him, her beautiful eyes shimmering with tears. His heart ached, but still he spoke in a bitter voice, 'If I stay here with you, which is what I want more than anything in the world, then I will spend the rest of my life knowing that I acted selfishly, that I went against my word. But, if I leave and return to heaven, I'll spend eternity wishing I was down here with you. Tell me, Draupadi, which tragedy should I choose?'

But Draupadi didn't reply. In fact, she didn't move at all. Arjuna frowned and took a step towards her. 'Draupadi?'

'She can't hear you right now, Arjuna.'

Arjuna whirled around. The childlike voice had come from the small Krishna statuette on the table. Upon closer inspection, he saw that the statuette's face had come to life.

Krishna's cherubic face grinned at him, his cobalt-blue eyes shining with their usual, impish turquoise sparks. 'Hello, my brother,' he said in a gentle voice.

Arjuna kneeled on the floor next to him and smiled. 'My god and brother. It's good to see you.'

'I see you have been happy.'

Nodding, Arjuna replied, 'I have.' He turned to look at Draupadi. 'Is she all right?'

'She's fine. I just stopped time for her temporarily. It's better she doesn't see me right now.'

'Why not? I'm sure she misses you.'

Krishna said softly, 'That's exactly why she shouldn't see me. Mortals are always happier when god is at the back of their minds, rather than the front.'

Arjuna looked down at the floor and sighed. 'Tell me what to do.'

'I can't do that.'

'You've always told me before, my brother. Guided me when my mind was at odds with my heart.'

'And what did I tell you to do during those times?'

'You told me to do my duty, whether perfect or imperfect.'

'Where does your duty lie?'

'With Subhadra.'

'Why?'

'Because I made a promise.'

'But?'

Arjuna looked up into the statuette's eyes. After a moment, he replied, 'But I want to stay with Draupadi.'

Krishna smiled. 'What if you were to remove yourself from the equation, Arjuna? Your body, your soul, your heart and your promises, your desires, choices and opinions. What is left?'

'Duty.'

'Where does your duty lie?'

'With perseverance, with action, with the greater good. With detachment to the outcome.' His eyes widened as he recalled a conversation with Krishna on the edge of a battlefield, in another life. 'Or the effects of that outcome on others, be they family or foe. Or both.'

'Where does your duty lie?'

'Where I am most useful. Where I can fulfil my karma.'

'Where does your duty lie?'

'On earth.' Arjuna sucked in a breath and held it for a moment. Then, he exhaled. 'On earth.'

He looked into Krishna's eyes, his own spilling over with tears. 'But Subhadra?'

'She has her own journey. You have made your decision, Arjuna. You must move forward now.'

He sighed and then nodded. 'You'll keep an eye on her?'

Krishna laughed. 'I keep an eye on all of you. Tell Draupadi. She gets angry with me sometimes.'

Arjuna looked into Krishna's infinite eyes. 'Thank you, my god and brother. For everything.'

'Enjoy your second chance, Arjuna. I will be with you, always.'

And with that, Krishna's face disappeared, and the statuette was restored to its blank uniformity. He was gone.

Arjuna stood up, relief engulfing his body in its warm wrap. He closed his eyes, and for the first time in his entire existence, he felt truly at peace with the universe.

He felt free.

He laughed out loud.

'What the *hell* are you laughing about?' Arjuna heard Draupadi's voice, still furious, behind him.

He laughed harder.

'That's it. I'm done with you!' she shouted and began to march towards the door.

Arjuna moved so fast she didn't see him coming. Grabbing her hand from behind, he pulled, whirling her back into his arms. Then, just as Draupadi opened her mouth to yell at him again, he covered it with his own, kissing her and laughing at the same time. Outraged, she kicked his shin. Hard.

'Ow!' he exclaimed.

'Don't you dare touch me ever again,' she hissed, pushing away from him.

'Draupadi, listen to me,' he said as she slipped away and headed for the door. 'I have to tell you—'

A piercing scream came from the kitchen.

36

'I'm free. *I'm free!*'

Narad Muni was dancing around the kitchen in glee, dressed in the sage habit he had donned for millennia. Leaping over pots and pans, and twirling in the air, he looked like he was in a Bollywood film song. One hand was automatically playing his signature tanpura, the other one was pointed towards the group now gathered around him. Arjuna, Draupadi, Nakula, Sahadeva and Kunti had all come rushing to the kitchen when he had screamed, imagining the worst.

'Ha hah! Thought you could push me around, did you? Guess what, my magical powers are back, mortals!' He turned to Bhima, barely concealing a grin. 'Hmmm, should I turn you into a toad or a snail, I wonder?'

Bhima looked completely unruffled. 'Take your pick. I'll be extra happy when Krishna sends you here for another month of repentance.'

That made a worried scowl appear on Narad Muni's face. The last thing he wanted was to return to this hellhole. Everyone watched as his expression went from unease to anger at his inability to seek revenge for the worst thirty days of his life.

'Fine,' he declared. 'I will refrain from meting out any retributions. But, let me just say, you people are fools! Giving up heaven for *this*?' He waved an arm around the kitchen in disgust. 'You will regret it, mark my words. But by then, it will be too late!' His glee returned and he did a little shimmy.

Then, he squinted at the Pandava brothers and said in the condescending tone he always adopted towards mortals, 'I have a quick errand to run, but I'll be back in a few minutes, so you better say your goodbyes fast.' With a snap of his finger, he disappeared in a puff of smoke.

'I thought I'd never get rid of him,' muttered Bhima as he stood up.

The five brothers faced each other. None of them seemed to know what to say.

Kunti finally spoke, which was when everyone noticed that she had silent tears running down her cheeks. 'I was dreading this day.' She looked at Yudhishtra, Arjuna and Sahadeva, and said, 'Your brothers, Bhima and Nakula, have already informed me they are staying, but I'm going to miss the three of you so much.'

Arjuna smiled at her and then at Draupadi, who also looked like she was about to burst into tears. 'Actually, I'm staying too.'

Draupadi's jaw dropped. 'What?' she whispered.

'That's what I was trying to tell you before you kicked me.' He chuckled. 'I'm staying.'

'Are you sure?' she asked.

'I'm sure.' He leaned towards her and whispered in her ear, 'I had a little chat with Krishna. Remind me to tell you what he said later.'

Draupadi let out a cry that bordered on the hysterical, and threw her arms around his neck. Burying her face in his chest, her shoulders heaved with sobs.

Embarrassed, Arjuna cleared his throat and patted her back awkwardly, all too aware of the eyes upon them. His mother was in the room, for god's sake. In fact, his mother was gaping at them with her mouth hanging open.

'You two?' Kunti pointed at them and then asked, 'You two?' again, seemingly incapable of producing more words.

Arjuna was saved from having to answer when Draupadi turned, still sobbing, to Kunti and blubbered, 'I'm sorry I didn't tell you!'

Tears were already streaming down her face. So we could just say that she began to sob too. 'No, no. I'm so happy for you both! This is how it should have been!'

The two women hugged each other tightly and wept, both taking turns to cry out, 'I'm sorry!' and, 'No, *I'm* sorry.'

Meanwhile, the five men in the room, having no idea what to do next, just stayed where they were and waited. Minutes passed. Then, Bhima shook his head and went back to his cooking, muttering, 'Women.'

Finally, Yudhishtra ventured a few words. 'Narad Muni will be back soon, ladies.'

His words snapped Draupadi and Kunti out of their embrace and back to the situation at hand. Kunti wiped her tears with her sari and reached out to Yudhishtra.

'My son,' she said. 'While I am thrilled that your younger brothers have decided to make their lives here, I am now more worried about you. How will you fare without them?'

Yudhishtra touched her feet respectfully and then let her enfold him in a long hug. He patted her back and stepped away. 'Don't worry about me, Mother. It's about time I learnt how to manage without them. It's overdue, in fact.'

'What will you do?' she asked.

He smiled. 'Train for the war, make myself useful in heavenly court. Think. Find out about myself. I still don't know who I am without my brothers. That will be a purpose in itself.'

Draupadi walked back to Arjuna's side, slipping an arm around his waist, as if reassuring herself that he wasn't going anywhere. She looked at Yudhishtra and said, 'Why don't you stay? You would do very well for yourself as a guru. A proper one, this time.'

Yudhishtra laughed. 'I think I'll leave being a guru to the professionals. Besides, if there is anything I have learned down here, it's that I have a lot to figure out before I can begin to advise others.'

He turned to Kunti. 'Mother, I have something to admit. Before I came here, I was angry. Because I felt you had abandoned us. I've only lately realized how wrong I was, and come to respect and admire your decision. However, because of my anger, I haven't spent as much time with you as I could have. I'm sorry. I should have been here, helping you, from the start.'

Kunti shook her head pulled him in for another hug. She cupped his face and said, 'We will always be together, in our minds, our hearts and our memories.'

BOOM!

'Ah, I missed this!' Narad Muni appeared from the middle of a cloud of smoke, his bony hand waving it away from his face. 'Nothing like a dramatic entrance to begin one's day!'

At this point, Bhima stood up again and said, 'We haven't finished yet.'

Narad Muni cackled, 'Too late, boy! Now, which of you are coming with me? Chop, chop, I'm running late.' He snapped his fingers impatiently.

'You know,' Arjuna stepped forward, 'I just had a chat with Krishna in the other room. I think he would like us to say our farewells in peace.'

At that, Narad Muni gave him a nasty glare and muttered, 'Fine. But that is the last time you get to use Krishna's name.' He snapped his fingers again. 'Hurry up!'

Kunti turned to Yudhishtra and smiled. 'Bless you, my son. Farewell.'

Yudhishtra smiled back. 'Goodbye, Mother. Don't worry, I'll be fine.' He walked over to Draupadi, smiled and took her hand in his. 'Goodbye, Draupadi.'

Draupadi pulled him into a hug. 'Goodbye, Yudhishtra.'

He turned to Arjuna, who was trying desperately to fight a ball-sized lump in his throat. 'Brother.'

Arjuna bent down and touched his feet. 'Brother,' he whispered. They hugged.

Bhima stepped forward and touched Yudhishtra's feet as well, lifting him in the air when they embraced. Nakula and Sahadeva joined them, exchanging hugs and respects.

For a few endless moments, the five of them just stood in a circle and looked at each other, unspoken words passing between them. Everything had been said, yet it wasn't enough. There were still adventures to be acknowledged, lifetimes to be remembered, missions and wars won and lost, companionship, comfort and counsel that was always at hand. Trials and triumphs, always shared. Friendship. Brotherhood. A collective destiny.

Till now.

They would always be the Pandavas. Each would hold their memories close, carry the others in their hearts while they walked different paths. Forged different futures.

'Right. While this is all very heart-breaking and tragic,' drawled Narad Muni while tapping his foot, 'I've been out of commission for a month, and have a million things to do. So could we move it along?'

Sahadeva turned to Nakula and clasped his forearms tightly. Nakula did the same.

Sahadeva said, 'You will be happy, my twin. And, because of that, so will I. No regrets.'

Nakula nodded, swallowing heavily. 'No regrets. I'll see you back in heaven. I plan on being really good.'

Sahadeva laughed. Then, he turned to Yudhishtra and nodded.

Stepping towards Narad Muni, Yudhishtra said to him, 'Sahadeva and I will return with you.'

'Sensible chaps,' said Narad Muni, putting a hand on each of their shoulders. 'God, I hope I never have to see this bloody kitchen again.'

And with that, all three of them disappeared in a loud puff of smoke.

For a long time, right up until there was virtually no smoke lingering in the kitchen, all of the remaining occupants stood staring at the spot where the trio had disappeared from. Almost as if any kind of action or comment would mean that they were really gone. That all of this had really happened.

Eventually, Bhima uttered a rather choked-sounding grunt and resumed cooking.

Arjuna lightly kissed the top of Draupadi's head, making her look up at him with a smile. 'Any regrets?' she asked softly.

'None.' He grinned back. This had been the right thing to do.

'I'm never going to forgive you for putting me through the last few days, you know.'

He shook his head, chuckling. 'As long as you forgive everything before that, I'm fine.'

She moved up on her toes to give him a kiss, but he widened his eyes. His mother was in the room! Draupadi laughed and replied, 'The slate has been wiped clean.'

'Thank god.'

'Except for that last one, of course.'

'Of course.'

Kunti came up to them. 'I really am so happy for both of you. I suppose you'll start playing cricket now, Arjuna?'

He nodded. 'Yes. I can take over the orphanage expenses as well. They're paying me a lot of money.'

His mother smiled. 'That will be helpful once this batch of money runs out.'

'Hopefully, it won't,' said Bhima from the corner. 'We're going to expand the lunch service and invest the remaining funds. What you can do with your cricket money, Arjuna, is buy a house for Mother, Karan and myself.'

'Of course,' replied Arjuna.

Kunti frowned. 'But, Bhima, the children need me here.'

Bhima nodded. 'Yes, while they're awake. But we are going to hire people to live here now, and you can come every morning. I want a proper home, Mother, and I'm not going anywhere without you.'

Kunti took a minute to think about it. 'Maybe just a small apartment, near Karan's school,' she said, warming up to the idea. 'So I can take him out of the boarding house.'

Bhima's lip twitched. 'Whatever you want, Mother.'

Nakula dusted the smoke off his clothes and fidgeted. 'If everything is under control, could I maybe take off for a bit?'

'Of course, son,' replied Kunti.

'Tell Angela I said hi,' said a smiling Draupadi.

Nakula winked at her and hugged Kunti before walking towards the door. Then, just as he was about to exit the room, he turned with a thoughtful expression on his face.

As he observed Draupadi standing within the circle of Arjuna's arms, Nakula scratched his head. 'So, technically, if Draupadi has already told everyone that she is Kunti Kuru's daughter and Arjuna is now going to be Kunti Kuru's son ...,' He wagged a finger between Draupadi and Arjuna. 'How exactly are we explaining this?'

Everyone stared back at him, stumped.

Acknowledgements

I wrote down the idea for *Ms Draupadi Kuru* and *The Misters Kuru* in 2005, long before the mythological book wave hit the country. The first words in my idea note were, 'Modern Mahabharata? A new Mahabharata for a new age? Clichéd. Draupadi drops down from heaven? They all drop down from heaven?' and voilà, my journey with the Kuru family began. I've lived with these characters for so long and have so many people to thank for prying them out of my head, onto the page and sending them into the world.

First and foremost, to all the readers who have read, reviewed, commented and messaged over the last few years, you have my heartfelt gratitude. You guys make me want to keep writing, get better. I really hope this book was everything you hoped it would be. And I really, really hope you'll let me know what you think – your words mean so much to me!

HarperCollins India and all the wonderful mortals there, both past and present, who gave the Kuru family a home. My editors in 2016 – Karthika V.K. and Ajitha G.S., who brought Draupadi and her gang to life. My editors since then – Diya Kar and Swati Daftuar, who've brought the Pandavas to join in the fun. Shabnam Shrivastava, Shreya Dhawan, Jyotsna Raman, Akriti Tyagi, Bonita Shimray, Amit Malhotra and Surabhi Banerjee. Ananth Padmanabhan and Rahul Dixit. Thank you all from the bottom of my heart – I'm incredibly fortunate to have collaborated with you.

So grateful to have Jayapriya Vasudevan from Jacaranda Lit batting in my corner and being a diplomat when I'm being a toddler.

Mr Rajiv Mehrotra, who listened to a 23-year old's rambling ideas as if they were important. You will always have my gratitude.

Shoutout to Radhika Shukla for saying, 'You should send the Pandavas to jail,' over coffee and then laughing as if it was a ridiculous idea. Be careful what you say to authors.

My various mini tribes, from relatives and friends to fellow authors and more, for your steadfast affection, support and encouragement.

My late grandparents, for enriching my life with stories and instilling in me a love for books.

Vir, for getting me when no one else does.

Poppy, who always said, 'You can do whatever you want as long as you do it well.'

Ma, who always said, 'No matter what, I'll always have your back.'

Deeps, who always knows exactly what to say and for whom I thank the universe every day.

R & J, the loves of my life.

b, as always.

About the Author

Trisha Das is the author of *Kama's Last Sutra, Ms Draupadi Kuru: After the Pandavas, The Mahabharata Re-imagined, The Art of the Television Interview* and the internationally acclaimed *How to Write a Documentary Script*. She has also written columns and short stories for *Magical Women* and publications like *Cosmopolitan, Harper's Bazaar, Grazia India, Hindustan Times* and Scroll. In her film-making career, Trisha has directed over forty documentaries and won an Indian National Film Award. She was also UGA's International Artist of the year for 2003. You can find Trisha dancing around her study on most days or contact her on Facebook @trishadasauthor, Twitter @thetrishadas, Instagram @trishadas or via email at trishadasauthor@gmail.com.